P9-CQM-795

JOAN ELLIOTT PICKART
presents the powerfully emotional story
of a woman who lost her faith in love
and the rugged detective who wins her trust...
and her heart. This is one MacAllister story
you won't want to miss!

* * *

Why did Jessica MacAllister push his sexual buttons like this?

Just saying her name brought to mind the kiss they'd shared. That incredible kiss that had created a heated, aching want of Jessica deep within him.

Maybe he was making too big a deal out of their kiss, Quinn mused. Maybe it wasn't Jessica.

But...

Just *any* woman wouldn't have big, chocolate-brown expressive eyes and golden hair that made his fingers itch to sift his fingers through it. Just *any* woman wouldn't, he somehow knew, send him up in flames by returning his kiss with sensual abandon. Just *any* woman wouldn't nestle against him as though custom-made only for him.

Just *any* woman wouldn't be Jessica.

* * *

Praise for Joan Elliott Pickart

"Joan Elliott Pickart weaves a sensitive love story..."
—*Romantic Times Magazine*

"Joan Elliott Pickart leaves you breathless
with anticipation."
—*Rendezvous*

Also available from

JOAN ELLIOTT PICKART

and
Silhouette Books

Available February 2001
HER LITTLE SECRET
(Silhouette Special Edition #1377)

Available July 2001
SINGLE WITH TWINS
(Silhouette Special Edition #1405)

Available December 2001
"A Wish and a Prince"
A brand-new MacAllister short story available in
CROWNED HEARTS
(Silhouette Books)

JOAN ELLIOTT PICKART

Party of Three

Silhouette Books

Published by Silhouette Books

America's Publisher of Contemporary Romance

If you purchased this book without a cover you should be aware
that this book is stolen property. It was reported as "unsold and
destroyed" to the publisher, and neither the author nor the
publisher has received any payment for this "stripped book."

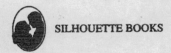 **SILHOUETTE BOOKS**

ISBN 0-373-48431-3

PARTY OF THREE

Copyright © 2001 by Joan Elliott Pickart

All rights reserved. Except for use in any review, the reproduction
or utilization of this work in whole or in part in any form by any
electronic, mechanical or other means, now known or hereafter
invented, including xerography, photocopying and recording, or in
any information storage or retrieval system, is forbidden without
the written permission of the editorial office, Silhouette Books,
300 East 42nd Street, New York, NY 10017 U.S.A.

All characters in this book have no existence outside the imagination of
the author and have no relation whatsoever to anyone bearing the same
name or names. They are not even distantly inspired by any individual
known or unknown to the author, and all incidents are pure invention.

This edition published by arrangement with Harlequin Books S.A.

® and TM are trademarks of Harlequin Books S.A., used under
license. Trademarks indicated with ® are registered in the United States
Patent and Trademark Office, the Canadian Trade Marks Office and in
other countries.

Visit Silhouette at www.eHarlequin.com

Printed in U.S.A.

In memory of
DANA BOLSTAD
So loved...so missed...
...by so many

Chapter 1

The night wind chased the cold rain in a frenzied game of tag, causing the downpour to beat against the windows of the old house as though seeking entry, a place to hide from its pursuer.

Jessica MacAllister shivered as she glanced at the rattling pane of glass in the warped window frame in the small office. After taking a sip of hot coffee, she wrapped her hands around the mug and propped her elbows on the dented metal desk, wiggling slightly in a futile attempt to find a comfortable position on the wooden folding chair.

This poor place needed an overhaul, she thought, frowning. It was held together by a hope and a prayer, and very little money.

She shifted her gaze to the thick tan envelope on the corner of the desk. The package had arrived at her office that day and she hadn't had an opportunity to do more than take a quick look at the inch-high stack of papers inside.

Jessica set the mug on the desk and leaned back in the torturous chair with a weary sigh. She'd had no idea when she sent for the material to apply for a grant for The Peaceful Dove that there would be so much paperwork involved in trying to obtain funding for the women's shelter. The form letter on top of the stack had listed a half-dozen books that would be helpful in filling out the papers accurately.

Somehow, she would have to find the time in her busy schedule to obtain at least some of the books from the list, study them, then tackle the daunting project of applying for the grant that held the key to the shelter staying open.

The donations they were receiving from various service groups just weren't enough to cover the on-going daily expenses, let alone do any much-needed repairs to the ancient two-story house.

Above the noise of the storm raging outside, Jessica heard a cheer and a smattering of applause. She smiled as she got to her feet and straightened the waistband of her red sweatshirt over her jean-clad hips. She left the office, then crossed the narrow hallway to enter the living room.

The room was fairly good-sized and sparkling clean, the white walls having been painted recently. The gray carpet was worn through in spots and the various pieces of furniture had definitely seen better days.

Four women were rising from the faded sofa, several sniffling into tissues. One of the women turned off the small television, gave it an appreciative pat, then popped a video out of the VCR resting on the bottom shelf of the metal stand.

"I take it that *Sleepless in Seattle* was wonderful," Jessica said, smiling. "Again."

"It's just so romantic," one of the women said, then dabbed at her nose. "I could watch that movie a dozen times."

"You *have*," another woman said, laughing.

Another of the women stretched and yawned. "It's nearly eleven o'clock and I'm off to bed. My Jeff will be awake at dawn looking for his bottle. He's just like his father when it comes to wanting his breakfast on time and—"

"Don't go there, Chrissy," another woman interrupted. "Don't give one thought to that bum who beat you to a pulp. He doesn't deserve to even be on the same planet as you and your Jeff."

"I know," Chrissy said quietly, wrapping her hands around her elbows. "I thought, I really believed, when I married Sonny that we'd be so happy, just like the couple in the movie."

She laughed, the sound holding an echo of unshed tears. "What a joke. After a year of Sonny hitting me and... I just couldn't take any more and came here last night and... Oh, God, I'm so scared. Sonny is going to be furious when he gets back into town from his sales route and discovers that I'm gone and that

I've taken his son with me. What if he finds me? What if he…''

"Chrissy." Jessica closed the distance between them and wrapped one arm around the young woman's shoulders. "Sonny will have no idea where you are. You're safe here. You and Jeff are out of harm's way and no one is ever going to hit you again. Understand?''

Chrissy nodded as she struggled against threatening tears.

"It's cold in here," one of the women said. "I'm going to my warm bed. Do you want me to unplug the Christmas tree, Jessica? That is the scrawniest tree I've ever seen, but I think it's beautiful because I'm here at The Peaceful Dove to look at it and not home waiting for the next pop in the chops from the sleaze-ball.''

"Yes," Jessica said, smiling. "Go ahead and un-plug our gorgeous tree, Kathy, and turn off the lamps. I'll be spending the night in the office, per usual, ready to answer the telephone and hopefully get caught up on some work I brought along from my office.''

"I wouldn't want to stay up all night in this place," Kathy said. "It's creepy.''

Jessica laughed. "It is a bit eerie, but I'm only here one night a month so…" She shrugged. "The ghos-ties haven't shown themselves yet. I—''

"Shh," Chrissy said, raising one hand. "Do you hear something?''

"It's just the storm," Kathy said. "The wind is

causing the branches from that big tree out front to hit against the windows along with the rain.''

"No, no," Chrissy said, the color draining from her face. "Listen. There's someone pounding on the front door. Don't you hear it?"

The women all turned at once in the direction of the front door they couldn't see from where they stood. They strained their ears to listen for any sound that wasn't caused by the storm.

"Uh-oh," Kathy whispered. "There *is* someone knocking on the front door and none too gently, I might add."

"Okay, stay calm," Jessica said, her own heart racing. "Whoever it is can't get in unless we want them to. We spent money on a sturdy door with heavy-duty locks. I'm going to go ask who it is in case it's a woman seeking shelter."

"We're going with you," Kathy said decisively. "There's safety in numbers." She paused. "Isn't there?"

No one answered Kathy's question as they moved into the hallway, then closer to the front door. They took a step backward as the pounding resumed.

"Chrissy!" a man bellowed, his booming voice muffled slightly by the noise of the storm.

"Oh, God, no," Chrissy said, her voice quivering. "It's Sonny."

"I know you're in there," Sonny yelled. "I found the pamphlet you dropped on the kitchen floor explaining all about this damn place. You come out here right now and bring my son with you. Damn it, Chrissy, I'm not telling you again. You get your butt home where you and Jeff belong. I'm not putting up with this ridiculous crap.''

Chrissy covered her ears. ''No, no, no. Oh, please, no.''

''Don't fall apart, sweetie,'' Kathy said to Chrissy. ''The creep can't get in. Let him huff and puff, but he can't blow that door down.''

''This is all my fault,'' Chrissy said, tears spilling onto her cheeks. ''I was so nervous and upset when I left the house. I didn't know I dropped the pamphlet and...I'm sorry, so sorry. Maybe I should just get Jeff and go with Sonny and...''

''No!'' the women said in unison.

''Chrissy!'' Sonny yelled, pounding on the door. ''I have my gun with me. I'll use it if I have to. You have three minutes to get out here with my boy.''

''That does it,'' Jessica said. ''I'm calling the police. Sonny is threatening Chrissy with a weapon and that's enough to get him picked up and, hopefully, have him spend the night in jail.''

''Whip some of your fancy lawyer jargon on the cops,'' Kathy said. ''Let them know they're dealing with a highfalutin attorney and they'd better get over here on the double.''

''Go back into the living room and away from the door,'' Jessica said over her shoulder as she hurried into the office. She grabbed the telephone receiver on the desk and punched in 9-1-1.

* * *

The Homicide and Domestic Violence Divisions of the Ventura Police Department were in a large room with two rows of desks, the majority of them piled high with files and papers. Several men were sitting behind desks, two talking on the telephone. On top of one of the numerous filing cabinets was a scanner turned to low volume as it broadcast all the calls between city dispatchers and on-duty police officers.

Daniel Quinn slid one hip onto the edge of his desk, rotated his neck back and forth, then dragged his hands down his beard-roughened face. He was so tired he was punchy, he thought. He was thirty-six years old and had just gone thirty-six hours without sleep, a matching numbers combination that obviously no longer worked.

"Come on, partner," Mick said, whopping him on the shoulder. "Let's call it a night. I can hardly remember what my own name is. I'm getting too old for this kind of stretch."

Daniel chuckled. "That's the very thought I just had, Mick. I'm really feeling my age tonight. But, damn, every lead we followed up on this homicide produced zero. The puzzle is definitely not coming together."

"Yeah, well," Mick said, then yawned, "maybe we'll have a brilliant idea after we get some sleep. My bed beckons. I wonder if Rosemary and the kids remember who I am."

"Why would they want to?" Daniel said. "You're a total dud."

"*I* know that," Mick said, smiling, "and *you* know that, but I'm hoping my family never figures it out. Let's hit the road."

"Sounds good to me," Daniel said, shrugging into his sport coat. "I'm really beat and...hold it. Did you hear that?"

"Hear what?" Mick said, frowning.

"On the scanner," Daniel said. "There's a man with a weapon threatening the occupants of The Peaceful Dove." He narrowed his eyes and a muscle ticked in his jaw. "I'm going over there."

"Danny, no," Mick said. "Don't do it. The uniforms will handle it. It's not our call and you don't belong there. It's only going to dredge up stuff that you don't need to deal with. Go home, buddy, and get some sleep."

Daniel shook his head. "No, I'm going to that shelter."

He spun around and started toward the door. "I'll see you tomorrow."

"Hell," Mick said, starting after his partner. "I'm coming with you to be sure you don't do something nuts, Quinn."

Nature's game of tag had apparently exhausted the storm, and only a chilly, misty rain was falling as Daniel and Mick drove across town, Daniel at the wheel of the unmarked dark sedan.

"Crummy neighborhood," Daniel said, shaking his head in disgust. "Why do they always open these shelters in high-crime areas? The women aren't safe from the scum walking the streets over here, let alone from the men they're hiding from.''

"They probably can't afford a classier area of town," Mick said. "Plus the people in the better places don't want a shelter near them. They go to the city council and holler their heads off about the danger and how it diminishes the value of their property."

"They bury their heads in the sand is what they do," Daniel said. "If they don't see abused women and kids, then they don't exist. Hell."

"Man, look at that up ahead," Mick said. "The uniforms responded with four squad cars. They still have their lights flashing, and I bet they came in with sirens wailing, too. That's good work." He paused. "Danny, things are obviously in control at the shelter. Why don't we turn around and...''

"No."

"Then keep your cool," Mick said. "You stay twenty feet away from the bozo who was waving the weapon around. No, make that thirty feet. Got it?"

Daniel stopped the car in the middle of the street in front of the shelter and got out, his detective shield already in his hand. He sprinted around the front of his vehicle and the patrol car next to it, holding his badge at shoulder level. A uniformed officer was putting a handcuffed man into the back seat of a police car. Another officer stepped in front of Daniel and looked at his shield.

"Lieutenant," the officer said, nodding. "What brings you to our fun and games?"

"You got him?" Daniel said, jerking his head in the direction of the man in the car. "Did he hurt anyone in the shelter?"

"The women are fine," the officer said. "Scared, but fine. The jerk is going downtown."

"No bail," Daniel said, narrowing his eyes. "Understand?"

"Hey, I'll do the best I can in my report," the officer said, then shrugged. "But if he gets himself a smooth-talking lawyer, he'll probably be out in a few hours."

"Damn it," Daniel said, "he threatened those women, or at least his wife, with a gun."

"I'll write it up, Lieutenant," the officer said. "That's all I can do. He dropped the gun the minute we arrived so we can't get him on attempted assault of a police officer. If he'd turned that weapon on us, he'd be a dead turkey."

"He doesn't deserve to be breathing," Daniel said, taking a step in the direction of the patrol car.

"Whoa," Mick said, grabbing Daniel's arm. "We're done here. Besides, I'm getting soaked through from this rain and it's cold. Show's over, Danny."

"Not...quite," Daniel said, yanking his arm free of Mick's grasp. He slid the leather folder holding his badge onto the lapel of his jacket so it could be clearly seen. "I want to talk to whoever is in charge of this place."

"Oh, hell," Mick mumbled, trudging slowly after Daniel as he strode toward the front door of the house.

* * *

Jessica sank onto the chair behind her desk, acutely aware that her trembling legs were about to refuse to support her for another minute. She drew a shuddering breath and mentally ordered herself to get a grip.

She was suffering from aftershock, she thought. She'd been calm, cool and collected through the terrifying event of Chrissy's husband arriving at the shelter with a gun. But now the whole thing was over, Sonny was in custody, she'd sent the women off to bed and she was very close to falling apart.

No, she thought, patting her cheeks. She was fine. Granted, she was about a breath away from bursting into tears, but she was ignoring that fact. She'd...yes, she would get a fresh cup of coffee, then concentrate on the work she'd brought from the office. Good plan.

As she got to her feet, a man came barreling into her office. His sudden appearance shattered the last thread of her frayed nerves and she plunked back down in the chair, staring at him with wide, terror-filled eyes.

"Are you in charge of this place?" the man said, none too quietly.

Jessica blinked. "Pardon me?"

"Is that a tough question, lady?" he said. "Are you, or are you not, running this shelter? Because if you are, you're doing a lousy job of it."

Three realizations tumbled one into the next in Jessica's beleaguered brain.

One, this rude individual was a member of the Ventura Police Department.

Two, this rude individual was, without a doubt, one of the most ruggedly handsome men she'd ever seen in her thirty years of life. He had wavy black hair that was wet from the rain, dark eyes and tawny skin, shoulders as wide as a city block, and masculine features that appeared as though they'd been chiseled from stone.

And three, this rude individual had replaced her terror with rip-roaring, mad-as-hell anger.

Jessica planted her hands flat on the top of the desk and rose to her feet slowly, her narrow-eyed gaze focused on the rude individual. She straightened and folded her arms beneath her breasts.

"Just who do you think you are, Mr. Whatever Your Name Is," she said, "coming in here telling me this shelter isn't managed well? You've got a lot of nerve, do you know that? Or is that too tough a question for *you?* I want you to leave. Now."

She was beautiful when angry, Daniel thought, his gaze riveted on the irate woman before him. Her big dark-brown eyes were flashing like laser beams, her cheeks were flushed a pretty pink, and her kissable lips were pressed tightly together, just waiting to be teased apart.

She was blond. Natural? Maybe. And her hair was in a long braid that lay over her right breast. Her full right breast. Pushing against the soft material of the sweatshirt she was wearing and—

"Hello?" Jessica said. "No, cancel that. The word I want is goodbye. You're leaving."

Daniel thudded back to reality from the rather hazy,

sensual place he'd floated off to and matched the woman's pose by crossing his arms over his chest.

"I'm Lieutenant Daniel Quinn," he said. "Homicide. Ventura Police Department. And you are?"

"Insulted to the maximum," Jessica said, lifting her chin. "I'm also Jessica MacAllister, Attorney-at-Law, since you feel it's important to fling titles around. Homicide? What are you doing here? No one was hurt, let alone killed, for mercy's sake."

"No one was killed *this time,*" Daniel said, nearly shouting. "But what about the next episode like this and the one after that? Why in the hell isn't there an armed security guard on duty at this place twenty-four hours a day? That's the bottom line question here, Mrs....Miss..."

"It's *Ms.,* Lieutenant," Jessica said tightly, "and we have no security guard because there aren't funds to pay one."

"Then you should close this place down until you have the money to hire one," Daniel bellowed. "Without an armed guard these women and kids are sitting ducks, fish in a barrel, easy pickings. This isn't a shelter, it's a tragedy waiting to happen."

"Oh-h-h, you are so off-base, it's a crime," Jessica said, nearly sputtering. "You should arrest yourself, Lieutenant."

"Now that," Mick said, strolling into the room, "was funny."

"Super. Just great," Jessica said, rolling her eyes heavenward as she saw the badge clipped to the new arrival's jacket. "There are two of you. Flick and Flack. Ding and Dong. Abbott and Costello."

And as different as day and night, she registered absently. This second man was blond, shorter than Daniel Quinn by several inches, more slight, with wholesome, cornflake-box features.

"Please tell me that you outrank this rude individual," Jessica said to the second man, "and that you're here to haul him out of this building and my life."

"Sorry, ma'am," Mick said, raising both hands. "*Sergeant* Mick Smith at your service." He paused. "However, I do agree that it's time that Danny and I exit stage left. Right, partner?"

"No," Daniel said.

"Listen to him," Jessica said, pointing to Mick. "He's the one of your dynamic duo who has the brains."

"Oh, Lord," Mick said, with a burst of laughter. "Oops," he added, as Daniel shot him a dark glare. "Sorry, buddy."

Daniel directed his attention to Jessica again. "You just don't get it, do you, Ms. MacAllister? To bring these battered women and kids under this roof, then not provide an armed guard to protect them around the clock is irresponsible. And tack stupid on there for good measure."

Jessica marched from behind the desk and Mick backed up quickly to get out of her way. She halted in front of Daniel Quinn and poked him in the chest with one finger, absently registering the fact that said chest was hard as a rock.

"You are the one who just doesn't get it, Lieutenant," she said, continuing to stab him with her finger. "There…is…no…money…for…an…armed guard. Is it clear yet? Should I somehow tell you that in smaller words that you can understand? At least the women and children are safer here than at home where they are beat up whenever the mood strikes the lunatic they're living with."

Daniel snagged Jessica's hand in mid-poke and held it still against his rain-dampened shirt.

"You're wrong, Ms.…Jessica," he said, his voice suddenly quiet and weary-sounding. He looked directly into her big brown eyes as he spoke. "What happened here tonight should have proved that to you. If that guy would have gotten inside this building before the uniforms arrived, someone, maybe a lot of someones, would be dead now.

"Dead is…dead is forever, Jessica. No second chances. No way to undo it, change things, turn back the clock and handle it differently. You've got to listen to what I'm saying to you."

"I…I am, but…" Jessica started, then stopped speaking as she totally forgot what she was going to say.

Dear heaven, she thought, she could hardly breathe, let alone think clearly. Her hand was splayed on the rock-solid wall of Daniel's chest and completely covered by his large callused hand.

She could feel the steady thump of his heart beneath her palm and…and heat. There was such a tremendous heat radiating from him and traveling up her arm and across her breasts, causing them to feel strangely heavy and achy.

His eyes were so dark that the pupils were hardly discernible and he was pinning her in place with his mesmerizing stare, causing her heart to flutter and that heat…that incredible heat…to shift, swirl and pulse throughout her entire body.

"May I…" she said, then cleared her throat as she heard the funny squeak that used to be her voice. "May I please have my hand back, Lieutenant?"

No, Daniel thought hazily. He was going to keep Jessica MacAllister's hand exactly where it was. It felt good there, pressed against his chest…soft and feminine, and…her lips. Oh, man, those lips of hers were soft and feminine, too, tormenting him, teasing and taunting him to capture them with his and—

"Thank you," Jessica said, yanking her hand free and glaring at Daniel.

"Look," Jessica said, then sighed. "We could stand here and argue about this all night and it wouldn't accomplish a thing. I'm exhausted. This hasn't exactly been a peaceful night at The Peaceful Dove. I usually stay up all night when it's my turn to volunteer for duty here, but I'm going to stretch out on the lumpy sofa in the living room for a while. Just go. Please."

"So you can forget everything that I've said?" Daniel said, narrowing his eyes.

"Come on, Danny," Mick said. "That's enough. Ms. MacAllister is obviously wiped out."

"Yeah, I know," Daniel said. "Fear, being terribly

frightened, can do that. If there had been an armed guard on duty here..."

"All right, Mr. Know-it-all," Jessica said, "I've had it with you." She turned and snatched up the heavy envelope from the top of the desk. "See this? They're the papers needed to apply for a grant, which I intend to do to hopefully obtain funds for The Peaceful Dove. I have approval of the board of directors to undertake this project, and since you're so determined that there should be an armed guard on staff at all times, then you can help me fill out these forms and make your pitch for money for the salary to pay that person. So how do hours and hours of tedious paperwork sound, Lieutenant?" Jessica smiled rather smugly as she tossed the heavy envelope back onto the desk with a thud. "I think you're about to sing a different tune."

"Wrong," Daniel said. "I'll be in touch with you very soon and we'll make arrangements to get together and start working on that application."

Jessica's smile disappeared and her eyes widened. "What?"

"Good night, Ms....Jessica," Daniel said, smiling. "I think since we're going to be spending hours and hours together doing tedious paperwork we ought to be on a first-name basis, don't you?"

"But..." Jessica said.

"Ready to go, Mick?" Daniel said, jerking his head toward the door.

"But..." Jessica repeated.

"Yep," Mick said. "Good night, ma'am. Be sure to lock up behind us."

The two men turned and strode from the room. Jessica blinked and shook her head slightly as she stared after them.

"But..." Jessica said weakly, then threw up her hands in defeat.

Chapter 2

The building that housed the office of Cavelli and MacAllister, Attorneys-at-Law was one of a group built in a square around a grassy courtyard with a tall mulberry tree in the center.

Jessica MacAllister and Mary-Clair Cavelli had been roommates in college and were best friends. They'd completed law school, passed the California State Bar at the same time, and immediately decided to take the plunge and open their own firm. A flip of a coin determined that Mary-Clair's name would be listed first.

They specialized in women's issues and were gaining a reputation for being savvy, hard-hitting and impeccably honest. To their relief and delight their client list grew bigger each month.

Following the Saturday night episode at The Peaceful Dove, Mary-Clair was tied up in court. It wasn't until late Wednesday morning that Jessica had an opportunity to relate the gruesome tale to her friend and partner.

Mary-Clair's dark eyes grew wider and wider as Jessica told her nerve-jangling story while the pair sat in Mary-Clair's office.

"Oh, my stars," Mary-Clair said finally, sinking back in the chair behind her desk and covering her heart with both hands. "I would have been scared out of my mind and died on the spot just knowing that Sonny guy was out there waving a gun around. It's as though you're telling me about a bad movie you saw, Jessica, rather than what actually happened." She shivered. "Oh, I have goose bumps just thinking about it."

"It wasn't the highlight of my life, believe me," Jessica said, as she sat in one of the chairs opposite Mary-Clair's desk.

Mary-Clair laughed. "I would have loved to have seen you on your rip when you took on that Lieutenant Quinn. It's not like you to lose your temper like that. Me? Yes, I go off like a rocket all the time, but you're usually so calm under pressure."

"I was on emotional overload at the time," Jessica said, smiling. "Besides, Daniel Quinn was rude and I'm not one bit sorry I gave him a piece of my mind. He was sinfully, ruggedly handsome as all get-out, but definitely rude."

Mary-Clair leaned forward. "Sinfully, ruggedly handsome? How handsome is sinfully?"

"Forget it," Jessica said. "I know your rules. No men over five-nine or ten maximum, because you feel like you're talking to their belt buckle. Daniel Quinn is about six feet tall, I'd guess."

"Drat," Mary-Clair said, leaning back in her chair again. "Just like my five older brothers...and my father, too, for that matter." She laughed. "I complained to my mother about being only five foot two, and she said that since I was her sixth baby in nearly nine years, she was so worn-out I should be grateful I'm as tall as I am."

"I adore your parents," Jessica said, "and your mother has a valid point there, Ms. Cavelli. Gracious, I shudder at the thought of how many diapers she has changed in her life."

"Isn't that the truth?" Mary-Clair said, then sighed. "I'd settle for one cute little bambino created by incredible lovemaking with a fantastic five-foot-ten-inch man. He would have, of course, declared his eternal love and devotion to me and slipped a rock the size of Toledo on my third finger left hand."

Mary-Clair waved the hand in question. "Enough of my yearnings. Let's get back to sinfully, ruggedly handsome Daniel. He'd be the perfect height for you, Jessica. Since you refuse to become a Cavelli by falling in love with any of my brothers who are still playing the dating game, one must not dismiss any eligible candidates."

"Hello?" Jessica said. "This is me, remember? I have no desire to marry. I'm..."

"Devoted to my career," Mary-Clair finished for her. "I've heard the spiel."

"Well, it's true," Jessica said. "And don't start in on me with your bit about how women can combine marriage, babies and careers. Been there, heard that a zillion times, thank you very much."

"You'll change your tune when the love bug bites," Mary-Clair said. "So, anyway, back to the story. You and Daniel Quinn are going to work together on the grant application for The Peaceful Dove?"

"No," Jessica said, shaking her head. "I haven't heard one word from him. Quinn was all bluster and blow and he fizzled out in the light of the new day, which doesn't surprise me."

"Well, drat," Mary-Clair said.

"Thank goodness is closer to the mark. I never want to see him again."

Jessica only wished her mind would cooperate. Daniel Quinn was driving her crazy; he kept flitting into her mental vision during the day. He was also disrupting her sleep as vivid and embarrassingly sensual dreams about the man continued to plague her ever since their meeting. Enough was enough.

"...don't you think?" Mary-Clair was saying.

"Pardon me?" Jessica said. "I'm sorry. I drifted off."

"To where?" Mary-Clair said. "Your cheeks are suddenly flushed a pretty pink."

"Forget it," Jessica said, then cleared her throat as

she felt the remembered heat from Daniel's hand covering hers. "What were you saying?"

"Just that while I didn't get everything I wanted for my client in the divorce case I just finished, I believe I did well enough by her to pat myself on the back a little."

"More than a little. You were up against one of the toughest divorce attorneys in Ventura. Remember that case last year where the husband he represented walked away with a bundle and the wife got her clothes, a car and the dog? You did a super job, Mary-Clair."

Mary-Clair laughed. "I got my Mrs. joint custody of the dog, by golly. I'm a force to be reckoned with." The telephone on the desk rang and she frowned. "Can't we afford a full-time secretary yet, instead of just occasional temps when we're both in a crunch?"

"Just about, I think. Very soon, I hope," Jessica said. "Answer that thing, Ms. Secretary."

Mary-Clair picked up the receiver and pressed it to her ear as she rolled her eyes heavenward at the unwelcomed title Jessica had given her.

"Cavelli and MacAllister," she said, ever so sweetly. "May I help you? ...Is the MacAllister in the listing a Ms. Jessica MacAllister? Yes... You wish to speak with her? I believe she's still with a client but let me check. Who shall I say is calling?" Her eyebrows shot up. "Daniel Quinn?"

Jessica stiffened in her chair and her heart started to beat in a rapid tempo, which she ignored. She shook her head and waved her hands as she mouthed, "I'm very busy," at Mary-Clair.

"My, my," Mary-Clair said, "Ms. MacAllister is now free to speak with you, sir. Will you hold for just a moment, please?"

Mary-Clair pressed a button on the telephone console and replaced the receiver.

"You can take the call from the sinfully, ruggedly handsome lieutenant in the privacy of your own office, Jessica," she said, grinning.

Jessica got to her feet and pointed a finger at Mary-Clair. "You'll pay for this, Cavelli. I'm going to eat three jelly doughnuts right in front of you."

"That's cruel. Would you really do that, tempt a dear, dieting friend? Raspberry jelly?"

"Raspberry," Jessica said decisively, then headed for the door. "The frosted ones with sprinkles."

"Oh-h-h," Mary-Clair moaned, as Jessica disappeared from view. "Not fair, not fair, not fair."

Jessica entered her office and sank into the chair behind the desk. As she reached for the telephone receiver, she hesitated and frowned.

Get a grip, she ordered herself. She was behaving like an adolescent who had just been told that the captain of the football team was waiting to talk to her on the phone. This was ridiculous.

Well, not totally ridiculous. She hadn't expected to hear from Daniel Quinn so it was understandable that she was a tad jangled. He was probably calling to deliver some lame excuse as to why he couldn't help with the grant application after all. The conversation would take sixty seconds max and that would be that. She could handle this.

Jessica nodded, then pressed the blinking button on the console as she picked up the receiver with her other hand.

"Jessica MacAllister," she said breezily.

"Hello, Jessica. Daniel Quinn."

Oh, good night. Jessica plunked her elbow on the desk and rested her suddenly flushed forehead in the palm of her hand. The sound of Daniel's deep, rumbly voice had caused a shiver to slither down her spine, then change into pulsing heat low in her body. She was back to acting ridiculous and was furious at herself. What on earth was the matter with her?

Jessica straightened, lifted her chin and narrowed her eyes. "Lieutenant. What can I do for you?"

Daniel chuckled, a rumbly, male chuckle that convinced Jessica that her bones were dissolving right there on the spot.

"Now that's an interesting question," Daniel said. "Is it multiple choice?"

"I'm extremely busy, Lieutenant," Jessica said coolly. "Would you get to the point, please?"

"Yes, ma'am. Whatever you say, ma'am. This is the first free moment I've had at a reasonable hour to contact you regarding that grant application. Would you by any chance be free this evening to get together and start tackling the thing?"

Jessica's eyes widened. "You really intend to take part in filling out the application?"

"I said I would."

"Yes, I know, but…"

"You'll discover in time that I always mean what I say, Jessica."

She really, really wished that Daniel would quit saying her name in that…that male-beyond-belief voice of his, Jessica thought frantically.

"I see." Jessica cleared her throat. "Yes, well, all right. I suppose I could free up a couple of hours this evening."

"Good," Daniel said. "My apartment. Seven o'clock. I'll give you the address."

Not a chance, buster, Jessica thought. She wasn't about to go tromping blissfully into the spider's web. She'd meet with the man on *her* turf.

"I think my apartment would be best," she said. "I went to the library and checked out a whole stack of recommended books to help in the preparation of the application. It would be much more efficient for you to come to me. What I mean is, to where the reference material is located."

"That won't be possible tonight," Daniel said. "I have to be at home."

Jessica frowned. "Why?"

"I don't have time right now to explain," he said. "Do you have a pen? I'll give you my address."

No! Jessica thought. Forget it.

"Yes," she said, then sighed. "Go ahead."

She wrote down the information that Daniel rattled off, then smacked the pen onto the pad of paper.

"Fine," she said. "I'll be there promptly at seven, Lieutenant."

"It's Daniel, remember?"

"Da...Daniel," she said, telling herself that her voice had *not* sounded all breathy and weird.

"Goodbye for now...Jessica," Daniel said.

The dial tone hummed in Jessica's ear before she could deliver her own farewell and she replaced the receiver with more force than was necessary. She leaned back in her chair and pressed her fingertips to her temples.

That man, she thought, had given her a stress headache. Why, why, why did Daniel Quinn throw her so off-kilter? Unless...yes, that made sense.

She dropped her hands into her lap and stared into space.

Of course, that was it. She associated Daniel with the terrifying events at The Peaceful Dove on Saturday night. While he had been very rude at the time, because he was a police officer, she had subconsciously labeled him a hero to the rescue, a knight in shining armor, giving him unwarranted larger-than-life qualities because she'd been an emotional and physical wreck.

"Ta-da," she said. "I've figured it out. Oh, what a relief."

When she saw Daniel tonight, she would be in complete control of herself, and would function as she normally would. Daniel was just another man. Handsome, yes. Built like a dream, yes. Possessed a voice that could melt ice cream in a snowstorm, yes. But...still...he was just a man.

*   *   *

Daniel stared at the telephone receiver long after he'd completed his conversation with Jessica Mac-Allister.

Damn, he thought. He'd been so certain that once he spoke to Jessica again he would be free of the nonsense that had been driving him nuts since he'd met her Saturday night. She'd taken up residency in his brain, had refused to leave him alone during the day, and had crept into his dreams at night with regularity.

He knew that Jessica's strange effect on him was due to the emotionally charged event that had brought them together in the first place. Hearing her voice on the phone was supposed to have placed her in proper perspective as just another attractive woman, one of the multitude he knew.

Well, the sound of her voice hadn't done the trick. Not by a long shot. The pictures in his mind of Jessica MacAllister had become more vivid, more tantalizing, causing heat to coil low in his body.

Daniel mumbled an earthy expletive and got to his feet so quickly that his chair rolled back and crashed into the desk behind him.

Man, this was annoying, he thought, shaking his head. *Seeing* Jessica again this evening would take care of this ridiculous business. Regaining control of his mind and body had been postponed for a few more hours, that was all.

"Damn straight," Daniel said, rapping the knuckles of one hand on the corner of the desk.

"You're talking to yourself?" Mick said, as he stood beside Daniel. "You're awfully young for senility, Danny, but..." He shrugged. "You never know about stuff like that. It can sneak up on you."

"On *you* maybe," Daniel said. "Me? When you see me come in here tomorrow morning, you'll be looking at a man who is in total command of his...his person."

"Do tell," Mick said, with a burst of laughter.

"I just did. Pay attention."

"So what's on your agenda for tonight," Mick said.

"Reality, buddy," Daniel said. "A good old-fashioned dose of reality."

Jessica stood on the sidewalk edging the parking lot of Daniel's apartment building and swept her gaze over the seven-story structure clearly visible in the light from a multitude of lampposts along pathways leading in several directions.

The members of the family firm, MacAllister Architects, Inc., would label this building "cookie-cutter crap." It appeared to be fairly new and the grounds were well-maintained. It was also located close to a main street that afforded Daniel a straight, swift drive to the police station. He had no doubt selected this residence for the convenience it provided, rather than for any aesthetic appeal.

Okay, Jessica, she thought dryly as she started forward, she'd stood there like an idiot long enough, postponing the inevitable. She was now marching toward the entrance, would zoom up in an elevator to the sixth floor, then knock on Daniel Quinn's door and greet him politely.

Then, mature woman that she was, she would spend the following hours calmly and methodically starting the preparation of the grant application with Daniel by her side.

Close by her side. Where she would probably be able to inhale his male aroma. Where she would be acutely aware of his incredible masculinity compared to her own femininity. Where he would speak to her in that black-velvet voice of his and cause a flash-fire of heat to consume her yet again.

"Oh-h-h, for Pete's sake," she said, as she left the elevator on the proper floor and stomped down the carpeted hallway. "Get a grip. Right now."

She refused to dwell on how long it had taken her to decide what to wear to this meeting with Daniel. She'd dithered between staying in her suit or changing into casual clothes.

Thoroughly disgusted with herself, she'd finally grabbed a pair of faded jeans and a chocolate-brown sweater. Yes, okay, she happened to know that the sweater was the exact shade of her MacAllister brown eyes, but so what? Daniel Quinn didn't come across as the type of man who would notice such a thing, anyway.

She wore her hair in a single braid and brown loafers on her feet. She probably looked about sixteen years old, instead of presenting the image of a successful attorney. Was that good? Bad? Oh, what difference did it make? She was driving herself nuts.

Jessica found the door she was seeking, lifted her chin and knocked sharply, telling herself that her heart was racing due to the fact that she was lugging an extremely heavy briefcase.

She drew a steadying breath and waited for Daniel to answer her summons. A moment later the apartment door was flung open and Jessica produced a smile that was supposed to be followed by a pleasant greeting. Instead, the smile dissolved, her eyes widened and she stared at Daniel with her mouth forming an astonished O.

There he was, she thought foggily, Lieutenant Daniel Quinn, wearing snug faded jeans that were white at the knees and accentuated his long muscular legs to perfection. The navy-blue sweater did marvelous things for his broad shoulders, midnight-dark hair and tawny skin.

Jessica catalogued all that information in an instant, then focused on what was causing her to have difficulty breathing.

In the crook of one arm Daniel Quinn was holding a baby in a fuzzy pink sleeper.

A baby. A baby?

"A baby?" Jessica said, then shook her head slightly. "I didn't know you..."

Oh, good grief, she thought, the man was married. She'd never even considered the possibility, which was really dumb on her part.

How mortifying! She'd had sensual dreams about this...this husband and father. She was so embarrassed she could just die right there on the spot.

No, now wait a minute. Daniel didn't know about her…her wanton dreams and…if she got her act together in the next three seconds, she could pull this off with him being none the wiser.

"Yes," she said, "that certainly is a baby, isn't it? A girl, I think. She's very cute. Looks just like you with her dark hair and eyes and…does she have a name? Well, of course, she has a name. All babies have names. What's her name?"

She was babbling like a moron, Jessica thought dismally. So much for trying to recover with class.

"Her name is Tessa," Daniel said. "Would you like to come in, Jessica?"

No, thanks, she thought sheepishly. She was just going to scoot on home, jump into bed, pull the covers over her head and not emerge for five years. She had lusted in her heart about a married man!

"Certainly," she said, walking into the living room. She wiggled one of Tessa's pajama-clad feet as she zoomed past the baby and Daniel. "Hi, Tessa. How old are you, sweetie pie?"

"She's seven months and she's very grumpy because she's teething," Daniel said.

He closed the door and turned to look at Jessica where she stood in the center of the room. "I know you come from a very large family," he said, "because I've seen articles about the MacAllisters in the newspapers over the years. You must be a real expert on babies. What's your take on one that's teething?"

"They're grumpy," Jessica said.

"No joke," Daniel said, frowning. "I've already

figured out that much. Do you know what I can do to make her more comfortable?''

''I assume it was necessary for us to meet here this evening because you're on baby-sitting duty,'' Jessica said. ''Didn't your wife leave you any helpful hints about what to do before she went out for the evening?''

''I'm not married,'' Daniel said. ''I've been divorced for a good many years, in fact.''

Jessica frowned. ''Then whose baby is that?''

''Mine. I have custody of Tessa. We're a family, just the two of us. I have a live-in nanny who tends to Tessa, but it's the nanny's night off so...'' He shook his head. ''I forgot to ask her what to do for Tessa's teething problem before she left.''

''Oh, I see,'' Jessica said, nodding. But she really didn't. Why did Daniel have custody of Tessa? Was he the baby's father? Where was her mother? Well, there was only one way to find out the answers to her questions. ''Is Tessa your daughter?''

''No.'' Daniel paused. ''Well, yeah, now she is. I'm not her biological father, but I'm her...her dad and she's my...kid. Yes, I guess you could say she's my daughter...now.''

''I'm totally confused,'' Jessica said. ''Where's her mother?''

Daniel's jaw tightened slightly. ''I'd rather not get into all that tonight. It's...complicated and...no, not tonight. Look, we're not going to get started on that grant application if I don't figure out some way to calm this kid down. If I don't hold her, she wails loud enough to be heard in Chicago.''

Jessica set her heavy briefcase on the floor. ''Don't you have any teething toys?''

''What do they look like?'' Daniel said, then cocked his head slightly to one side. ''That sweater you're wearing is the exact same shade as your eyes.''

''It is? Well, my, my, isn't that interesting?''

''You look very nice, Jessica,'' he said. ''Anyway, back to the teeth.''

''Teeth,'' Jessica echoed, still savoring the warmth that had tiptoed around her heart as she gathered in Daniel's compliment. ''Oh. Yes. Tessa's teeth that are trying to pop into existence. Poor baby. Give her to me, then go look in the refrigerator and freezer and see if there are any plastic toys in there.''

''In the refrigerator?'' Daniel said incredulously.

''Trust me,'' Jessica said, reaching out her arms for the baby.

''Whatever,'' he muttered, then placed Tessa into Jessica's embrace and strode across the room.

Jessica snuggled the baby close, and filled her senses with the wonderful scent of a baby fresh from her bath.

''Who are you?'' she whispered to the infant. ''Why are you here? Oh, I wish you could talk, Tessa, because it's very apparent that your...your daddy is not about to share that information with me tonight. You, sweet baby, are a mystery waiting to be solved.''

Chapter 3

Daniel found several teething toys in a plastic bag in the refrigerator, all of which Tessa rejected with wails that increased in volume with each offering.

She also refused to have anything to do with her bottle, pushing it away as Daniel attempted to pop the nipple into her mouth.

He finally placed the baby on a quilt on the floor and planted his hands on his hips as he frowned at her.

"Now what?" he said, loud enough for Jessica to hear him over Tessa's crying. He shifted his gaze to Jessica. "That noise should be considered a tool to interrogate the bad guys at the station. They'd be willing to spill it big time just to have that screeching stopped. What in the hell am I supposed to do for her?"

"Don't swear in front of a baby, Daniel," Jessica said. "You never know what they're storing up in their tiny minds." She lifted Tessa into her arms and jiggled her as she patted her on the back. "There, there. Calm down. I'd sing to you, but that would probably scare you to death."

Tessa stiffened and hollered even louder.

"But I'm desperate," Jessica said.

She began to walk around the living room, crooning a very off-key rendition of "Twinkle, Twinkle, Little Star." Daniel slouched onto the sofa and watched the pair, his frown still firmly in place.

As Jessica trekked, she scrutinized Daniel's living room, deciding she liked his choices of large, puffy furniture upholstered in earth tones with oak tables as accessories. The room definitely had a masculine flair, but that stood to reason since Daniel was an extremely masculine man.

Don't go there, she ordered herself. The last thing she needed was to start dwelling on Daniel Quinn's masculine magnetism. Her hope that Daniel would appear as just another man fizzled the moment he'd opened the door and she'd catalogued every blatantly sexual inch of him.

"You don't like that song, Tessa?" she said. "Okay, let's try 'The Bear Went Over the Mountain.'"

Tessa definitely didn't like the ditty about the dumb bear, nor the one where the baby, cradle and all, came crashing down from the tree, which Daniel said sure sounded like child abuse to him, and didn't Jessica know lullabies that weren't so violent? Jessica glared at him.

"Okay, Daddy," she said twenty minutes later, "it's your turn. My arms are aching because this kiddo is no lightweight. She's starting to get tired because she's rubbing her eyes. *You* walk her for a while."

Daniel got to his feet and took the screaming baby from Jessica.

"If she's so tired, why does she still have the energy to holler her head off?" he said, tucking Tessa in the crook of one arm.

"If I knew the answer to that one," Jessica said, sinking onto the marshmallow-soft sofa, "I'd be the wealthy woman who solved the mystery that began at the beginning of babies." She flapped one hand in the air. "Walk. She gets louder if you stand still. Go."

"Cripe," Daniel said, then started across the room.

His singing was even more off-key than Jessica's and his choice of "A Hundred Bottles of Beer on the Wall" caused her to roll her eyes heavenward.

When Daniel counted down to seventy-five bottles of beer, Tessa took a shuddering breath, poked her thumb in her mouth, and fell asleep.

An almost eerie silence fell over the room.

Daniel stopped and stared at the baby, Jessica, then back at Tessa.

"Now what?" he whispered.

Jessica got to her feet and matched his whisper

when she spoke. "Don't make any sudden moves," she said. "Where's her bedroom?"

"Down the hall on the left."

"Okay," she said, nodding. "Is there a night-light in there?"

Daniel nodded.

"I'll walk in front of you and turn it on," Jessica said, still whispering. "You bring her, but whatever you do, don't jostle her awake, or I will personally strangle you with my bare hands."

"Got it."

The nursery was a feminine delight decorated in pink and white. Daniel eased Tessa into the crib, then slowly, very slowly, slid his arms from beneath her. Jessica stood next to him, hardly breathing, as they both stared at the peacefully sleeping baby.

"She's so beautiful," Jessica said.

"Yeah, she's cute for someone who has lungs like a linebacker," Daniel said, dragging both hands down his face. "Man, she wiped me out. How do people with three or four kids survive?"

"Shh," Jessica said, tiptoeing toward the bedroom door. "Shh, shh, shh."

Back in the living room they sank onto the sofa, rested their heads on the top, and stared at the ceiling.

"I'm exhausted," Daniel said.

"So am I," Jessica said.

Daniel chuckled and Jessica turned her head to look at him, ignoring the heat that had traveled down her spine as she heard the oh-so-sexy sound.

"What's funny?" she said.

"The fact that a tiny bundle like that can totally blitz two adults," he said, smiling as he met Jessica's gaze. "It's amazing. Ridiculous, but amazing."

"True," Jessica said, laughing.

They continued to look directly into each other's eyes, their smiles fading slowly as the humor they found in the situation began to shift to a different plane.

It was a sensuous place that drew them in and seemed to encase them in a misty sphere that literally crackled with sexuality, acute awareness and heat...a burning heat deep, and hot within them.

Jessica's heart quickened, and a trickle of sweat ran down Daniel's chest.

Dear heaven, Jessica thought, what was happening, what was Daniel doing to her? She'd never experienced anything like this before. It was frightening... and exciting...and very, very dangerous. She had to leave here...now. Go home...now. Tear her gaze from Daniel's mesmerizing dark eyes...right now.

But she couldn't move! Could hardly breathe and...oh, God, now Daniel was lifting one hand and extending it toward her face. He was going to touch her with strength she just somehow knew was going to be tempered with infinite gentleness.

No! her mind hammered.

"No," she said, then got to her feet, immediately aware that her legs were trembling.

Daniel blinked, shook his head slightly, then rose to stand in front of Jessica.

"Jessica…" he started.

"No," she said, slicing one hand through the air. "Don't say my name. Don't say anything." She glanced at her watch. "It's getting late. We'll have to work on the grant application another time. I've got to go before…I have to leave now."

"You've got to go before…what?" Daniel said, staring at her intently. "Before I kiss you and you kiss me back because that's what you wanted a minute ago as much as I did? Before that happens, Jessica?"

"Daniel, don't," she said, hearing the shaky quality of her voice. "Just…don't. I can't explain what just took place between us. I have never felt anything so…but it's best forgotten, ignored, as though it never happened."

Daniel shoved his hands into the back pockets of his jeans. "Why?"

"Do you always ask so many questions?" Jessica said.

"I'm a detective, remember?" he said, smiling. "I'm set on an automatic question-asking mode."

"Well, go detect somewhere else," Jessica said crossly, "because I'm not playing this game."

Daniel's smile turned into a deep frown. "Let's get something straight right now. I don't play games, Jessica. Yeah, sure, I perform the good-cop-bad-cop bit with Mick when we're interrogating someone and we think it will work. But in my personal life? With women? No. I don't play games. Never."

"Fine. However, I'm not a woman." Jessica

sighed. "Oh, for Pete's sake. What I mean is, you're speaking of women you're romantically involved with, I assume. You and I are meeting only to secure funds for The Peaceful Dove. I am not, therefore, for all practical purposes, a woman, in the sense that you're referring to."

"Do they teach you to talk like that in law school? Or are you lawyers just born that way?" Daniel pulled his hands free of his pockets and crossed his arms over his chest. "I've often wondered about that. You attorneys don't speak in sentences, you deliver entire paragraphs at the drop of a hat."

"Ah, yes," Jessica said, nodding. "Now you're being the Daniel Quinn I remember so well from our meeting on Saturday night. Rude."

Daniel raised both hands in a gesture of peace. "Sorry. I apologize if I was rude. Okay? Good. Now, let's get back to the subject. Why should we ignore our physical attraction? We're normal, healthy adults, so…"

"Let's have sex?" Jessica interrupted.

"Damn it, I didn't say that," Daniel said, nearly shouting.

"Keep it up, Quinn," Jessica said, with a burst of laughter. "Go right ahead and wake Tessa. I, however, am going home before I have to listen to you demolish seventy-five more bottles of beer on the wall."

"Oh, cripe," Daniel said, looking quickly in the direction of the hallway leading to the baby's bedroom. "Do you hear her? Do you think I blew it?"

Jessica listened intently for a moment. "No, all is quiet on the western front, or whatever direction her bedroom is in." She paused. "Well, I must be going."

"Wait a minute," Daniel said. "You're avoiding the subject under discussion here, Ms. MacAllister. I still want to know why you believe we should ignore the attraction...and that word doesn't even cut it... between us. And don't say it's because you're not a woman, because, lady, you are most definitely a woman."

Jessica sighed. "Yes, I'm a woman. Yes, I am attracted to you. Yes, I wanted to kiss you and wanted you to return that kiss. But the truth of the matter is, I simply don't have the time, nor the desire, to become involved with anyone right now. I feel as though I'm burning the candle at both ends as it is without complicating my life further. Is that clear enough?"

"Ladies and gentlemen of the jury," Daniel said, flinging out his arms, "are you buying this spiel?"

"Consider it bought, Quinn," she said, "because that's the way it is. End of story. I wouldn't think you'd be interested in adding anything more to your life at the moment, either. I mean, heavens, you have a very demanding career, and you're a single father trying to figure out what makes your baby tick. Isn't that enough on your plate?"

Daniel opened his mouth to reply in the negative, hesitated, then pursed his lips and nodded slowly.

"You're right, I suppose," he said. "I've had

Tessa for four months and all I've learned is how to heat a bottle and change a diaper. Her nanny can tell what's wrong with Tessa by the way she cries, for Pete's sake, but I'll never figure that out.''

"Sure you will...in time," Jessica said.

"I doubt it." Daniel paused and ran his hand over the back of his neck. "Hell, speaking of a full plate, the nanny just gave me two weeks' notice because a relative of hers is ill and she has to go take care of her. Isn't that dandy? Do you know anyone who qualifies as a nanny who is looking for work?''

"No," Jessica said thoughtfully, "but I have a large extended family, remember? I'll put the word out among the MacAllister clan for you.''

"Thanks. I'd appreciate that.''

"No problem," she said, smiling.

Their gazes met again. The heat sizzled again. Hearts raced again.

"Must go," Jessica said, taking a step backward. "Where's my briefcase? Oh, there it is. Yes. Well, before we meet again to tackle the grant application, I'll hopefully have had time to study some of the books I have on the proper way to do this project.''

"Could I take a look at that reference material for a minute?" Daniel said.

"Well, sure, if you want to.''

Jessica retrieved her briefcase and set it on the sofa. She snapped it open, lifted the lid, and swept her arm through the air.

"There you go," she said. "I wonder if these au-

thors got grants to finance writing books on how to
apply for grants?''

"Mmm," Daniel said, taking each book out and
placing them on the sofa. After looking at all the titles, he repacked the briefcase. "They're probably
fine, but that's a lot of information to plow through."

"I know," Jessica said with a weary sigh.

"I'll be right back," Daniel said, starting across
the room.

"What..." Jessica started, then shrugged as Daniel
disappeared from view.

She wrapped her hands around her elbows and
tapped one foot as she waited for Daniel to return.
Her glance fell on the sofa cushions where she and
Daniel had sat after putting Tessa to bed. She *had*
wanted Daniel to kiss her, she thought. She'd been so
consumed with that incredible heat, with desire, with
the want of that man, the burning need to feel his lips
capture hers and—

Jessica closed her eyes for a moment and shook
her head.

Oh, he was dangerous, this Lieutenant Quinn. Being in close proximity to him caused her to behave
like a Jessica MacAllister she hadn't even known existed. For all she knew, she'd been a breath away
from tearing off her clothes and yelling, "Take me.
I'm yours!"

"Here we go," Daniel said, as he came back into
the living room.

Jessica jerked in surprise at the sudden sound of
his voice.

"Did I wake you?" Daniel said, smiling.

"No, I...never mind. What is that?" she said, nodding toward the inch-thick paperback book he was holding.

"This, my dear Ms. MacAllister," Daniel said, appearing very pleased with himself, "is the magic formula. It's the only reference needed to apply for a grant and get the money...guaranteed." He laughed. "What's really amazing is that I kept it and could actually find it."

"I don't understand."

"Several years ago," Daniel said, "my captain volunteered me to be on a public relations committee. I represented the cops, and along with a firefighter, parole officer and social worker, we were to apply for a grant for funds to turn an inner-city vacant lot into a playground. We had a stack of books like those you have, and then we found this pamphlet. This little beauty did the trick. It's all we'll need to get the job done. We were approved in less than a month, but it can take much longer if they're really busy. Anyway, this pamphlet is the magic wand."

Jessica's eyes widened. "Are you serious?"

"Yes, ma'am."

"Oh, Daniel, this is fantastic. Let me see it. I can't believe this."

"Believe it," he said. "We got our money and the playground is still filled with kids every time I drive by it. I definitely deserve a reward." He tapped one cheek with a fingertip. "Plant one right here."

Jessica hesitated for a second, then closed the dis-

tance between them and stood on tiptoe to give Daniel
a quick kiss on the cheek.

At the exact moment that her lips brushed his face,
he turned his head and captured her mouth with his.
He dropped the pamphlet to the floor, wrapped his
arms around her and nestled her close to him as he
deepened the kiss.

No! Jessica thought, stiffening in Daniel's arms.
She didn't want Daniel to…but then again…no…
but…oh…dear…heaven…yes.

Jessica's arms floated upward to encircle Daniel's
neck and she returned the kiss in total abandon, blank-
ing her mind and just savoring the taste, the feel, the
aroma of Daniel.

The kiss was ecstasy. The kiss was heat rekindled
into raging flames that consumed them. The kiss was
real, and earthy and rough.

And then the kiss was over.

Daniel raised his head slowly, reluctantly, but kept
Jessica pressed against his aroused body. He drew a
ragged breath and looked directly into her eyes, seeing the smoky hue of desire that he knew was reflected in his own eyes. Jessica's lips were moist and
slightly parted and her cheeks were flushed.

Beautiful, Daniel thought hazily. And he wanted
her. He wanted to make love with her through the
entire night, wanted to wake up next to her in the
morning, to reach for her again and—

Daniel cleared his throat and eased Jessica away
from him. She blinked, then took an extra step backward, tearing her gaze from Daniel's to concentrate

on straightening the waistband of her sweater over her jeans.

"I knew it would be like that," Daniel said, his voice raspy. "Sensational."

"Yes," Jessica whispered, then raised her head to look at him again. "Yes, it was. I could rant and rave in anger and say you tricked me, then forced me to…but I won't because that's not really true. I was an equal partner in that kiss and I'll admit I wanted it to happen as much as you did."

"For the record," Daniel said quietly, "I didn't set you up when I said to kiss me on the cheek. I told you I don't play games, Jessica. But there you were, close to me, so damn enticing and… I guess the question is, so now what?"

"So now…nothing. Neither of us has time to devote to…to a relationship, an affair." Jessica shook her head. "And I don't do one-night stands. So now…nothing."

Daniel looked at her for a long moment.

"We'll see," he finally said.

A wave of fatigue suddenly swept through Jessica and she realized she didn't have the energy to challenge Daniel's statement. She was exhausted and just wanted to go home.

She retrieved the pamphlet from the floor, placed it in the briefcase and snapped the latches closed. "Now that I have your magic formula book," she said, dragging the heavy briefcase off the sofa, "I imagine I can complete the grant application myself."

"No," Daniel said quickly and a tad too loudly.

"What I mean is, I said I'd help and I will. We'll stick to our plan of doing this together. You could study the pamphlet in the meantime, of course, and I'll contact you about meeting again to..." His voice trailed off.

"Don't ever get on my case again about speaking in lengthy paragraphs," Jessica said, rolling her eyes heavenward. "You were babbling, Lieutenant."

Jessica started toward the door with Daniel right behind her.

"Yeah, okay, so I got a little carried away," he said, "but do you agree not to submit the application until I have a chance to see it?"

"Yes, all right." Jessica gripped the doorknob. "Good night, Daniel."

"Jessica," Daniel said, his voice low and rumbly, "look at me."

"No."

"Please."

Without releasing her hold on the doorknob, Jessica half turned to meet Daniel's gaze, her heart fluttering as she saw the raw desire in his dark, dark eyes.

Before Daniel could speak, an earsplitting wail reverberated through the air, causing him to cringe.

"Ah," Jessica said, smiling, "your master's voice. Enjoy the seventy-five bottles of beer you have left on the wall."

"Hell," Daniel said, his shoulders slumping. "I can't handle this."

"Sure you can," Jessica said breezily, as she opened the door. "It just takes practice, practice,

practice, and Tessa obviously intends to see that you get plenty of that. Ta-ta, Lieutenant."

As the door clicked shut behind Jessica, Daniel didn't move. He stared at the door and allowed himself the luxury of reliving the kiss he'd shared with her to the point that heat coiled low and painfully in his body.

Tessa cried louder.

"I'm coming, I'm coming," he said, trudging toward the hallway. "I wish I really did have seventy-five bottles of beer in the refrigerator. Teeth. Whoever would have believed that tiny little baby teeth could cause so much trouble?"

Daniel changed Tessa's diaper and fed her, then she fell asleep again when the bottles of beer on the wall numbered twenty-two. He eased the baby gently into her crib, covered her with a blanket, and literally tiptoed from the bedroom, feeling like a thief skulking in the night.

When he returned to the living room, he stretched out on the sofa, resting his head on the arm. This time the remembrance of the kiss shared with Jessica made an unwelcomed appearance in his mind and he frowned.

He really hadn't intended to kiss Jessica, he thought. He'd just been messing around when he'd told her to reward him with a peck on the cheek. It was something his mother had done when he and his sister were kids after she'd baked them chocolate chip cookies, or let them stay up late as a special treat. Thank you, Mama, they'd say, and she'd smile and tap her cheek with a fingertip as she said, ''Plant one right here for my thank-you, my sweeties.''

No, he hadn't been pulling a fast one on Jessica. But when she'd been so tantalizingly close to him, he'd lost it. His self-control went south and he'd been kissing her before he realized he was doing it.

And then he hadn't wanted to stop.

The now familiar heat rocketed throughout Daniel's body and he groaned and dragged both hands down his face.

He didn't know what it was about Jessica Mac-Allister that threw him so off-kilter. He couldn't remember ever being turned inside out by a woman the way he was by her.

Why? Why her? Why Jessica?

Hell, he didn't know.

Yeah, sure, she was pretty. No, correct that. She was beautiful, really exquisite. And intelligent. Had a sense of humor. She liked Tessa and probably went nuts over kittens and puppies, too. But, hell, a lot of women had those attributes.

So why did he want to make love with Jessica so badly that he went up in flames at the mere thought? And why had he nearly tripped over his own tongue to get across that he still wanted to be included in the completion of the grant application? He knew damn well that Jessica no longer needed his help because the book he'd given her spelled everything out, step-by-step, loud and clear.

So much for being a totally together guy, a man in control of his person. He was a complete wreck.

Chapter 4

Two evenings later while the swinging singles of Ventura were out seeking fun on a Friday night, Jessica sat curled up in the corner of her sofa reading the pamphlet Daniel had given her.

She'd spent a long day in court in a custody battle that now awaited the decision of the judge, and had come home to her apartment to soak in a long, relaxing bubble bath. After slipping on her comfortable, rose-colored velour robe that covered her from fingertips to toes, she'd prepared a dinner of salad, toast and cup of cinnamon tea.

Once the kitchen was again spotless, she put easy-listening music on the stereo, snuggled into the corner of the sofa that was upholstered in bright colored flowers, and began to read the information.

A short while later Jessica closed the pamphlet,

gave it a pat and slipped it onto the coffee table front-
ing the sofa. "Excellent material," she said aloud.
"I'm ready to start filling out the grant application."

She didn't have to wait until she could meet with
Daniel again.

But she wanted to.

"Oh, Jessica," she said, pressing her fingertips to
her temples, "you're hopeless."

If she had a dollar for every time she'd thought
about Daniel Quinn in the past forty-eight hours,
she'd probably have enough money to go on a luxury
cruise. She'd relived that exquisite, desire-evoking
kiss over and over, causing flashes of heat to consume
her during each replay.

Her preoccupation with Daniel had long since gone
beyond ridiculous and was now in the stage of bor-
derline crazy. She really was behaving like an adolescent with a hormone rush.

Jessica sighed, raised her arms above her head in
a stretch, then glanced at the small clock on the end
table, her eyes widening in surprise as she saw that it
was already eleven o'clock.

Fine, she thought, getting to her feet. She would
watch the late local news on television and keep her
mind on current affairs instead of on Lieutenant
Quinn. The sinfully, ruggedly handsome Daniel. The
Daniel who kissed like a dream and caused her to be
consumed with a heated want and need like nothing
she'd experienced before in her entire life.

Jessica turned off the stereo, pressed the remote to

bring the television alive, then sat back down on the sofa, yawning as she sank into the plush cushions.

"Good evening, Ventura," a pretty anchorwoman said, smiling.

"Hi," Jessica said, waving one hand breezily in the air and yawning again.

She shifted lower on the sofa, and watched the screen through half-closed eyes as she vaguely registered that the city council had approved funding for a much-disputed sculpture that was to be placed in one of the city parks. A picture of the artwork appeared on the screen.

"Weird," Jessica mumbled.

"In other news," the anchorwoman went on, "the citizens of Ventura can rest easier tonight. A man has been arrested and confessed to the brutal murder of businessman R. W. Benson whose body was discovered last week in a canal. We have an interview taped earlier today with Lieutenant Daniel Quinn of the Homicide Division of the Ventura Police Department."

Jessica sat bolt upright on the sofa, wide awake again as Daniel filled the screen. He was standing on the steps of the police station and a reporter had a microphone pointed toward him. Jessica leaned forward, her gaze riveted on Daniel.

He looked exhausted, she thought, frowning. His tie was pulled down a few inches, he had a stubble of beard on his face and dark smudges of fatigue beneath his eyes. His hair, that gorgeous, black, sink-your-fingers-into-it hair, was tousled as though he'd been dragging a restless hand through it.

"There was nothing fancy about it," Daniel was saying. "It was just plain old-fashioned police work. My partner, Sergeant Mick Smith, and I checked, rechecked, and checked again every scrap of evidence we had until the puzzle came together. As the saying goes, we got our man."

"And the motive for the murder?" the reporter said.

"Drug money," Daniel said, frowning. "The man in custody has signed a confession and the rest is up to the District Attorney's staff."

"It's my understanding that you took the time to call on the widow of the victim to inform her that her husband's killer was behind bars," the reporter said. "Is that correct, Lieutenant?"

Daniel nodded. "She deserved to have as much closure on this tragedy as we could give her."

"Thank you for your time, Lieutenant," the reporter said. "I'm sure that the citizens of Ventura join me in expressing gratitude for your diligence in solving this horrendous crime."

The scene switched again to the anchorwoman who began to give background information on the man now in custody.

Jessica sank back on the sofa and pressed one hand to her racing heart.

Oh, good grief, she thought, she was in worse shape than she'd imagined. The image of Daniel on a television screen had sent her body into a tizzy. Even tired and disheveled he was so blatantly, sensuously male it sent her into a tailspin and brought the remembrance of the kiss they'd shared front row center in her mind.

There would be no one waiting for Daniel when he returned home. No one to rush into his embrace, tell him how grateful she was that he was safe and was there with her once again. No one to prepare him a meal and sit with him while he unwound from the tension of the past days.

Would he be too exhausted to fix himself something to eat? Would he toss and turn in bed, unable to relax and get the sleep he so desperately needed? Would Daniel Quinn be lonely?

"Jessica MacAllister," she said, jumping to her feet, "you are totally bonkers."

She pressed the remote to turn off the television, snapped off the lamp, and went to her bedroom, having no trouble maneuvering the familiar path despite the darkness. A short time later she lay in bed, staring up at a ceiling she couldn't see.

Well, dandy, she fumed, now she was wide-awake. *She* would probably be the one to toss and turn all night while Daniel slept as peacefully as baby Tessa.

Oh-h-h, she was furious at herself. She'd created a scenario in her mind that could qualify as a silly soap opera. The big, strong, handsome hero comes home to face four walls taunting him with his aloneness. Hungry, exhausted and miserable, he shuffles to a bed that literally screams its emptiness and spends a seemingly endless night yearning for the woman of his dreams to be nestled close to him, his heart aching.

"Aakk," Jessica yelled, covering her face with her hands. "I'm certifiably insane."

She rolled onto her stomach, punched her pillow into a fluffy ball, then dropped her head onto it, closing her eyes. Three seconds later her eyes popped open again, and she flopped onto her back.

"Sleep," she ordered herself, tapping her forehead with a fingertip. "Right now."

An hour later, out of desperation, Jessica began to mentally sing "A Hundred Bottles of Beer on the Wall." She finally drifted off into a restless slumber, leaving eighteen bottles of beer behind.

On Saturday morning, Daniel woke in an upbeat mood after a rejuvenating ten hours of dreamless sleep. He showered, shaved, dressed and headed for the kitchen, his stomach rumbling in agreement with his mind that it was time for food.

As he crossed the living room he stopped dead in his tracks when he saw two large suitcases and a shopping bag sitting by the door.

"Uh-oh," he said, frowning as he went into the kitchen. "Mary?"

A plump woman in her mid-fifties looked up from where she sat in front of a high chair feeding Tessa her breakfast.

"Oh, Lieutenant Quinn," Mary said, getting to her feet, "I've been waiting for you. I didn't want to waken you because I know how hard you've been working and…well, you see, my great-aunt has taken a turn for the worse and I must go to her immediately.

"There's no one but me to care for her and if I don't go, she'll be placed in a nursing home. There's no reason for that to happen since I'm willing to tend to her and...I'm so sorry to just leave you and Tessa like this, but I have no choice."

Daniel's cheerful state of mind crashed and burned, and he frowned as he hooked one hand over the back of his neck.

"Sure," he said, "I understand, Mary. Family comes first and that's the way it should be. I'll get you a check so you can be on your way."

"Thank you so much. You're very kind," Mary said, then glanced at her watch. "Yes, I must be going. I have a plane to catch. I want you to know that I've enjoyed working for you, Lieutenant, and Tessa is such a sweet baby. You won't have any trouble finding another nanny because one look at this little sweetheart and someone will be eager to care for her."

"Yeah, right," Daniel muttered. "I'll get your check and be right back."

A short time later Mary was gone and Daniel was spooning cereal and fruit into Tessa's mouth, then scraping it off her chin and pushing it back in as the baby smacked her hands happily on the high chair tray.

"We're in deep trouble, kid," Daniel said, shoveling in another spoonful of applesauce. "The agency where I found Mary doesn't have anyone for me to interview right now." He paused. "Would you mind looking a little upset by this crisis?"

Tessa grabbed the sticky spoon from Daniel's hand and plopped it on top of her head, laughing merrily.

"Ah, cripe," Daniel said, retrieving the spoon. "Jessica MacAllister, if you're still sleeping, wake up, call everyone in that big family of yours and find me a nanny. Fast."

That was dumb, he admonished himself, as he wiped Tessa's hair with a wet paper towel. He'd managed to go almost twenty-four hours without thinking about Jessica since he'd been so busy at the station.

So what did he do? Like an idiot, he just up and said her name out loud, which immediately produced a vivid image of her in his mind's eye.

And with that picture came the remembrance of the kiss they'd shared. That incredible kiss that had created a heated, aching want of Jessica deep within him with an intensity like nothing he'd experienced before.

Why, damn it, did that woman push his sexual buttons like this?

Daniel deposited Tessa in the playpen, then searched through the refrigerator for something to fix for his own breakfast.

Maybe he was making too big a deal out of this, he mused, as he scrambled some eggs. Maybe it wasn't Jessica who was tying him up in knots. Maybe it had simply been a helluva long time since he'd been with a woman.

Yeah, that made sense. It stood to reason that any reasonably attractive female he was in close proximity to for a length of time would set off sparks in him.

But...

Just *any* woman wouldn't have big, chocolate-brown expressive eyes and golden hair that was making his fingers itch to untangle it from the braid she wore and sift his hands through it. Just *any* woman wouldn't, he somehow knew, send him up in flames by returning his kiss with sensual abandon. Just *any* woman wouldn't nestle against him as though custom-made only for him.

Just *any* woman wouldn't be Jessica.

The odor of burning eggs brought Daniel back to the moment at hand and he swore as he yanked the frying pan off the burner on the stove.

The eggs went into the trash and he settled for a bowl of cereal, six slices of toast and a cup of coffee.

He had agreed with Jessica, Daniel mused, as he ate the dull meal, that he was in no position, nor was she, to become involved in any kind of a relationship. But acceptance of that fact hadn't done one damn thing to keep Jessica MacAllister out of his thoughts, or extinguish the simmering desire for her that was always present deep and low within him, driving him right up the wall.

No, his theory of having been too long without a woman didn't cut it. It was Jessica, herself, who was hanging him out to dry and he wanted to know why. Maybe, just maybe, if he could solve the mystery of how she was capable of continually casting the strange, sensuous spell around him, he would be able to dismiss it, and her, and that, by damn, would be that.

* * *

Daniel tended to Tessa on his own the remainder of Saturday and was so exhausted by ten o'clock that night he fell onto his bed fully dressed and didn't stir again until the baby wailed the arrival of Sunday morning.

On Sunday afternoon he pleaded his case to Rosemary, Mick's wife. She agreed, after dissolving in laughter over Daniel's frazzled state, then regaining her composure, to baby-sit Tessa for several hours while Mick and Daniel went to the station to finish the paperwork on the arrest that had made the local news.

Mick was still grumbling as he settled onto his chair at the desk next to Daniel's in the squad room. "This could have waited until tomorrow, Danny," Mick said. "I was planning on having a full day at home with my family for a change."

"I owe you one," Daniel said. "I figured I had a better chance of Rosemary agreeing to tend to Tessa if I said we really had to get this stuff to the District Attorney's office. Take pity on me, man, I'm totally worn-out. That kid has me jumping through hoops. Teeth. I will never again think kind thoughts about little tiny teeth."

Mick laughed and shook his head. "Rosemary knew you were blowing smoke, buddy. I'd already told her I was free all day, but since she planned to visit her mother and knew I didn't want to go, she let me off the hook."

"Oh."

"You shouldn't be here typing," Mick went on,

"you should be out beating the bushes for a new nanny."

"On a Sunday?" Daniel said. "None of the agencies are open today. Besides, I'm hoping that Jessica will come through, that someone in her family will know of a nanny who is looking for work."

"Jessica?" Mick frowned, then raised his eyebrows in the next instant. "Jessica from The Peaceful Dove? *That* Jessica?"

"Yeah," Daniel said, peering at the computer screen on his desk. "We...we got together at my place to tackle the grant application. Well, that was the plan, but Tessa's teeth had other ideas. Anyway, Jessica comes from a big family and...you know, *the* MacAllisters that have been written up in the newspapers time and again for various stuff, and she's going to see if any of that clan knows a nanny."

"Amazing," Mick said, chuckling.

Daniel looked at his partner. "What is?"

"You. And women," Mick said. "I was at The Peaceful Dove, remember? That lady was ready to do you bodily harm. Now? She's going to take time out of her busy schedule to canvass her family to find you a nanny. Yep. Amazing."

"Give it a rest, Smith," Daniel said. "You make it sound like I have women falling at my feet and climbing into my bed."

Mick nodded thoughtfully. "That about covers it, I'd say."

"Knock it off," Daniel said, glaring at Mick. "Jessica MacAllister and I are partners on a project."

"Right," Mick said, with a burst of laughter. "And

you didn't even notice that she is one very attractive female because you were so focused on that grant application, or Tessa's teeth, or something.''

''Well,'' Daniel said, lifting one shoulder in a shrug, ''sure, Jessica MacAllister is pretty...beautiful, actually...and those big brown eyes of hers are...and her lips...forget lips. I'm not having this discussion. Just type, damn it, and quit talking to me.''

Mick hooted with laughter. Daniel glowered at him. Then they both began their hunt-and-peck two-finger style of typing.

On Monday morning, Lieutenant Daniel Quinn arrived at the detective's squad room of the Ventura Police Department with a diaper bag hooked over one shoulder as he pushed Tessa in a stroller.

The big, strong, tough detectives who were on duty were immediately reduced to grinning, baby-talking softies who jostled for a turn to entertain the darling infant, who was obviously enjoying all the attention she was receiving.

With Tessa happy and very occupied, Daniel sank onto the chair behind his desk and dialed the number of Jessica's office, absently realizing that he knew it by heart. He drummed his fingers immediately on the desktop as the ringing started on the other end of the line.

''Cavelli and MacAllister. May I help you?''

A bolt of heat rocketed through Daniel as he heard Jessica's voice instead of the secretary he'd expected to answer the telephone. He shot a quick glance at the other men and women in the squad room, having the irrational thought that they might be able to detect the reaction he'd had to the sound of Jessica's greeting.

"Hello?" Jessica said. "Is anyone there?"

"This is Daniel Quinn, Jessica."

She knew that, Jessica thought, pressing one hand to a suddenly flushed cheek. From the top of her head to the tip of her toes, she was extremely aware that this deep male voice belonged to Daniel.

She cleared her throat and sat up straighter in her chair.

"Good morning, Daniel," she said.

"Where's your secretary?" he said gruffly.

Jessica frowned in confusion. "You want to speak with the secretary?"

"No, no, I was just wondering where she was, why you answered the phone."

"Oh," she said. "Mary-Clair and I use temps when we get really snowed under, but we should be able to hire a full-time secretary very soon."

"Mary-Clair Cavelli," Daniel said, smiling. "Your partner is definitely Italian. My mother was Italian."

That explained Daniel's thick, yummy black hair, dark, dark eyes and tawny skin, Jessica thought rather dreamily, then blinked and shook her head slightly.

"Was?" she said.

"My parents are deceased and so is my..." Daniel's voice trailed off.

"Daniel?" Jessica said, frowning.

"My sister," he said, a rough edge to his voice. "My sister, Karen, is deceased. Dead. She died. Karen was...she was Tessa's mother."

"Oh, Daniel, I'm so sorry," Jessica said, her eyes widening in shock. "Was it an accident, or was your sister ill? Was she married?"

"Her husband is dead, too. Tessa and I are it, a family, just the two of us. She looks so much like Karen it's like the clock has been turned back to when I was ten and had a new baby sister who…hell, forget all this. I don't know who put a nickel in me."

"Thank you for sharing with me, Daniel," Jessica said softly. "I really am so very sorry about your sister and her husband."

"Her husband isn't worth feeling badly about," Daniel said. "Not for a second. Look, I know you're busy and there's a reason for this call besides giving you my life history."

"Oh?"

"Tessa's nanny quit," Daniel said, dragging a restless hand through his hair. "She's gone already, because her relative took a turn for the worse. I was hoping you'd had a chance to check with all your MacAllisters and see if anyone knows of a nanny who might be available for me to hire right away."

"Yes," Jessica said, "I did ask the troops, but no one knows any nannies. However, my cousin, Patty, said… Well, she isn't really my cousin but we grew up together and I call her parents aunt and uncle because…" She sighed. "Never mind all that. Patty said she would baby-sit Tessa for you during the day until you could find a nanny. Patty has a year-old son, Tucker, and stays home with him."

"That's terrific," Daniel said.

"Well, not exactly," Jessica went on, "because I

thought your nanny wasn't leaving for two weeks. Patty, her husband, Peter, and the baby left last night for Chicago to have an early Christmas with Peter's parents. They won't be back until Saturday morning.''

Daniel sank back in his chair. "Hell."

"What did you do with Tessa today?"

"I brought her to work with me," Daniel said. "Everyone is having a grand old time, but it would lose its cuteness if I did it again tomorrow." He paused. "Listen, I really appreciate your going to the trouble to contact your family about this and I'm very grateful to Patty for being willing to care for Tessa until the agency finds me another nanny. I'll figure out something for this week. I have some vacation time coming, but..." He chuckled.

"What's funny?" Jessica said, ignoring the frisson of heat that slithered down her spine as she heard the rumbly sound.

"I don't believe I can survive a week of taking care of Tessa all day," Daniel said. "The kid wipes me out. Totally." His smile changed into a frown. "I don't think she likes me much. She stiffens up when I hold her and...I don't know."

"She probably senses that you're not completely comfortable with her," Jessica said.

"No," he said quietly, "I'm not. Not at all. It's difficult for me because...never mind."

"Lieutenant!" a man yelled from across the room.

"What?" Daniel hollered.

"Your turn, Daddy. Your kid needs a clean diaper...fast. Cripe, someone open a window."

Jessica laughed. "I heard that. Daniel, before you go to the duty that calls, we're having our annual MacAllister Christmas tree-trimming gathering at my grandparents' house Saturday night. Would you like to come? It would give you a chance to meet Patty and give Tessa an opportunity to interact with the person who is going to care for her."

Daniel nodded. "Yeah, that sounds good. Thanks. Where and what time?"

"Why don't you pick me up at my apartment? That way we won't run the risk of your arriving before me and not knowing anyone."

"Sounds like a plan."

"Lieutenant!"

"I'm coming!" he yelled. "Keep your pants on."

"It's not *my* pants that have the problem," the man shot back.

Jessica rattled off her address, they agreed on seven o'clock Saturday night, then quick goodbyes were exchanged. Daniel dropped the receiver back into place and got to his feet.

"You guys are wimps," he said, starting across the room. "Haven't any of you ever changed a diaper before? Whew. Tessa, you're setting records here. Open that window wider, would you?"

Jessica sat statue-still in her chair, the telephone receiver still pressed to her ear, the dial tone humming.

What on earth had she done? she thought incredulously. She couldn't believe this. She'd asked Daniel Quinn to join her at a traditional MacAllister family event. She hadn't considered doing any such thing, then suddenly the invitation was coming out of her mouth.

Oh, she was insane, she really, really was.

She'd never brought a...a date to such a special event as the tree-trimming party. When she walked in with Daniel and Tessa, the MacAllister clan would go nuts, fast-forwarding the whole thing to wedding bells.

No, no, she had to calm down.

She also had to hang up the receiver, she thought, clanging it back into place.

Okay, she was getting a grip. From the moment she walked into her grandparents' home, she would make it clear that Daniel was *not* her date, that he and Tessa were there to meet Patty. Fine. That would make perfect sense to everyone in attendance and nip the speculative looks and whispers in the bud.

Excellent.

But why had she invited Daniel to the event in the first place, knowing full well she could have arranged a meeting between him and Patty for the afternoon before the party?

Why?

She didn't have a clue.

Chapter 5

He was aging before his very eyes, Daniel thought late Friday night, as he stared at his reflection in the mirror above the bathroom sink. He swallowed two aspirin for his throbbing headache, then walked slowly toward the kitchen, knowing he should eat but wondering if he had the energy left to chew.

Without a doubt, he thought as he peered into the refrigerator, this had been the week from hell.

Dinner was a peanut butter and jelly sandwich and a glass of milk, which Daniel ate while leaning against the kitchen counter.

Before he could put in for vacation time to tend Tessa, his captain was called away on a family emergency. Rotten luck. That had left him, the next highest ranking officer, in charge of all divisions, with detectives reporting to him and asking advice on their cases in a seemingly endless stream.

He'd had no choice but to put Tessa in an extended-hours day-care center, something he had been determined not to do. He didn't want his niece—correct that, his *daughter*—to be lost in the shuffle, one more in a herd of kids.

So, okay, the place was sparkling clean and cheerful, the people had been nice enough, and Tessa had appeared no worse for wear, but still…

Daily calls to the employment agency had gotten him the repeated message that they had no one for him to interview for the job of live-in nanny. They were so sick of hearing from him that they were willing to call other agencies to see if that produced what he so desperately needed. That effort had resulted in nothing, nada, no one, zip.

Daniel stuck his empty glass in the dishwasher, realized the machine was full, then scrounged through three cupboards before he found the soap.

He transferred a load of wash to the dryer, started another without bothering to sort whites from colored garments, then stretched out on the sofa and decided he felt very sorry for people who lived to be a hundred because every bone in their body must ache as his did.

And he felt sorry for stay-at-home mothers, too, who must be so beat at the end of each day they could barely move. No, maybe not, because they knew how to properly care for their child, just stepped up and did it. Not only that, they weren't carrying around a heavy load of guilt that got instantly bigger every time they looked at their baby. Guilt that was definitely taking its toll on him.

"Look at the bright side, Quinn," he said aloud. And he would, just as soon as he could remember what it was. Oh, yeah, he had it now.

Tomorrow night he would see Jessica.

He would spend the entire evening with her at her grandparents' house, hear her voice, her laughter, be able to inhale and savor her feminine aroma, watch her move with her special elegance and grace.

And then, when he took her home after the tree-trimming party, they'd—

"Say good-night in the parking lot at her apartment because Tessa will probably be asleep in her car seat," Daniel said aloud. "Hell."

He'd allowed himself to indulge in the momentary fantasy that he had a *date* with Jessica MacAllister, which was not the case. She'd invited him to the party so he and Tessa could meet Patty before Tessa was left in the woman's care.

Big, boring deal. Because, damn it, he wanted to nestle Jessica to his body, to kiss her senseless, then make love to her for hours. Man, how he wanted that woman.

Forget the party. He wasn't going. He'd be out of his mind to subject himself to a series of torturous, look-but-don't-touch hours spent in close proximity to Jessica. That was masochistic to the max. He'd come up with a story about having to be on duty and suggest that he and Tessa meet Patty on Sunday.

Yeah, that was good.

No, that was terrible.

Daniel Quinn did not run and hide...from anything. Never had. Never would. He'd focus on his plan to figure out why Jessica had such an impact on him and once he knew he'd no longer be susceptible to her...her charms, for lack of a better word.

He'd come away from the party with at least temporary arrangements made for Tessa's care and regained control of his libido.

"Works for me," he said decisively. "Okay, the Christmas tree-trimming gig is once again on my social agenda."

He frowned. How many years had it been since he'd helped trim a Christmas tree? A lot of years, going all the way back to his short, disastrous marriage that should never have taken place to begin with. A cop was *not* husband material the majority of the time. Well, he sure as hell hadn't been.

He glanced around the living room and his frown deepened.

There wasn't one thing in this place that indicated that Christmas was only a few weeks away, he thought. Was that bad? He was depriving Tessa of the excitement and hype of the holiday. Was she old enough to care one way or another? Did it matter? Hell, he didn't know, but he guessed he'd better find out.

Daniel swung his feet to the floor and sat up. He rested his elbows on his knees and made a steeple of his fingers, resting the tips against his lips.

Christmas. He could remember sneaking into Karen's room and waking her before dawn, telling her he'd heard Santa's reindeer prancing on the roof.

She'd crawl into his gangly teenage arms and stare at him with wide eyes, asking him if he was really sure that Santa had come and brought her presents. Was it true, Danny? You bet, baby girl, he always told her, then they'd go to wake their parents, only to find that their mother was already waiting for them, her dark eyes sparkling.

They'd all pounce on his father, who would pretend to be a grump, then he would leap up and sweep Karen into his arms and ask her if it was time to see if Santa had come.

"He came, Daddy," Karen would say, splaying her tiny hands on her father's beard-roughened face. "Danny told me and Danny always knows what's right."

Daniel covered his face with his hands as the vivid pictures of those Christmas mornings of years before hammered against his mind.

"Danny always knows what's right," he said, his voice choked with emotion. "But not when it really counted, Karen. I failed you. *I failed you.* I'm so sorry, Karen. I'm so damn sorry, baby girl."

Time lost meaning as Daniel relived haunting memories over and over in his mind, feeling as though he was being pummeled by punishing blows.

He heard a noise. As he pulled himself back to the here and now, he realized that Tessa was crying. He got to his feet, drew a shuddering breath, then hurried down the hall to the baby's room, coming to a halt by the crib.

"Hey, hey, what's the matter?" he asked, patting Tessa on the back. "Are your teeth hurting you again? I don't know how to make it…make it right. I couldn't make things right for your mother and I can't do it for you, either."

The baby cried louder and Daniel lifted her into his arms, swaying slightly to hopefully soothe her. He finally stilled when the motion did nothing to comfort Tessa. Daniel's shoulders slumped and he simply stood there, holding Tessa close and feeling very old, very tired, and very, very defeated.

Chapter 6

Jessica clipped on tiny, diamond chip earrings that her grandparents had given her for her sixteenth birthday, then stepped back from the floor-length mirror hanging inside her closet door to critically view herself from head to toe. She turned one way, then the other, finally nodding in approval.

She frowned in the next instant. A shiver coursed through her as her mind flew back in time to when she couldn't bear to even see those earrings because she'd been wearing them during the horror of....

No, she thought. She wasn't going to do that to herself, refused to relive it all again. She'd think about the evening ahead, not torture herself with images from the past.

She liked her new outfit purchased for this important holiday event, she decided. The black silk pa-

jama-slacks were topped by a stylish red silk jacket
cut like a man's smoking jacket and cinched at the
waist by a matching sash. She wore evening sandals
that allowed her toes to peek from beneath the hem
of the slacks. Very classy. Very trendy.

And so expensive she'd gritted her teeth when
she'd signed the charge slip, adding the outrageous
price to a balance-owed that was growing almost
daily due to Christmas gifts for her huge family.

But she looked darn good for thirty years old, she
decided. She was as slender as she had been at twenty
but, in actuality, there was no excuse not to be since
she'd never had a baby.

That thought had come out of left field, she mused,
closing the closet door. Well, no, maybe not. She'd
had baby Tessa on her mind off and on during the
entire week, hoping a Mary Poppins-type nanny
would drop out of the heavens and solve Daniel's
problem.

She crossed the room to the bed and began to place
what she needed in a small evening purse.

And, of course, she thought with a sigh of self-
disgust, with every fleeting remembrance of Tessa
had come a vivid picture of Daniel Quinn in her mental vision. And each and every time the images of
Daniel had produced the incredible heat.

Before leaving the bedroom, Jessica returned to the
mirror to study her hair, pursing her lips in the process. She was toying with the idea of cutting it, she
mused, turning so she could see the tumble of waves
that fell to the middle of her back. Granted, when she

wore it in a bun at the nape of her neck, or twisted it into a figure eight, it created a sleek professional appearance. But when it was in a single braid hanging down her back, or floating free as it was tonight... well, perhaps it was just too youthful for a mature woman of thirty.

"Maybe I'll ask the family," she said, smiling. "Heaven knows that MacAllisters are always ready to offer an opinion whether they've been asked for it or not."

The sound of a brisk knock at the front door caused Jessica to spin around and stare at the open doorway to the bedroom.

Daniel, she thought, feeling her heart begin to beat wildly. Daniel was here.

"No kidding," she said dryly. "This is where Daniel is *supposed* to be to pick me up so we can go to the Christmas party."

But not as a couple, she reminded herself as she walked down the hall. This was not a date. Nope, not even close. This was an efficient means by which Daniel and Tessa could meet Patty, and vice versa. That fact was something she was going to make very clear to her family immediately upon arriving at her grandparents' home.

Jessica crossed the living room and smiled as she opened the door.

"Merry..." she said, then her mind went completely blank and she could not for the life of her remember what came after Merry.

All that she was capable of comprehending was

Daniel. Daniel, who was holding Tessa. Daniel, in a dark suit that did scrumptious things for his thick, black hair, dark eyes and tawny skin. A dark suit, crisp white shirt, and a whimsical red holiday tie dotted with minuscule reindeer.

Daniel Quinn was here.

And Jessica MacAllister was suffused with such heated desire that it caused her cheeks to flush a pretty pink.

Daniel felt a sharp pain in his chest and only then realized that he'd forgotten to breathe.

Lord, he thought, look at her, look at that vision of loveliness standing before him. Jessica. Her hair. Oh, man, he was guilty of daydreaming about what her hair would be like falling free and there it was... golden and soft, calling to him to sink his hands into it and—

"Baa," Tessa said, smacking Daniel on the cheek. "Baa, da, baa."

Daniel and Jessica jerked at the sudden baby sound, blinked, and drew much-needed air into their lungs.

"Christmas," Jessica said. "Merry Christmas." She stepped back. "Come in."

Daniel entered the apartment and Jessica closed the door, turning to direct her attention to Tessa.

"Well, my gracious," she said, "aren't you Christmassy tonight, Tessa? What a pretty red velvet dress you're wearing, and your coat and bonnet match it, and you have on all-grown-up white tights, and teeny-tiny black patent leather shoes and...your daddy certainly knows how to shop for baby girl clothes, doesn't he?''

"The nanny bought this outfit and all of Tessa's other clothes, too," Daniel said, frowning. "I just gave her the money and said to get what Tessa needed. I don't know the first thing about buying kid's stuff and I can't say I have a yearning to learn, either. Shopping is not my thing and... Jessica, you look beautiful, absolutely fantastic, and your hair is sensational and..." His voice trailed off as a bolt of heat rocketed through him.

"Thank you, Daniel," Jessica said, shifting her gaze slowly from Tessa to look directly into his eyes. "You're very...handsome, too, and...I like your tie...and...I'm contemplating the idea of cutting my hair, but then again...I think we should get going."

Jessica tore her gaze from Daniel's, dashed around him to pick up her purse from the sofa and rushed back to the door.

"I'm not going to bother with a coat," she said. "It's not that cold out, is it? No, I'll be fine. Off we go to meet Patty and stick some ornaments on a tree and..." She smacked the door with one hand and turned to face Daniel again. "This has got to stop. It's so juvenile and ridiculous and...it just has to stop. And you're not helping the situation one bit, you know, when you look at me with those dark eyes of yours as though you can see right through my clothes, and then the heat...that damnable heat...you didn't hear me swear, Tessa...are you listening to me, Daniel Quinn? This...has...got...to...stop."

"Hey," Daniel said, frowning. "Don't dump this all on me. I'm not the one who's wearing one of the sexiest outfits I've ever seen with a top held together with a sash that could be slipped free so easily.... I don't have gorgeous blond hair that's only missing a pillow to be spread over. I'm just standing here in a plain old black suit holding a kid, for crying out loud.

"And if you cut your hair, I'll have you arrested for malicious destruction of valuable property."

"Oh."

"This has got to stop?" Daniel went on, none too quietly. "Okay, fine. You tell me how to do that, Ms. MacAllister. You lay it all out for me. How do I stop wanting you, desiring you, thinking about making love to you? How do I do that, Jessica? I'm a man, not a machine with a button I can push that will...ah, hell."

"Don't swear in front of—"

"Yeah, yeah, I'm sorry. I won't swear in front of Tessa." Daniel paused. "I was going to try to figure out what it is about you that turns me inside out all the time. I thought it was a big mystery. But it isn't. Nope. It's very simple. Look at you. You're beautiful and classy and...I can't help but want you, Jessica, and I don't plan to apologize for that fact."

"Well." Jessica drew a steadying breath. "That's certainly plain enough, isn't it? Yes, it is. And as long as we're being so candid here, I'll admit that...that I want you, too, Daniel. However...that doesn't mean I intend to succumb to my...my lust."

"Now *that*," Daniel said, glaring at her, "is a very

tacky word. It's desire we're both feeling, Jessica. Desire.''

''We don't know each other well enough for it to be desire,'' Jessica said, ''because that indicates there are emotions involved. No, it's lust.''

''You're wrong,'' Daniel said, his voice suddenly very low and very, very male. ''It's desire. If I made love with you, Jessica, there would definitely be emotions involved. There would be caring, sharing, a driving need to assure your pleasure before my own and…''

''Daniel, don't,'' Jessica whispered, as a shiver coursed through her. ''Just…don't.''

''Think about it,'' he said. ''It's getting late. Let's hit the road.'' Daniel glanced around. ''I like your apartment, by the way. It's big, bright, looks like a garden with those flowers on the sofa. It makes my place seem sort of dark and dull.''

''Oh, no, your home suits you,'' Jessica said. ''You walk in and know that a man lives there.''

''Mmm,'' Daniel said, sweeping his gaze over the room again. ''And this apartment shouts the fact that a man *doesn't* live here. It's very feminine, very you.''

Jessica frowned. ''Would you be uncomfortable here? Is it too…girly?''

Daniel looked directly into Jessica's eyes again. ''If I was spending time here with you, I wouldn't be concentrating on the furniture.''

''We're leaving,'' Jessica said firmly. ''Now.''

''Good idea.''

When they emerged from the high-rise building, the cool night air felt good against Jessica's heated skin and she willed her racing heart back to a normal tempo.

When she was settled into her seat in Daniel's sports vehicle, she gave him directions to her grandparents' home without looking at him. She then spent the entire drive pointing out Christmas lights to Tessa, while pretending not to be aware that the baby had dozed off in her car seat in the back seat.

The senior MacAllisters lived in an older, affluent neighborhood that boasted large, well-kept homes with sweeping lawns of lush green grass. Jessica nodded toward a house that had a circular drive already filled with vehicles. Cars were also parked on the street and Daniel had to settle for a spot halfway down the block.

He turned off the ignition, unsnapped his seat belt, but made no move to open the door. He folded his arms on top of the steering wheel and looked over at Jessica, who was clearly visible from the old-fashioned lamps lining the street.

"Do you plan to pretend I don't exist the entire evening?" Daniel said.

A flash of anger coursed through Jessica, but fizzled in the next instant. She sighed and met Daniel's gaze.

"I'm sorry," she said. "I was...unsettled by our conversation and I behaved badly during the entire drive over here. I apologize."

"Okay," Daniel said, nodding. "I might mention

that Tessa slept through your entire Christmas light tour of Ventura.''

"Oh," Jessica said, glancing back at the baby, who was now awake and sucking her thumb. "That's too bad, because I thought I did a job that the Chamber of Commerce would have approved of." She paused and sighed again. "Look, let's just go inside and have a good time. It really is a fun party and I think you'll enjoy my family."

"Sounds good to me," Daniel said. "I don't want to argue with you, Jessica."

"Fair enough. Shall we go?"

"Wait a minute," he said, straightening in the seat. "Before I meet this Patty who is going to take care of Tessa, maybe I should know why she's your cousin, but not really your cousin, or however that goes."

"Oh, that," Jessica said, laughing. "Well, my uncle Ryan, who is really my uncle, was a Ventura police officer for many, many years before he retired. During that time, his partner on the force was Ted Sharpe. We all grew up calling him Uncle Ted, because he was like a member of the family and, hence, his and Hannah's children, Patty and Ryan, were our cousins. Uncle Ted and Aunt Hannah adopted Ryan from Korea when he was six months old. Ryan is over in Korea right now, but should be home in time for Christmas."

"Okay, that makes sense now. You've got retired cops in the family?"

"Sure do. I remember them being called away from

various celebrations a great deal. They were uniformed officers who drove a squad car. Neither one wished to move up to detective at any point.''

Tessa stiffened in her car seat and began to cry.

''Oops,'' Jessica said. ''Madam is tired of being buckled in that thing. I'll carry the diaper bag, you get the unmerry princess.''

''Yep,'' Daniel said, opening the door. ''I've never packed a diaper bag before. I just stuffed a bunch of junk in there.''

''Did you remember diapers?'' Jessica said.

''Sure I did,'' he said, getting out of the vehicle. ''I think.''

Jessica laughed, Daniel chuckled, and Tessa gurgled happily when Daniel released her from her seat. A lighthearted mood replaced the strain between Jessica and Daniel and they were smiling as they approached the house that was decorated with a multitude of bright Christmas lights.

''Someone spent a lot of time on a ladder,'' Daniel said, as they walked up the driveway. ''That's a lot of lights on that house.''

''Aunt Margaret refuses to allow Uncle Robert to do it anymore,'' Jessica said. ''They hire a professional service to come because Robert said the MacAllister homestead would have Christmas lights as always, by golly, even if he couldn't put them up himself. I love my grandparents so much. They're wonderful people. Well, my parents are, too.'' She laughed. ''The whole clan is super. Ugh. Do I sound syrupy sweet, just gushing ad nauseam?''

"No," Daniel said, "you sound like someone who loves her family. There's nothing wrong with that. It's nice. Poor Tessa is stuck with just me, which is the short end of the stick."

"Numbers don't matter," Jessica said. "If the love is there, it makes no difference if your family is two people or twenty-two, or...you love Tessa so...don't you? Love your...your daughter?"

"I...I don't know her very well," Daniel said quietly, as they approached the front door. "I don't use the word love lightly, Jessica. I care about Tessa, but I need more time with her to...never mind."

Something is wrong here, Jessica thought, as she reached the front door of the house. How could Daniel not *love* that adorable, innocent baby? Tessa had been with him for several months now and he still only *cared* about her?

Even a man like Daniel, who had no experience with babies, should have lost his heart to sweet Tessa by now. Oh, yes, something was definitely not right in the Quinn household.

Over the next half hour, Daniel learned that the MacAllisters were warm, friendly people, who gave no hint by their behavior that they were wealthy, powerful members of the upper-crust level of society in Ventura.

The MacAllisters, and all those whom they considered to be members of their large family, were some of the most attractive people he had ever seen gathered in one place at one time.

The senior MacAllisters' home, while enormous, had a comfortable aura that was welcoming to anyone who stepped through the front door.

Tessa, who'd had little contact with people, was a natural-born party girl, and beamed at everyone as Patty carried the baby around the room.

And the MacAllisters, Daniel thought finally, attempting to curb his smile, were having a marvelous time speculating as to what his relationship was in regard to their Jessica.

Sure, Jessica had called for everyone's attention the moment they'd entered the house, explaining that Daniel and Tessa had accompanied her to the event in order to meet and get to know Patty, who was going to tend to Tessa until Daniel could find a new nanny.

Polite smiles and nods were the response to Jessica's announcement, but within minutes Daniel saw heads come together and glances slide his way, along with smiles that changed into rather smug, knowing expressions.

While he found the whole thing rather amusing, he could tell that Jessica was none too pleased as she introduced Daniel to the multitude, telling each person that attending the party together was an extremely efficient way for Tessa to become acquainted with Patty.

"You sound like a broken record, sweetheart," Forrest MacAllister said. "I may be your old daddy, but I'm not hard-of-hearing yet. We get the message. It's a pleasure to meet you, Daniel. I saw you on the news the other evening. That was nice police work you did tracking down that sleazeball who killed that businessman.''

"Thank you, sir," Daniel said. "I couldn't have done it without my partner, Mick.''

"Spoken like a true cop," a man said, joining the group.

"Daniel," Jessica said, "this is my uncle Ryan, who was a police officer for many years.''

"Still miss it, too," Ryan said, smiling as he shook Daniel's hand. "If I can tear you away from Jessica long enough, Ted and I would like to talk shop with you. Ted was my partner the entire time we were uniforms on the force. Those were the good old days. Grab a drink and come with me.''

Jessica laughed. "Go ahead, Daniel. They won't rest until they've exchanged war stories with you.''

As Daniel was led away, Jessica watched him go, marveling at how at ease Daniel seemed to be among her family, while she was a wreck due to the scrutinizing, narrow-eyed looks she and Daniel were receiving.

"Relax, sister mine," a woman said. "They won't gobble him up.''

Jessica turned to see her sister, Emily, who was the second-born of the identical triplet girls, Jessica, Emily and Alice, known as Trip, who had been born to Jillian and Forrest MacAllister thirty years before.

"Hello, hello," Jessica said, then hugged her sister. "You look lovely this evening, Emily.''

"No, I don't," Emily said, frowning. "I'm impersonating a fat sausage in this dress. It fit a month ago when I bought it for this shindig, and now it's much too snug. I can hardly breathe. No, no, don't say a word. No one puts a gun to my head and makes me eat like a piggy. How I look is my fault and I know that. In case I ever forget it, I have a twelve-year-old son only too willing to remind me of that fact.'' She sighed. ''I embarrass Trevor, Jessica, by being fifty pounds overweight. He's ashamed to be seen with me in public for fear that his friends will get a glimpse of his mother the blimp.''

''Oh, Emily, I'm sure that Trevor—''

''No, it's true, but I didn't mean to go on and on about me. What I'm interested in is your gorgeous hunk. My goodness, Jessica, Daniel Quinn is so handsome he's to die for. How did you meet him?''

''First of all,'' Jessica said, ''he isn't *mine*, as you implied. I told everyone why Daniel came to the party with me tonight.''

''Yeah, right,'' Emily said, laughing. ''Want to sell us a bridge, too? Come on, Jessica, you and Daniel and that precious baby could have met with Patty anytime. Hey, if I had a man like that, I'd want to show him off, too. Makes perfect sense to me.''

''Emily,'' Jessica said, a warning tone to her voice.

''How did you say you met him?'' Emily said, raising her eyebrows.

''Daniel…stopped by The Peaceful Dove when I was there on my volunteer night,'' Jessica said, averting her gaze from her sister's and picking an imaginary thread off her jacket. ''That's how I met him.''

Emily frowned. "Why would he stop by a women's shelter? Did he know someone who was staying there?"

Change the subject, Jessica, she thought frantically. She wasn't about to tell Emily what had happened that night at The Peaceful Dove with Sonny and the gun and…her family worried enough about her overnight stint at the shelter without them getting wind of that disaster. Oh, good grief, she'd forgotten to ask Daniel not to mention what had taken place at The Peaceful Dove to anyone this evening.

"No, Daniel didn't know any of the women at the shelter," she said. "He's a cop, remember? He…he checks up on places like The Peaceful Dove to be certain everything is all right and…is Trip coming to the party?"

"No, she's busy in New York City doing whatever it is she does and doesn't tell us about," Emily said, frowning. "She phoned and told Grandma she'd be here for Christmas, which I'll believe when I see her face, which is a duplicate of yours and mine, only mine is fat and—forget it, I'm not going off on that tangent again."

"Emily," Jessica said gently, "you're so unhappy about your weight. Why don't you make a New Year's resolution to go on a diet…and stick to it this time."

Emily shrugged. "I might. Then again, I might not. How I look isn't all that important to me, Jessica, except it does bother me that Trevor is ashamed of my appearance. I work at home, no one sees me much, so...what the heck.''

"But Aunt Kara, our family doctor extraordinaire, says that it's not healthy for you to carry around those extra pounds," Jessica said. "You're a single mother, Emily, and you have a responsibility to your son to—''

"Yes, yes, I've heard all that a thousand times from Aunt Kara," Emily said, waving one hand in the air. "Let's go back to the subject of the scrumptious Daniel Quinn. Okay, he dropped by the shelter when you were there and...and then what?''

"Oh, well, we just..." Jessica started.

"A gun!" Ryan yelled from across the room. "Forrest, are you hearing this? Some bozo with a gun threatened his wife and the other women at The Peaceful Dove the night your daughter was staying there. That's how Daniel met Jessica. Jessica MacAllister, why didn't we know about this, young lady?''

"Oh, damn," Jessica said, closing her eyes for a moment. "Daniel blew it. No, I did, because I forgot to tell him not to—''

"Jessica!" her father bellowed.

"You're in trouble," Emily said in a singsong voice. "I'm gone. I see frosted brownies on the table that are calling my name. Good luck getting out of this one, Ms. MacAllister.''

"Emily," Jessica said, planting her hands on her hips, "are you actually planning on deserting me in my hour of need?''

"Yep," Emily said, "in a New York minute. I'm outta here."

"Mmm," Jessica said, glaring at Emily's back as her sister hurried away.

"Jessica!" Forrest MacAllister said. "Would you come over here for a moment, please?"

An attractive woman in her late fifties slipped her arm through Jessica's, then kissed her on the cheek.

"Hello, Mother," Jessica said. "Are you friend, or foe?"

Jillian MacAllister laughed. "I don't know yet, sweetheart. I haven't heard all the details about this gun-toting varmint at the shelter your uncle Ryan is blustering about. Let's go face the music, shall we?"

The men were sitting in a grouping of chairs in front of a fireplace where leaping flames danced and crackled. Daniel got to his feet as Jessica approached with her mother.

"We were just chatting," he said, "and they asked how I met you, and I told them about…I didn't know that they didn't know…but now they know." Daniel frowned. "Did that make sense? Anyway, I'm sorry, Jessica."

Jessica smiled up at him. "It's not your fault, Daniel. I should have mentioned that I hadn't shared the news of my little adventure with my family."

"Little adventure?" Forrest said. "You call nearly being shot a little adventure?"

"Dad, calm down," Jessica said. "I did *not* come even remotely close to getting shot, nor did anyone else at The Peaceful Dove. Sonny…the man with the gun...was apprehended by Ventura's finest before he even entered the shelter.''

"The uniforms nabbed him," Ryan said, nodding.

"Of course they did," Ted Sharpe said. "The uniforms are the boys to get the job done...no offense intended, Daniel. Detectives have their uses, too.''

"Oh, thanks a lot," Daniel said, chuckling.

"This is *not* a laughing matter," Forrest said.

"Forrest," Jillian said, "you're forgetting that Jessica is a thirty-year-old woman, who has the right to make her own choices, dear.''

"Thank you, Mother," Jessica said.

"I don't care how old she is," Forrest said, "she's still my baby girl and the thought of a man with a gun...damn it, Jessica, I want you to stop doing volunteer stints at that shelter. It's far too dangerous. You call whoever is in charge and tell them that you are no longer available and they'll have to find someone else to—''

"Excuse me, sir," Daniel said, "but Jessica and I are attempting to solve the problem in another manner. In a grant proposal we're in the process of filling out, we're requesting funding for armed guards who would be on duty at The Peaceful Dove around the clock. Well, Jessica has started the paperwork, I guess, but I'm going to zero in on the armed guard part.''

"Oh," Forrest said, nodding. "Well, that idea has merit.''

"There will be no need for Jessica to stop doing something that is obviously important to her," Daniel went on, "because her safety can be assured if the grant money comes through. I just can't imagine that our request will be denied, because what The Peaceful Dove provides is far too important. I just feel that guards should be on duty at all times to protect the women and children, as well as the people who work there. I feel very strongly about that, believe me.''

"Very good," Forrest said. "Yes, this is good. Keep me posted on this grant application thing, Jessica.''

"The bomb squad could use you, Daniel," Ryan said, laughing. "You just defused a big one right here in this house.''

The group's attention was diverted by the arrival of Mary-Clair and her date, a rather nice-looking man who stood about five feet nine inches tall, with thinning brown hair and wire-rim glasses.

"There's my little Italian darlin'," Forrest said, moving around Jessica and Daniel and starting across the room. "Mary-Clair Cavelli, it's been far too long since you've visited your Uncle Forrest and Aunt Jillian, young lady.''

Jessica looked up at Daniel and smiled. "Thank you, Daniel. You rescued me again.''

"Hey, my big mouth got you into that jam," he said, matching her smile. "The least I could do was try to get you out of the trouble I caused.''

"My father is a tad overprotective.''

"No, your father loves you very much," Daniel said seriously. "He sure wouldn't want anything to happen to you." He paused and drew his thumb lightly across Jessica's lips, causing a shiver to course down her spine. "But then, neither would I.''

Chapter 7

When Jessica introduced Daniel to Mary-Clair, Daniel greeted her in Italian, which resulted in a squeal of delight from Mary-Clair. She rattled off a reply in Italian and Daniel laughed.

"Enough," Mary-Clair said, smiling. "We're being rude to carry on a conversation that no one else can understand, but this is such fun. I didn't have a clue that you were Italian, Daniel. Your name certainly doesn't shout that fact like mine does."

"My mother was Italian," he said, smiling. "She insisted that my sister and I learn her native language and be proud of our heritage." He shrugged. "I've never forgotten how to speak Italian, but I don't have much occasion to use it. I probably mangled half of what I said to you."

"Nope," Mary-Clair said, "it was textbook perfect, right on the mark."

"What did you say to Daniel that caused him to laugh like that?" Jessica said. "Knowing you, Mary-Clair, it was probably naughty."

"It was not," she said, with an indignant sniff. "I simply said that if he wasn't so tall, I would have snagged him for myself instead of letting you have him." Mary-Clair gave her date a quick peck on the cheek. "No offense, Jerry. I was just blithering."

Jerry laughed. "No offense taken, Ms. Cavelli, due to the fact that Daniel *is* far too tall for you and he obviously does belong to Jessica. I'm safe for the moment, at least." He glanced around the room. "Do you people have a secret formula or something? Every guy in the house is at least six feet tall. I'm feeling extremely vertically challenged at the moment."

Mary-Clair kissed him on the cheek again. "You're just the right size for me. And Daniel is perfect for Jessica, so everyone is happy, happy, happy."

"Jerry," Jessica said, glaring at Mary-Clair before directing her attention to her friend's date. "It's a pleasure to meet you. However, let me clear up a misconception, if I may. Daniel does not *belong* to me, nor do I *belong* to him. He came with me tonight for the sole purpose of meeting my cousin Patty, who is going to take care of Daniel's daughter, Tessa, until Daniel can employ a new nanny for said infant."

"She's gone into her lawyer mode, Jerry," Daniel said, slipping one arm across Jessica's shoulders.

"She just can't help herself when the mood strikes and she delivers a sermon instead of a sentence."

"Ah," Jerry said, nodding.

"I do believe I'll interrupt," a man said, joining the foursome, "before Jessica pops someone in the nose."

"My nose thanks you, Mr. MacAllister," Daniel said, laughing.

"Oh, call me Robert, Daniel," he said. "We're all family here."

"We are not!" Jessica said, then shook her head. "Never mind. I'm obviously outnumbered and I'm going to give up. Daniel, would you please remove your arm from...from my person? You're giving everyone the wrong impression of our relationship. What I mean is, we don't *have* a relationship, but standing here with your arm around my shoulders makes it appear as though we do and...is anyone even listening to me?"

"Not really," Robert MacAllister said. "It's time to start trimming the tree. That's what I came over here to say, but after those long dissertations of yours, Jessica, it's a wonder I can remember what my mission was. Mary-Clair, how are you, sweetheart? It's been too long since we've seen you. How are those big strapping brothers of yours?"

Mary-Clair laughed. "They're driving me crazy. They can't get it through their thick skulls that I'm all grown up, and don't need hovering bodyguards anymore."

"That's what we believed was true about Jessica,

too," Robert said, "but then she nearly got herself shot at The Peaceful Dove."

"I know," Mary-Clair said, her eyes widening. "She scared the bejeebers out of me just telling me what happened that night."

"Well, Daniel is on the scene now," Robert said, "so we can rest easier about Jessica's volunteering at The Peaceful Dove."

"Oh, now wait just a minute here, Grandpa," Jessica said.

"No time to wait," Robert said. "Come along, children. We have a Christmas tree to trim."

Jessica threw up her hands in defeat, glowered at Daniel when he chuckled, then they followed everyone into the huge family room beyond the living room where an eight-foot tree stood in the center of the expanse.

Boxes of ornaments were set out on the furniture and the children were handed plastic and wooden ones for the lower branches of the tree. The adults began to hang their choices on the higher limbs. Lights had already been strung on the tree, but weren't turned on.

It was bedlam. The noise level was high as opinions were given freely as to another's choice of what went where, and bodily harm threatened when one person moved another's ornament to a different spot. Great quantities of delicious desserts were consumed during the project to turn the bare tree into a gorgeous, fairyland creation.

It was loud and it was fun, and despite the cacophony, Tessa and two other babies fell asleep on a puffy quilt that had been spread on the floor.

Daniel made no attempt to hide his constant smile as he did his share of bantering about no one changing where he had placed an ornament. Jessica moved around the tree, searching for exactly the right spot for what she wished to hang on a limb, but somehow always managed to return to Daniel's side, a fact that he was very aware of and could not deny that he liked... very much.

This was an incredible family, he thought. They were warm, friendly, and made a stranger like himself feel as though he belonged right there among them. Jessica was very fortunate to have been raised in the midst of the MacAllister clan.

Suddenly Forrest's words echoed in Daniel's mind and he frowned.

She's still my baby girl, Jessica's father had said. His *baby girl. Baby girl...baby girl...baby...*

Images of his sister, Karen, centered in Daniel's mental vision.

That was what he'd called Karen, he thought, feeling a knot tighten in his gut. *Baby girl.* He'd wanted to protect her and care for her, just as Forrest MacAllister wanted to do for his daughter, Jessica. But baby girl Karen was dead. She was dead, and it was his fault and—

"Daniel?" Jessica said quietly. "Are you all right? You're rather pale all of a sudden and...aren't you feeling well?"

"What?" he said, snapping himself back to the

moment at hand. "I'm...I'm fine. It's just...warm in here."

"Oh, well, take off your jacket. All the other men have."

"Yeah, okay, I'll..."

"Tessa is a doll," Patty said, joining Daniel and Jessica before the tree. "I'll enjoy caring for her, Daniel." She paused and laughed. "Tessa looks so much like you. Anyone just coming into the room would be able to tell that she's your niece...well, your daughter now. Yes, she certainly does take after you."

No, she doesn't, Daniel thought, his mind racing. Tessa is a miniature Karen. Looking at that baby was like being flung back in time to when Karen was small and he was the protective big brother, keeping his sister out of harm's way.

He'd done his job well back then, taking Karen with him whenever possible. His friends had given him a hard time about always having a baby in tow, but they'd finally shrugged and accepted the fact that their buddy Daniel was devoted to his little sister. *His baby girl.*

But the years passed, Karen grew up, and when it mattered, really mattered, Daniel had failed to protect her, failed to take the time to be certain that his baby girl was all right.

And because of him, Karen was dead.

"No," Jessica said, bringing Daniel from his tormenting thoughts. "I wouldn't even consider it, Patty."

Damn, Daniel thought, he'd been so focused on himself that he didn't have a clue as to what Jessica and Patty were talking about. He sure hoped neither one of them asked for his input on the unknown subject.

"Don't you think it's an idea that Jessica should at least think about, Daniel?" Patty said.

Oh…hell, he thought, scrambling for something intelligent to say.

"Well," he said slowly. "Well…um…"

"The subject is closed," Jessica said firmly.

Thank goodness, Daniel thought.

"But, Jessica," Patty said, "if you did volunteer work somewhere other than at The Peaceful Dove, you wouldn't be in danger…ever, and it would give such peace of mind to the family.

"All the MacAllisters do volunteer projects, that goes without saying, but you're the only one who chose a cause that could result in your being physically harmed. Why? Why do you have to go there? To The Peaceful Dove?"

A chill swept through Jessica and she wrapped her hands around her elbows as she looked at Patty.

"I…I need to be there, Patty," she said. "What I mean is, they need me there. Please…don't nag me about this. I won't change my mind."

"Oh-h-h, you're so stubborn," Patty said. "Well, we'll all have our fingers and toes crossed that you get the grant money and can hire armed guards for the shelter." She paused. "I'm starving. Sugar cookies, here I come."

As Patty walked away, Jessica took a shuddering breath, then looked up to see Daniel studying her intently.

"You *need* to be at The Peaceful Dove, Jessica?" he said. "Why?"

"No, no," she said quickly. "I said that wrong at first. What I meant was, they need me to be there, need volunteers to answer the phone and…if there's enough money from the grant, perhaps some salaried secretaries can be hired. But the armed guards are more important so…" She sighed. "Want a sugar cookie or something?"

Daniel leaned down to be certain that only Jessica could hear him speak. "What I want," he said, "is the truth. You meant what you said. You *need* to be there. Why? What's going on here, Jessica?"

"This is neither the time, nor the place, to discuss it," she said, frowning. "In fact, I don't intend to discuss it at all."

"Why not?" Daniel said.

"The tree is trimmed," Robert MacAllister yelled from across the room. "Nice work, family. Let's get these lamps turned off to get the full effect of the lights on the tree. Kara, will you get Andy?"

As people moved around the room, turning off the lamps, Jessica stood on tiptoe to whisper in Daniel's ear.

"Andy is my aunt Kara and uncle Andrew's adopted son. He was a crack baby, and unfortunately, there were far-reaching effects from the drugs. Andy has short-term memory problems, plus he can't handle all the noise and confusion of this party, so he stays in the kitchen, but it's his job to plug in the lights for the tree.

"He's twenty-five years old now, and an absolute whiz in math. He works for MacAllister Architects. He's so sweet and gentle and we all just love him to pieces."

Daniel nodded. "Andy is very fortunate to be a member of this family, to have so many people to love him, look out for him, be certain he's doing okay."

"That's what families are for," Jessica said, shrugging. "You know that, Daniel, because you stepped up and made a home for Tessa."

After failing to protect Tessa's mother, Daniel thought dismally. Too little, too late.

The room was suddenly pitch-black as the last lamp was extinguished. Daniel got a glimpse of a tall man backlit by the bright kitchen light as he came through the door.

"Are you ready?" a deep voice said.

"Ready, Andy," a chorus of voices answered.

"Oh, my," Jessica said, reaching for Daniel's hand as the Christmas tree came alive with a multitude of white fairy lights.

Daniel squeezed Jessica's hand as he drank in the sight of the magnificent tree. Then, by some unspoken directive, the group began to sing "Silent Night."

An achy sensation closed Daniel's throat and he dropped Jessica's hand to encircle her shoulders with one arm, nestling her close to his side. She slipped one arm around his waist as she sang.

When the beautiful hymn ended, Robert MacAllister began to speak in a voice that was deep and rich and ringing with reverence.

"And it came to pass," Robert recited from memory, "that a decree went up from Caesar Augustus..."

As Robert continued the story of the first Christmas, Jessica sniffled. Daniel reached into a pocket of his slacks without relinquishing his hold on her and produced a clean white handkerchief which he pressed into her hand.

He was so emotionally moved, Daniel thought dryly, that if he didn't get a grip, he was going to have to grab that handkerchief back for his own use.

What an incredibly beautiful tradition this family had. What fantastic memories were created in this room year after year. God, they were really something, these MacAllisters.

And Daniel Quinn, dud father of the year? He didn't even own a Christmas ornament, let alone have a tree waiting to be decorated for Tessa.

Well, he was going to fix that...tomorrow. He'd buy a tree and all the stuff to put on it, and when he plugged in the lights, he'd sing "Silent Night" to the baby and...no, cancel that part. He'd scare the diaper off of her with his voice. Well, maybe not. She didn't seem to mind his rendition of the beer bottles on the wall.

Maybe Tessa was too young to start a tradition like

that, but he didn't care. Karen would like it. Karen would want him to do it. His baby girl would be pleased. If she was here. If she wasn't dead.

"Amen," the group said, jerking Daniel back to attention.

The lights in the room were turned on and Daniel inwardly smiled when he saw that teary eyes were visible on as many men as women. He wasn't the only six-foot softy in the room, which was comforting.

"Oh-h-h," Jessica said, dabbing at her nose with Daniel's handkerchief. "I fall apart every year when Grandpa recites the Christmas story."

"With just cause," Daniel said. "It was very moving. I wasn't going to bother with a Christmas tree because I figured Tessa was too little to care one way or another, but...yeah, I'm going to put a tree up for her." He narrowed his eyes and stared into space. "Is that dumb? Does a seven-month-old baby give a hoot?"

"Daniel Quinn," Jessica said, stepping out of his embrace, "how could you have even considered not putting up a tree for Tessa? This is her first Christmas, for heaven's sake. No, she won't remember it, but you can show her the pictures when she's older."

Daniel frowned. "What pictures?"

"The ones you're going to take of her. With a camera. Photographs. Are you with me here?"

"I don't own a camera," Daniel said. "I had one once, but I think my ex-wife took it along with everything else she snatched up, including all our

Christmas tree ornaments.'' He nodded. ''Okay, I'll buy a camera, a tree, ornaments, presents for Tessa, gift wrap, tape, bows, and then I'll declare bankruptcy.''

Jessica laughed. ''You're such a Scrooge.''

''No,'' he said, running one hand over his chin, ''I'm just not a natural-born father. If you tell me I have to dress up in a Santa suit for the kid, I quit.'' He paused. ''Come to think of it, though, my father did that once for Karen when she was little. She was so terrified she scrambled right up my body...she really did...and buried her face in my neck until that scary guy was out of our living room.''

''Oh, what a special memory,'' Jessica said, smiling at him warmly. ''You're allowed to pass on the Santa suit, I guess.''

''Thanks a bunch. What kind of presents should I buy Tessa? Oh, man, I'm so out of my league it's a crime. I suppose I can ask the clerk in a toy department, huh? Unless...'' Daniel produced his best smile. ''Jessica, how would you like to go Christmas shopping with me tomorrow and help me pick out things for Tessa? Oh, and we'll get a tree and...''

Jessica laughed. ''Okay, okay, I'll take pity on you. I was going to put up my own tree tomorrow but it can wait another day. Don't forget to make that list of what we're buying.''

''Definitely busted broke,'' Daniel said, shaking his head. ''Cops don't make big bucks, you know.''

''Ain't that the truth?'' Ryan said, joining the pair. ''Cops aren't cops for the money, that's for sure. And you poor deprived detectives don't even get to wear a spiffy uniform.''

''I did my stint in the uniform,'' Daniel said, smiling. ''The only thing it had going for it was the fact that I didn't have to decide what to wear to work everyday. You uniforms just have to remember how to drive a car.''

Ryan hooted with laughter. ''Score one point for you, Lieutenant.'' He sobered in the next instant. ''Jessica, your Uncle Ted and I were talking. The next time you're doing your overnight thing at The Peaceful Dove, he and I will be there with you and we'll be carrying.''

Jessica frowned. ''Carrying what?''

''It's police jargon, kid,'' Daniel said, chuckling. ''Carrying means they'll be wearing guns. Sounds good to me, Ryan. You and Ted are still licensed to carry?''

''Until they close the lid on the coffin,'' Ryan said, nodding. ''Are we clear on this, Jessica? It's not open for discussion. Let us know when you're scheduled to be at the shelter again.''

''But...'' Jessica said.

''Ah, Mother Margaret is waving us over for the traditional eggnog. Now we're getting to the best part of the evening.''

As Ryan walked away, Daniel nodded. ''That's a good plan. Not bad thinking...for uniforms.''

''Yes, fine,'' Jessica said, ''but what about all the other nights at the shelter?''

''That's where the grant comes in,'' Daniel said,

his jaw tightening. "Once we get that money we'll know that no harm will come to any woman or child at The Peaceful Dove. *No one is going to die there.*"

But it was too little, too late, for his baby girl. Too little, too late, for Karen.

Chapter 8

Shortly before five the next morning, the telephone rang, waking Daniel from a deep sleep. He had snatched up the receiver on the nightstand next to his bed and mumbled, "Quinn" before he was even fully aware that he had done it.

A police officer on the other end of the line gave Daniel a report on a drug raid that had been conducted the previous night, saying they had just finished booking all the suspects they'd arrested. Since the captain was still away, the officer was filling Lieutenant Quinn in on what had taken place.

"Nice work," Daniel said, then yawned. "You and your guys go home and get some sleep. You've earned it. You can do the final paperwork on the raid on your next shift."

"Thanks, Loo," the officer said. "We're definitely

beat, but the whole thing went down exactly the way we planned.''

''Way to go,'' Daniel said. ''Bye.''

He dropped the receiver back into place, then dragged his hands down his beard-roughened face. In the next instant he listened intently, then smiled in relief when he didn't hear a peep from Tessa.

Daniel yawned again, then closed his eyes, delighted that the baby was apparently going to allow him to get some extra sleep on this Sunday morning.

Tessa must be all tuckered out from the big party last night at the MacAllisters, he mused. She sure did seem to enjoy herself, though, just as much as he had.

Yep, he thought sleepily, it had been a great evening, one he would remember for a very long time. The only glitch had come when he'd driven Jessica home and she'd insisted that he not waken a sleeping Tessa by taking the baby from her car seat. Jessica was perfectly capable of seeing herself to her own door safe and sound.

He, however, had wanted to kiss Jessica good-night at said door. Maybe even kiss her twice, or three times, or... But he'd had to settle for slipping one hand to the nape of Jessica's neck, capturing her lips and kissing her so intensely they'd both gasped for air when he'd finally released her.

Then Jessica had muttered a farewell, scooted out of the vehicle and disappeared into the apartment building. And that, as the saying went, had been that.

But one thing had been crystal clear to him as he'd driven home...it was *desire* that was coiling within him after sharing that sensational kiss with Jessica. Not *lust*, by damn, but desire.

"Damn straight," Daniel mumbled, then began to drift off to sleep.

I need to be there.

Daniel's eyes popped back open and he frowned.

He'd been aware that there had been something niggling at the edge of his mind last night, troubling him before he'd fallen asleep, but he hadn't been quite able to put a finger on what it was.

Now he knew.

When Patty had suggested that Jessica choose a different project to dedicate her volunteer hours to rather than the potentially dangerous shelter, Jessica had said *I need to be there* with passion ringing in her voice.

Yeah, sure, she'd attempted to backtrack by stating she'd meant to say that *they* needed her volunteer hours at the shelter. But he hadn't bought into her smoke screen, not for a second.

I need to be there.

Why?

What was Jessica keeping from him? What secret was she harboring that would cause her to make a heartfelt statement like that? Well, he was a detective so he'd do his thing and find out. But what would be more meaningful would be if Jessica told him on her own, trusted him enough to share whatever it was with him.

Oh, yeah? Daniel thought. What about tit for tat?

And what was good for the goose was good for the gander? Or however the hell that went.

When Jessica had approached the subject of what had happened to his sister, Karen, he'd refused to discuss it. The only person who knew the true facts surrounding Karen's death was Mick, his partner and best friend, who had listened quietly as Daniel had poured out his heart, his words often halted by the tears closing his throat.

Mick had offered his sympathy, then stated adamantly that Karen's death was *not* Danny's fault.

But it was, Daniel thought. Nothing Mick, nor anyone else might say, could change that godawful ugly truth. He hadn't protected his sister the way he should have, the way he had the entire time she'd been growing up. And because he'd failed to do that, his baby girl was dead.

How did a man tell a woman like Jessica something like that? How did he look her in the eyes and admit that he was a failure as a brother and would probably be a failure as a father to Tessa, as well? Each time he looked at Tessa he saw Karen and was forced to own up to his shortcomings.

How could he tell Jessica? He couldn't.

He couldn't divulge one damn word about it because he couldn't bear the thought of seeing the disgust and disappointment in Jessica's eyes, on her face, when she learned the truth about him.

I need to be there. Jessica had a secret. He had a secret.

He wanted Jessica to trust him enough to tell him

what was plaguing her, but he had no intention of returning that trust in kind. That was crummy, no doubt about it. But it was the way it was going to be. End of story.

"Quit thinking and go back to sleep, Quinn," Daniel said aloud. "You're wearing out what's left of your worthless mind."

A wail from Tessa split through the peaceful silence in the apartment and Daniel sighed as he threw back the blankets on the bed and got to his feet.

"I'm coming, kid," he said, reaching for a pair of jeans that were flung over the back of a chair. "Couldn't you tell your teeth to sleep for another hour?" Tessa cried louder in the distance. "Nope, guess not."

The day had officially begun, like it or not, Daniel mentally complained, as he left the bedroom, stifling yet another yawn.

A day, he thought, brightening in the next moment, that included spending the afternoon with Jessica MacAllister as they set out to empty his wallet to produce a memory-filled Christmas for Tessa. Yep, hours and hours with lovely Jessica.

Daniel entered the nursery, lifted the crying Tessa from the crib and held the baby high in the air to her laughing delight.

"Know what, kiddo?" he said, as he placed a smiling Tessa on the changing table. "This is going to be one helluva...oops, excuse me...one *heck* of a great day. Guaranteed."

*   *   *

The mall that Jessica selected for the shopping trip
with Daniel and Tessa was enclosed and had a huge
selection of stores. Christmas trees were being sold at
one end of the enormous parking lot.

Daniel pushed Tessa's stroller and they made their
way through the maze of people.

"I feel like a salmon swimming upstream," Daniel
said, frowning.

"Don't get grumpy," Jessica said, as they moved
slowly forward. "Any mall we went to today would
be this crowded. Don't you think it's beautiful in here
with all the decorations they've put up?"

"Mmm."

"Oh, look," Jessica said, "there's Santa Claus
over there. We should get Tessa's picture taken sitting
on his lap."

"Forget it, Jessica," Daniel said. "There must be
a hundred people in that line waiting to see the fat
guy. Besides, I'm a cop, remember? I'm not teaching
my...my daughter that it's all right to climb up onto
a stranger's lap. Nope. No way."

Jessica laughed and shook her head. "All right,
Daddy, maybe you'll soften up on the subject by next
year."

"Mmm."

What a strange thought, Daniel mused. Next
Christmas, a year from now. If someone mentioned
Daniel Quinn to Jessica twelve months in the future,
would she frown in confusion and say "Who?" then

vaguely remember having met him? Would she have only dim memories of the kisses they'd shared?

No, he didn't like that idea, not one little bit. But what could he offer Jessica to keep her in his life? Great sex? An ongoing affair with no real strings attached, no commitment to forever?

Yeah, well, maybe that just might be enough. Jessica had made it clear that she didn't want anything permanent with any man, just didn't have the time to devote to a serious relationship. So, okay, they'd have a not-serious relationship, a we'll-see-each-other-when-we-can thing that would include...well, great sex.

And that sounded so cheap, it was turning his stomach.

But, damn it, *he* didn't want to become seriously involved with a woman, either, so what else was there in the offering but a casual affair with Jessica?

Hell, forget it. He was thinking too much again, driving himself totally nuts.

"Toy store on the left," Jessica said, bringing Daniel back to attention. "Start steering the chariot over that way."

"How long before Tessa can play catch?" Daniel said. "You know, so we can toss a football back and forth?"

"Daniel, Daniel, Daniel," Jessica said, rolling her eyes heavenward. "Think teddy bears and rattles, musical toys with pretty lights that blink on and off, things she can chew on while she's teething."

"Boring," he said, as they entered the store.

"Not if you're seven months old," Jessica said, laughing.

The toy store was busy. Adults were attempting to control excited children who were announcing at full volume that they wanted this, and this, and this. Daniel frowned and inched the stroller forward slowly, wishing it had a horn he could blast to clear a path.

"Are the toys I saw in Tessa's playpen all she has?" Jessica said.

"Yes," Daniel said, nodding. "It's stuff that Mick's kids have outgrown. Tessa's favorite thing is the ball that jingles when it moves."

"See? Musical toys are great at this age," Jessica said. "Follow me and try not to run over any little people."

Jessica started down the aisle and Daniel dutifully followed until his attention was caught by a remote control police car that was on display and available to try. He set the car on the floor and began to press the buttons on the hand-held control bar.

Jessica found the baby section in the store and turned to speak to Daniel, only to discover that he was no longer with her. She made her way back down the aisle, then stopped and watched Daniel playing with the car, an instant smile on her face.

"Zoom," Daniel said, as Tessa hung over the side of the stroller to watch the car whiz by her. "We're chasing the bad guys, Tessa. Closing in now. Gonna get 'em. Zoom, zoom."

Tessa laughed in delight as Daniel drove the squad

car in a circle around the stroller, the lights on the toy flashing and a siren wailing.

A warm, tingling feeling invaded Jessica's heart as she continued to observe Daniel and the baby. Daniel was capable of being a natural, loving father, she thought, her smile fading. But he seemed to be holding his emotions in check in regard to Tessa. She was still disturbed by his reluctance to say that he loved the baby, having said something inane about not knowing Tessa very well yet.

But when he relaxed and let down his guard, as he was doing now, it was so easy to envision him as Tessa's daddy. They were so beautiful together, looked so much alike, father and daughter. All that was missing from the lovely picture was a wife and mother.

A chill swept through Jessica, replacing the warmth that had been there moments before as she suddenly became acutely aware of the distance separating her from Daniel and Tessa, and the special fun they were sharing.

They weren't just mere feet away from her, she thought, they were a world apart. The wife and mother missing from the little family made up of Daniel and Tessa was not her, would never be her.

She would not have those roles with Daniel and Tessa, or anyone else for that matter. That decision was etched in stone. She had loved once, given her heart away once, and the remembrance was a nightmare always lurking in the shadows ready to haunt her, to force her to relive the pain of the terrible choice she'd made.

Never again. No, dear heaven, never again.

But she didn't have to dwell on the past. Not now. Not today. She would just live for the moment, enjoy it, savor it, tuck the memories away in a special chamber of her heart. She would give herself this time with Daniel and Tessa as…yes, as a gift to be cherished.

Jessica made her way forward and was smiling when she reached the pair. "Do I get a turn?" she said.

"Are you a cop?" Daniel said, grinning at her.

"Well, no, sir, I'm just a regular citizen," she said, matching his smile.

"Then you can't drive the squad car, ma'am," he said, whizzing it around the stroller again as Tessa squealed and watched it go by her. "It's against regulations."

"Phooey," Jessica said.

"Phooey?" Daniel said, with a burst of laughter. On impulse he dropped a quick kiss on Jessica's lips. "Now, there's a great word. The next time you don't get the decision you want in court, you just stand up and yell 'phooey.'"

"I just might do that," Jessica said, laughing as she attempted to ignore the frisson of heat slithering down her spine from Daniel's kiss. "I hate to break up this party, but we *are* shopping for Tessa, you know."

"She needs this car," Daniel said.

"She's too young for that car," Jessica said.

"No, now, think about it. The next time she's all wigged out because her teeth are bugging her, I'll zoom the car around the living room and take her mind off her problems. It sure beats singing about beer bottles on the wall.''

''Get the car.'' Jessica narrowed her eyes. ''But be honest about it, Quinn. Put *your* name on the gift tag, because you know and I know that *you* want the car.''

''Whatever works, MacAllister,'' Daniel said. ''Hey, Tessa, we're getting this great car for Christmas.''

''We?'' Jessica raised her eyebrows and laughed. ''Oh, phooey.''

Daniel's laughter joined Jessica's, the happy sound swirling around them, accompanied by Tessa's happy babble. It was a special moment, a sharing moment, a moment of memories to keep.

Daniel made his purchases and as he was attempting to stuff the large shopping bag into the carrying compartment in the back of Tessa's stroller, Jessica wandered over to a display of teddy bears.

She picked up a brown bear with a pink bow around its neck, pink booties and a matching stocking cap. She smiled as she held the toy against her cheek, deciding it passed the soft and cuddly test.

''What are you doing?'' Daniel said, pushing the stroller to where Jessica was standing.

''I can't resist,'' Jessica said. ''I want to get Tessa a Christmas present, too, and this bear is perfect. Isn't it sweet?''

''No,'' Daniel said gruffly. ''I mean, yeah, it's nice, but don't get her that one. Pick one of the others.''

Jessica frowned in confusion. ''Why?''

Daniel grabbed another teddy bear and shoved it at Jessica.

"Take this one," he said.

"No. I want to know what's wrong with the one I selected, Daniel. You're acting so strangely and... what's going on?"

Daniel sighed and ran his hand over the back of his neck. "I bought Karen a bear just like that when she was little," he said, his voice flat and low. "It was her favorite toy and she carried it around, slept with it, ate with it. My mother washed it so many times it was faded and some of the fur was missing, but it still had a place of honor on Karen's bed even when she was a teenager."

"I see," Jessica said slowly. "Don't you think it would be nice later, when Tessa is old enough to understand, to be able to tell her that her mother had a bear just like this? It would be a special connection between them and—"

"No," Daniel said sharply. "Because Tessa might ask what happened to her mother's teddy bear. I don't want to have to tell her that her real father tore it to shreds and I found it when I went to close up the apartment where they had been living. Don't get her that bear, Jessica."

Jessica placed the bear back on the display, then looked at Daniel with wide eyes.

"Karen's husband destroyed her favorite keepsake?" she said. "Why would a man do that?"

"Good question," Daniel said, with a snort of disgust. "No answer."

"But..."

"I really don't want to stand in the middle of a crowded toy store and discuss this, Jessica. Let's go buy a Christmas tree before Tessa starts getting crabby because she needs a nap."

"Yes, all right," Jessica said, looking quickly at the bear one last time. "I'll buy her something when I'm shopping on my own." She paused. "Daniel, was your brother-in-law, Karen's husband, a violent man? Did he abuse your sister?"

"Not...here," Daniel said, his jaw tight. "We'll discuss this later."

Jessica placed one hand on Daniel's forearm. "Will we? Or will you refuse to talk about it again?"

Daniel looked at her for a long moment, then averted his gaze and turned the stroller around.

"Come on," he said. "I don't think Tessa is going to stay in this sunny mood too much longer."

As Daniel strode toward the entrance of the store, Jessica stared at his broad back, then started after him, feeling as though a dismantled puzzle was floating around in her mind, and she was unable to connect the pieces into any kind of order that made sense.

Jessica pushed the disturbing scene about the teddy bear to the back of her mind. For now, she thought, as they loaded the Christmas tree into the back of Daniel's sports vehicle. But the first time she got Daniel alone she was going to broach the subject again.

She'd seen anger reflected in the depth of his dark

eyes when he'd spoken of the special teddy bear being destroyed, but there had also been pain, raw pain.

Oh, why was she so determined that Daniel bare his soul to her, that he share his innermost secrets? Maybe she could help somehow by listening, comfort him at least a little, ease that haunting pain in his eyes, she thought, as they drove away from the mall.

Jessica sighed. No, it was more than that. She wanted, needed, Daniel to trust her enough to tell her what was plaguing him. Why? Why was that so very important to her? Why did it mean so much? She didn't know. She really didn't know.

When they were a short distance from the mall, Jessica suggested that Daniel swing by her house so she could get her car. "What for?" Daniel said, glancing over at her.

"Because by the time we get the tree up and decorated, Tessa will probably be ready for bed. You don't want to have to bundle her up and take her out again to drive me home. This is much more practical."

Daniel frowned. "I suppose it is, but...yeah, okay." He smiled, the first smile since the incident with the teddy bear. "Babies sure put a damper on a guy making his move when he takes his lady to her door. You know, he stalls, she finally invites him in for coffee, then..." He looked at Jessica and wiggled his eyebrows. "Get the drift?"

"To quote you, Lieutenant..." Jessica said, laughing. "...Mmm."

Daniel chuckled and the lighthearted mood they

had enjoyed at the beginning of the shopping trip returned, pushing the gloomy, tension-filled dark cloud into oblivion.

His lady, Jessica's mind echoed, as she looked out the side window of the vehicle. Daniel hadn't meant anything by saying that. He was just being silly.

His lady. And she was being equally silly, she admonished herself, by allowing the warmth those two little words had caused to tiptoe around her heart, then take up residency there.

Then again...maybe it wasn't so silly. It was quite understandable now that she studied it for a moment. They had been like a family during the shopping trip. Mother, father, baby. Wife, husband, child. And those roles would continue as they put up the tree and decorated it. So, for these few hours, she *was* Daniel's lady, in a manner of speaking.

When she drove home alone later that night, she would leave the fantasy behind where it belonged. But now? She was going to be self-indulgent and embrace the fantasy. There was nothing wrong with that.

She didn't even *want* to be a wife and mother on a permanent basis, so enjoying those roles for a short blip on the screen was harmless, just warm-fuzzy feelings she could keep as memories, or dismiss from her mind if she chose to do so.

It was something like...yes, like playing dress-up with her sisters when they were little girls. For a while they were princesses, or queens, or ballerinas. Then, when it was time, the clothes would be removed, put back in the box and they'd return to reality, to being the MacAllister triplets, nothing more.

There had been no harm done years ago by the fantasies, there would be no harm done today, either, because she knew exactly what she was doing.

When Jessica arrived at Daniel's after he'd dropped her off to get her car, he hollered for her to come in when she knocked on the door. She found Tessa crying in her playpen and Daniel struggling with a string of lights he was attempting to place on the tree. Jessica rescued the baby, held her against her shoulder and patted her on the back. Tessa quieted and stuck her thumb in her mouth.

"I had to put her in the playpen," Daniel said, "because she kept crawling over here and getting into everything. I'm not sure this is a good idea, Jessica. What if she pulls the tree over or...maybe we should just forget it for this year after all."

"Oh, no, you don't, Daniel Quinn," Jessica said. "You're not getting off the hook that easily. We'll just use a MacAllister trick of the trade."

"Oh? Which is?"

"Put the Christmas tree in the playpen."

"Huh?" Daniel said. "You're kidding."

"Nope. It works. Tessa will be able to satisfy her curiosity by crawling right up close, but she won't be able to reach the tree. She can't get hurt, the tree survives, and so do Mommy and Daddy. Well... um...in this case, just...just Daddy, of course, but you get the idea."

"Wait a minute," Daniel said, pointing one finger in the air. "For this nutsy plan you definitely get the title of the-mommy-who-suggested-it, because this daddy isn't taking the blame for it. It's nuts."

Tessa's *mommy,* Jessica thought, tightening her hold on the baby and relishing the fantasy. "I accept full responsibility for the tree being in the playpen, sir," Jessica said, dipping her head.

"You're going to get shipped to the farm one of these days, ma'am," Daniel said, as he began to toss toys out of the playpen.

"Oh, ye of little faith," Jessica said, laughing. "I think Tessa is hungry. I'll go feed her while you...ta-da...put the lights on the tree in the playpen. Try not to swear out loud, okay?"

"Mmm," Daniel said.

While Jessica fed Tessa, Daniel managed to string the lights on the tree that was now sitting in the playpen against one wall of the living room.

"You didn't hear that, Tessa," she said, smiling at the baby as an earthy expletive reverberated through the air. "Your daddy is losing his cool."

"I heard that," Daniel called from the other room. "And it's not my cool that I'm losing, it's my mind that's at risk here."

Jessica laughed in delight and shoveled another spoonful of pears into Tessa's mouth. Daniel appeared in the kitchen, asked Jessica what she liked on pizza, then telephoned a pizza parlor to order one delivered. Muttering under his breath, he stomped back into the living room.

Jessica gave Tessa a quick bath, then zipped her into her fuzzy pink blanket-sleepers. When she reentered the living room, the tree was about half-decorated and the pizza had just arrived. She set Tessa on the floor and the baby immediately crawled toward the playpen.

"This is the test," Daniel said, setting two glasses of soda on the coffee table next to the pizza box. "Ten bucks says she wiggles her fingers through the holes in the mesh and yanks on the tree."

"Won't happen," Jessica said, as she sat down on the sofa and opened the box. "Oh, that pizza smells heavenly."

Daniel settled next to her and as they each took a bite of the pizza, their attention was riveted on Tessa. The baby pressed her nose against the side of the playpen, patted the mesh, then plunked back on her bottom and stared up at the tree with wide eyes.

"You owe me ten dollars, Quinn," Jessica said, with a burst of laughter. "I told you it would work."

"I'll be damned," Daniel said, grinning and shaking his head. "Well, it looks dumb."

"Don't get picky."

"There isn't room in the playpen for the presents," Daniel said.

"Don't put them out until just before it's time to open them," Jessica said. "Quit trying to find something wrong with this genius-level plan. Just admit that you were wrong and I was right."

"Can't," Daniel said, taking a big bite of pizza. "My mouth is full."

The pizza was finished down to the last crumb, Daniel held Tessa and gave the baby her night bottle, and Jessica completed the decorating of the tree. She turned off the lamps, plugged in the tree lights, and looked at Tessa for the baby's reaction, only to discover that Tessa had fallen asleep in Daniel's arms.

"Well, phooey," Jessica said, planting her hands on her hips. "Tessa conked out before the big show. I guess our shopping trip caught up with her."

"Don't knock it," Daniel said, easing himself upward from the sofa. "She's asleep. She's quiet. Her teeth aren't adding their two cents worth. Life is good."

While Daniel went down the hall to put Tessa in her crib, Jessica cleaned up the pizza dinner, deciding not to turn the lamps back on so she and Daniel could enjoy the lovely glow of the multicolored lights on the tree. They reentered the living room at the same time and stood next to each other, looking at their handiwork and nodding in approval.

"It's not a bad Christmas tree," Daniel said, as they walked toward the sofa. "I don't think Martha Stewart would give it too many points, but I like it."

"Good." Jessica hesitated for a moment, then sat down close to Daniel. "That's what counts, because it's yours. Yours and Tessa's."

"And yours, too," he said, sliding one arm across Jessica's shoulders. "It wouldn't even be here if it wasn't for your nagging about it."

"Oh, thanks," Jessica said, laughing.

"Hey, I'm glad you pushed me on the subject,"

Daniel said. "Tessa deserves to have a real Christmas, or as real as I can make it. I'll get a camera and take a bunch of pictures of her, the whole nine yards." He paused. "Tessa's first Christmas, and her mother isn't here to share it with her." He shook his head. "Damn."

"Daniel..." Jessica said.

"Yeah, I know." He removed his arm from Jessica's shoulders, leaned forward and propped his elbows on his knees, then steepled his fingers against his chin while he stared at the glittering tree. "I've been avoiding the subject of what happened to Karen, refusing to tell you how my sister died."

"Yes, you have," Jessica said quietly, "but as I sit here I realize that I really don't have the right to demand to know. If you don't want to tell me, Daniel, I'll...I'll understand and—"

"No," he interrupted, his gaze still riveted on the Christmas tree. "It's time that I told you." He drew a shuddering breath. "Karen is...Karen is dead. My baby girl is dead...because of me. It's my fault."

"What?" Jessica whispered.

"If it wasn't for me," Daniel went on, his voice hoarse with emotion, "for what I didn't do for her, she'd be alive today. She'd be here to celebrate Tessa's first Christmas. Karen...Karen is dead, and when it gets right down to the bottom line, Jessica, I...I killed her."

Chapter 9

The fist that tightened in Jessica's stomach when she heard Daniel's chilling words was so painful that she gasped aloud, wrapped her hands around her elbows and bent over slightly.

Daniel turned his head to look at Jessica, then lunged to his feet. He crossed the room and stared at the Christmas tree, his back to her.

"Feeling sick?" he said, a rough edge to his voice. "I don't blame you. I asked myself how I could tell a woman like you the truth of what happened to Karen. My conclusion? I couldn't.

"I couldn't, without witnessing a reaction like the one you're having. Disgust. Disappointment. The knowledge that I was a failure as a protective big brother for Karen and will no doubt be a lousy father to Tessa as well.

"They're all there, aren't they, Jessica? Those emotions? I know they are, because it's how I feel about myself. I look at Tessa and I see Karen when she was a baby. I look at Tessa and know I can't measure up and I don't deserve the title of father, nor should I be the one to raise her. Tessa will hate me when she grows up and discovers the truth. I just can't..."

"Stop it, Daniel," Jessica interrupted, getting to her feet.

Daniel turned slowly to face her, pain etched so deeply in his dark eyes and on his rugged face that Jessica's breath caught.

"I...I just don't understand what you meant," she said. "I also don't know what you were referring to when you said a woman like me. A woman like me? What does that mean?" Jessica shook her head. "This is terribly confusing. Please, Daniel, don't leave it like this. I don't believe for one minute that you actually *killed* your sister, for God's sake. Talk to me."

Daniel stared up at the ceiling for a long moment to gather his raging emotions, then drew a deep breath, letting it out slowly. Jessica sank back onto the sofa, her trembling legs refusing to hold her upright for another second.

"Karen..." Daniel started, then cleared his throat, "Karen was about two months pregnant when she married Cliff. He was a handyman hired by the landlord of the apartment building where Karen was living here in Ventura. Cliff came to fix a warped door in

Karen's place, they started going out together and..."
He shrugged.

"Karen was thrilled about the baby and told me
that she and Cliff were very much in love. I went
with them when they were married at the courthouse.
I didn't like Cliff from the moment I met him, but I
told myself that was just me being a big brother, deciding no one was good enough for my baby girl."

Daniel returned to the sofa and sat down. He leaned
his head on the top and stared up at the ceiling.

"That was my initial mistake," he said, his voice
low and flat. "My first failure in this disaster. I should
have paid attention to my instincts as a brother, a
man, a cop. But I didn't. I just blew off my dislike
of Cliff and focused on how happy Karen seemed to
be."

"That was a perfectly natural and reasonable thing
to do, Daniel," Jessica said, shifting on the cushion
so she could look directly at him as he continued to
concentrate on the ceiling.

"Yeah, right," he said, with a snort of disgust.
"But it sure as hell wasn't *reasonable* that I accepted
Karen's explanation that she'd walked into an open
kitchen cupboard and that was why her face was
bruised. It wasn't *reasonable* that I was called to the
hospital by a cop friend because Karen was in the
emergency room with a broken wrist and a miscar-
riage threatening. Caused, she told me when I arrived,
by her slipping on the front steps of the apartment
building."

"Dear God," Jessica whispered.

"Cliff never showed up at the hospital that night," Daniel went on. "Karen said he was out of town doing some work he'd contracted for. She didn't lose the baby, but it was a close call.

"When I went back the next day to take her home, she'd already checked out, so I went to their apartment. Karen wouldn't let me in, just spoke to me through a crack in the door, saying Cliff had gotten home in the early morning and was sleeping. Hell, I bought it. Can you believe that? Big, tough, super detective me, I accepted what Karen told me."

"Why wouldn't you, Daniel?" Jessica said, a frantic echo in her voice. "She was your sister. You had no reason to think that she wasn't telling you the truth."

"I should have known something was wrong," Daniel said, raising his head and looking at her with haunted eyes. "All the signs were there. They were. But I ignored them, because I was neck-deep in work and centered on myself, my job, instead of being the kind of brother I should have been. Cliff was beating the hell out of my sister and I went merrily on my way solving violent crimes that involved total strangers."

Jessica shook her head. "Daniel, no, you mustn't do this to yourself. Women who are being abused are very convincing with their explanations for injuries. And the abusers are clever men. They hit…they hit their wives, their girlfriends, in areas of the body where bruises can't always be seen and…you're torturing yourself for something that wasn't your fault, and you mustn't do that.''

''It *was* my fault,'' Daniel said fiercely. ''I loved Karen so much, we were close, so close, and a part of me had to have known that she was lying to me. It was *easier* to accept what she was telling me, don't you see? I was too damn busy being super-cop Quinn to…hell. I should have listened to my inner voice, then talked to Karen, told her that I knew what was going on, convinced her to leave Cliff and come live with me.''

''She would have denied that she was being abused, Daniel,'' Jessica said wearily. ''She loved Cliff, was going to have his baby, and nothing you said would have made her leave him. She was convinced that he would change, that he was sincerely sorry that he had hurt her. Then he'd do it again, and she'd tell herself it was the last time, that he surely wouldn't harm her anymore.''

''You've really done your homework, haven't you?'' Daniel said, sarcasm ringing in his voice. ''I suppose you read up on all of this before you started volunteering at The Peaceful Dove. What chapter was that spiel in?''

''I…''

''I said I couldn't tell a woman like you what I had done, or to be more precise, what I *hadn't* done for my sister,'' Daniel continued. ''A woman like you who comes from a protected and perfect world, surrounded by a big, loving family. Any of those guys I met at your grandparents' house would go to the mat for you and you know that. You're encased in a safe bubble where nothing bad can happen to you. You don't know how to deal with what I'm telling you, Jessica, so you're reciting textbook paragraphs so you won't have to believe what a lousy failure I am.''

''No, I...''

''Well, believe it, because it's true,'' Daniel said, narrowing his eyes. ''Then go home where you want to be, because you can't stand to be close to me. But don't lay any more of that memorized book junk on me, because I don't want to hear it. The next thing you'll do is tell me what page it was written on.''

Jessica looked at Daniel for a long, breath-stealing moment, and when she finally spoke again, her voice was quivering. ''What I told you was written on a page...'' she said, hardly above a shaky whisper. ''...on a page from...from my own life.''

Daniel opened his mouth to respond to what Jessica had just said, then snapped it closed again, too stunned to speak.

''I haven't told anyone about this,'' Jessica said. ''Not my family, not my best friend, Mary-Clair, no one, because I'm too...too ashamed, so thoroughly disgusted with myself about my inability, my total lack of womanly wisdom in choosing who I gave my heart to.

''But I'm telling you what happened to me, Daniel, because I can't bear to see you torturing yourself like this when I know in my heart, my mind, my very soul, that what happened to Karen wasn't your fault.''

"I'm listening," Daniel said, his gaze riveted on Jessica.

"It was five years ago," Jessica said, struggling to control her emotions. "Five long years, yet sometimes the memories are so vivid it's as though it was yesterday. I was in love for the first time in my life, floating on Cloud Nine because William said he loved me."

Jessica clutched her hands tightly in her lap, looked at them for a moment, then met Daniel's gaze again.

"William and I had been together about six months and we were starting to talk about the future, about the possibility of getting married.

"One night we went out to dinner and William was upset because he'd lost a case in court that day. He was a criminal attorney and had a reputation for winning. He was edgy, very sharp and snappy with the waitress at the restaurant and with me. We cut our meal short and went back to his apartment. I suggested that we watch an old movie on television, thinking it would take his mind off his defeat. He...he erupted in anger, accused me of not caring about him, or his career. He screamed at me that I was so selfish and self-centered that I'd rather watch a movie than be a comfort to him.

"I told him that wasn't true, but that he needed to relax, to realize that he couldn't win every case he took on and...he..." Jessica stopped speaking and drew a quick, sharp breath. "He was so furious, Daniel, that he...he hit me. He punched me, actually, so hard that I fell to the floor in terrible pain."

"Damn it," Daniel said, taking Jessica's hands in both of his and holding them in a tight grip. "How badly did he hurt you?"

"My ribs on the right side of my body were badly bruised and seemed to take forever to totally heal. I was very careful around my family and friends to be certain that no one picked up on the fact that I was injured. I couldn't believe that William had done that. I had to face the horrifying fact that I hadn't paid close enough attention, didn't realize there was a part of him I didn't even know.

"My self-esteem was shattered, along with my confidence in my ability to know, as a woman, who was right or wrong for me as far as giving my heart away. I loved William, trusted and believed in him, envisioned spending the rest of my life with him and..." She shook her head as tears closed her throat.

Daniel released Jessica's hands and wrapped his arms around her. She hesitated, then allowed herself to be nestled against him. He moved one hand to the back of her hair and cradled her head on his shoulder.

"William who?" Daniel said, a rough edge to his voice. "What's the scum's last name, Jessica? I want to know because I'm going to—"

"No," she said, jerking her head up. "It's over. I told him if he ever came near me, I'd press charges against him and his reputation would be ruined."

"He never hit you again?" Daniel said, his jaw tightening.

Jessica averted her eyes from Daniel's. "William... William left Ventura," she said, "shortly after I threatened to go to the police.'' She looked at Daniel again. ''I'm telling you all of this, Daniel, because you need to understand that I've walked in Karen's shoes. You could have come right out and asked her if Cliff was abusing her and she would have denied it. I know, I've been there. If someone who cared about me would have sensed I was injured and asked what was wrong, I would have lied. I would never have admitted that the man I had chosen to love had physically harmed me.

''Oh, Daniel, please, don't you see? What happened to Karen wasn't your fault! It wasn't. You didn't tell me exactly how your sister died, but I assume that Cliff was to blame.''

''He shot her,'' Daniel said, then a chill ripped through his body. ''They moved north above San Francisco. Tessa was born and Karen kept making excuses why it wasn't a good time for me to come see my new niece. Karen said she was having difficulty recovering from the birth of the baby, then later Tessa had colic, or whatever. I don't know, she stalled me and I shrugged it off. I wanted to see Tessa, but if Karen said to wait, then I went with it like a damn fool. She'd sent me a whole stack of pictures of Tessa, but...

''Then when the baby was three months old, my world fell apart. I was at work when I got the call from a cop up there and he told me that...that Karen was dead. She'd taken Tessa to a women's shelter, but Cliff found out where she was somehow and broke into the building. He was drunk, waving a gun around, screaming and hollering, demanding to see Karen and Tessa. Karen confronted him and he told her to get the baby and come with him. Someone managed to call the police and they got there in record time but…''

''But it was too late,'' Jessica said, tears filling her eyes.

Daniel nodded. ''Karen refused to go with Cliff, told him she couldn't take any more and that when he'd threatened to harm Tessa at their apartment it had been the last straw. Cliff went berserk and he…he shot and killed Karen just as the cops came through the door. They blew him away.''

''Where…where was Tessa during all of this?'' Jessica said, dashing tears from her cheeks.

''She was asleep in a crib in a back room. The cop who called me said they found my name and phone number in Karen's purse and I needed to come up there and take care of arrangements for Karen's…funeral. They'd placed Tessa in a foster home but they would release her to me as soon as I arrived.''

Daniel shook his head. ''I told Mick, only him, what had happened, made up a lame excuse to my captain about a family emergency, then took off. I hardly remember driving up the coast, or much of what I did once I got there. I was in a fog, dazed, in shock, I guess. It was like being outside of myself, watching as I did everything I was supposed to do.

''I recall one of the cops saying how much he admired how well I was handling the situation and I just nodded at him. But my mind was a maze of voices, taunting me, yelling at me, telling me what a failure I was, that I had no right to take Tessa home with me because it was my fault her mother was dead, raging at me about my inadequacies as a brother, father, cop, a...a man.''

"No," Jessica whispered.

"Someday," Daniel said, "I'll have to tell Tessa the truth and she'll hate me, not for what I did, but for what I didn't do."

Jessica framed Daniel's face with her trembling hands. "No, she won't hate you, Daniel. Not if you help her through it, take her to talk to people who understand these situations. Someone...someone like me, who will tell her that..."

"That what?" Daniel said, moving his head back to force Jessica to drop her hands from his face. "That it was Karen's fault, not mine? Or just lay the whole thing on Cliff?"

"Daniel, it's not that black-and-white," Jessica said, the franticness creeping back into her voice. "It's hard to explain, even harder to comprehend, but with the proper guidance Tessa will come to understand how it happened, and find an inner peace about it. But that won't be possible if you don't quit blaming yourself, find your own peace, don't you see?

"You and Tessa will have established a loving bond of father and daughter by then, too, and there will be strength in that foundation that will hold you both in good stead. You will have had years together, sharing, caring, loving each other, that will make you a united front, a team, as Tessa deals with the truth of what happened to her mother and her biological father.''

''Maybe,'' Daniel said quietly. ''Father and daughter? A loving bond? I don't know, Jessica, I just don't know if that will ever take place. I look at Tessa and I see Karen, and it all comes rushing back and...'' He shook his head. ''Well, now you know why I'm so adamant about wanting armed guards on duty twenty-four seven at The Peaceful Dove. Hell, at every women's shelter in the country for that matter.''

Jessica nodded. ''We'll get the guards for The Peaceful Dove, at least. We'll write the best grant application they ever saw and get the funding we need.'' She paused. ''Daniel, you've got to bond with Tessa, see her for the wonderful child she is, not who she looks like. She deserves to be loved by you for herself.''

''Don't go there anymore tonight, Jessica,'' Daniel said wearily. ''I'm on mental overload right now.''

''Yes, all right, but promise me you'll think about what I've said?''

Daniel nodded. ''I guess what you told me answers my question about why you said you *needed* to be at The Peaceful Dove.''

''I didn't intend to put it like that,'' Jessica said, sighing. ''It just slipped out and I tried to smooth it over. But, yes, I *need* to be at The Peaceful Dove because I feel I can really be a help because I truly understand what those women have been through. And also because...'' Her voice trailed off.

"Because..." Daniel prompted.

"Because by going there I'm continually reminded that I mustn't become complacent, or overconfident. I do *not* possess the wisdom to see past the facade a man presents to me. It's a personal flaw of mine, and by being at the shelter I'm face-to-face with that fact. I will never again allow myself to become seriously involved with a man and run the risk of repeating my mistake. I'm focused on my career and that will be enough for me."

"Will it?"

"Yes." Jessica lifted her chin. "I've had these years since what happened with William to etch that in stone. Nothing, no one, will ever change my stand on the issue, Daniel."

"You're letting one incident determine your entire future," Daniel said, frowning. "That's wrong, so damn wrong."

"It's the way it has to be," she said. "I could never totally trust and believe in a man because I could never totally trust and believe in my ability to truly know who he is. I've accepted that."

"Yet you're so quick to tell me that I should change how I perceive myself in regard to what happened to Karen."

"It's apples and oranges, Daniel. When you really think about what we've discussed here tonight, you'll realize that. You don't have a flaw. You've done nothing to warrant the guilt you're carrying on your back. I hope and pray you'll come to know that. For your sake *and* Tessa's. If I didn't feel so strongly about that, I never would have told you about my past.''

''I'm...honored that you did,'' he said, drawing one thumb over her cheek. ''It must have been so difficult, so painful, to sit here and relive it, but you did it for me. I don't know if it will help me to...but I'm grateful for what you did. Thank you, Jessica. I mean that sincerely. Thank you very much.''

Daniel brushed his lips over Jessica's, then in the next instant gathered her into his embrace and captured her lips with his in a searing kiss. Jessica wrapped her arms around Daniel's neck and returned the kiss in total abandon. Heat consumed them and hearts beat in wild tempos as passion soared.

The kiss was rich and meaningful, expressing what would have been difficult to say in words. Then all thoughts fled as they savored the taste, the aroma, the feel of each other.

Daniel raised his head a fraction of an inch to draw a rough breath, then slanted his mouth in the opposite direction as his lips melted over Jessica's once again. His tongue sought hers in the sweet darkness of her mouth and she met his tongue boldly, stroking, dueling, the fire within them leaping higher and hotter.

Think about what you're doing, Jessica's mind hammered suddenly. She didn't conduct herself like this, didn't...but, oh, how she wanted Daniel Quinn, wanted to make love with him, have his powerful body possess her with what she knew would be infinite gentleness.

She *knew?* Oh, how foolish that was, to think she

knew the workings of a man's mind, the true persona beneath the outer facade.

But now, right now, in this exquisite tick of time, she wanted him. All that mattered was the moment at hand, the burning want and need, the desire. And, oh, yes, this was truly desire, not just lust. Desire born of secrets shared because she cared, and Daniel cared, and nothing beyond that was important. Not now.

Daniel broke the kiss and with hands that were not quite steady, he pulled Jessica's arms gently from his neck. He drew a ragged breath before attempting to speak, then looked directly into her eyes. "Jessica," he said, his voice gritty, "I have to stop before I can't, before I lose control. I want you. I won't even attempt to tell you how much I want you, but we're vulnerable right now, I think, because of what we shared here tonight and I won't take advantage of you, of that."

"Daniel…"

"But know this," he went on. "What I feel for you, what is sending me up in flames is *desire. It's not just lust.* Believe that, Jessica, please."

"I do," she said, hardly above a whisper. "I do believe that, Daniel, because it's how I feel, too. I want you, want to make love with you, *desire* you so very much. We can have this night with no regrets, no promises made, no thoughts of tomorrow. Just… this night, our night. Please, Daniel, make love with me."

Chapter 10

It was magic.

The Christmas tree created a cascade of rainbow colors that poured over Jessica and Daniel as they stood before each other and removed their clothes as quickly as possible, their fingers fumbling at times as they continued to gaze into each other's eyes.

Daniel lifted one hand palm up and extended it toward Jessica. She tore her gaze from his and watched from a dreamy, distant place as her own hand floated upward to meet Daniel's. He pulled her forward gently and she went willingly, eagerly, entwining her arms around his neck as he sought and found her lips.

Daniel held her close to his massive body and her breasts were crushed against his muscled chest in a sweet pain that heightened her desire even more.

Their tongues met in the darkness of Jessica's mouth, stroking, dueling, as Daniel lowered her carefully, so carefully, to the floor. He followed her down, never breaking the kiss, and stretched out next to her, catching his weight on one forearm, his other hand splayed on her flat stomach.

The rainbow danced over Daniel's tawny skin and thick, dark hair, and Jessica drank in the sight of him, etching every detail in her mind. His mouth melted over hers once more and she closed her eyes to better savor the exquisite, heated sensations rushing through her.

Daniel moved to one of her breasts and Jessica gasped in pure feminine pleasure as he drew the soft flesh deep into his mouth, laving the nipple with his tongue.

She was on fire, Jessica thought hazily. So hot. Burning. She wanted Daniel Quinn with an intensity like nothing she had ever known before.

Daniel moved to her other breast and Jessica whimpered as she sank her fingers into his moist hair and urged him to take more. Her hands fluttered over his back, feeling his muscles bunch and move beneath her fingertips.

Control, Daniel thought foggily. He had to regain control of his body, the raging want of this woman.

Jessica.

Jessica.

She was responding to him, holding nothing back. Her pleasure must come first. It was so important to him that she—

Heat. It was as though flames were licking through

him and...oh, how he wanted her. He couldn't remember ever desiring, needing, anyone the way he
did Jessica.

She was so beautiful. Her dewy skin tasted so
sweet, so feminine. The lights from the tree were
flickering across her with changing soft hues that
were...oh, he couldn't think, he could only want....

Jessica.

"Daniel," Jessica said, a near-sob catching in her
throat. "Please. Please, Daniel, I want you so much.
Now. Now, Daniel."

"Yes," he said, then kissed her.

He moved away only long enough to take steps to
protect her, then returned, arching above her, then
into her in one smooth motion, filling her, causing her
to whisper his name like a litany.

As Daniel began to move within her with an ever-
increasing tempo, Jessica gripped his shoulders,
tighter, tighter, as the heat within her began to spiral,
twist and turn, and pulse within her.

The rhythm of their melded bodies was wild, thundering, earthy and rich and real. It was ecstasy. Hearts
raced and breathing became labored as they climbed
higher, the flames growing hotter, the tension building, coiling, the exquisite pain of it all only causing
the anticipation of the wondrous moment yet to come
to increase.

Close...so close...

Hotter...higher...

"Daniel!"

"Ah...Jess...Jessica. Jessica."

And it was magic.

They were flung to the top of the rainbow waterfall with an explosion of senses and bright colors, hovered there as they held fast to each other, then slowly and reluctantly drifted back down.

Daniel collapsed, sated and spent, then rolled onto his back, taking Jessica with him and nestling her against his side. She rested her head on his shoulder and sighed. It was a womanly sigh, a sigh of contentment, fulfillment and awe that made words unnecessary.

"No joke," Daniel said quietly. "Incredible."

"Yes."

They lay still and silent, each reliving what they had just shared, each placing the memories in private places known only to themselves.

"Jessica," Daniel said finally. "I'm lousy at making profound speeches, or even finding the right words when...what I mean is...tonight was very special and all I can say, I guess, is thank you."

"I'm the one who supposedly speaks in lengthy paragraphs, according to you," she said softly, "but I don't have the words, either, Daniel, to...so, well, I thank you, too."

"No regrets?" he said. "You won't wake up tomorrow morning all safe and sound in your own bed and want to kick yourself around the block for—"

"No, Daniel," she interrupted, "no regrets. I promise you that. This was our night. Ours. Together. It was very beautiful, very meaningful, and I'll never forget it. Never."

"Good. That's good. But the way you're putting it, it sounds wrapped up, tidy, ready to be put away on a shelf, like a package of finished business." Daniel paused. "Don't you think we should be addressing where we go from here?"

Jessica wiggled out of Daniel's arms, sat up and began to gather her clothes.

"We're not *going* anywhere, Daniel," she said, starting to dress. "We agreed on that, remember? No commitments, no…no anything. Neither of us is interested in a serious relationship so…"

"So?" he said. "That doesn't mean we can't see each other, be lovers, be…come on, Jessica, we're consenting adults. We care enough for each other that what we'd have together wouldn't be remotely close to cheap."

Jessica got to her feet, slipped on her shoes, then sat down on the sofa. Daniel slid his hands beneath his head and remained stretched out on the floor.

"An affair," Jessica said. "You're proposing that we have a no-strings-attached affair, aren't you?"

Daniel got to his feet. "I'm not going to answer that, Counselor, until I'm certain that you're not setting me up. My definition of an affair as it pertains to you and me would not be tacky. Got that? It would be a mutually agreed upon…arrangement. *And* there is no way either of us could get hurt, because we're on the same wavelength. Are you following what I'm saying?"

"It's a tad difficult to concentrate, Lieutenant,

when you're standing there buck naked," Jessica said. "Put some clothes on so I can think clearly."

Daniel chuckled and reached for his jeans that lay in a heap on the floor.

"And don't make that sexy sound, either," Jessica said. "That's not fair."

Daniel zipped his jeans, raised both hands in a gesture of peace, then sat down next to Jessica on the sofa. She stared into space with narrowed eyes and pursed lips.

"You look like you just took a bite of a sour pickle," Daniel said.

"Shh," she said. "I'm getting into my zone."

"Oh, geez," he said, attempting and failing to curb his smile.

Fifteen seconds went by, then thirty, then Jessica suddenly burst into laughter.

"This is absurd," she said. "I've never in my life sat and contemplated whether to engage in an affair." She shook her head, still smiling. "This is about as romantic as a rock."

"Look," Daniel said. "The important thing is that no one will get hurt. Beyond that, everything falls into place. We have fun when we're doing stuff with Tessa, and when we're alone, just the two of us, we are really…"

"Don't start," Jessica said, poking him on the arm with one fingertip. "You'll scramble my brain again."

"It wasn't your brain I was thinking about at the exact moment I said that," Daniel said, grinning at her.

"Do tell."

"No, Jessica, it's *show* and tell. That's much better. Anyway, back to the subject. I want to see you again, be with you, enjoy your company, and when it's possible make love with you. So, yes, okay, I want to have an affair with you with absolutely no misunderstanding about the fact that I have nothing to offer you in regard to the future."

Daniel sighed. "Hell, I don't have anything to offer anyone and the real problem with that is I have a…a daughter to raise, who is going to get the short end of the stick."

"Daniel, please," Jessica said, "don't say such negative things about yourself. You have a great deal to offer Tessa and any woman you might…you might fall in love with and marry. You've got to change your mind-set, think about what I told you regarding what happened to me with William. Karen's choices are not your fault." She placed one hand on his bare back. Heat slithered up her arm and across her breasts and she snatched her hand away. "I've got to go home. It's getting late."

"I like your touch," Daniel said, turning to look at her. "You are so…feminine, so womanly and…I didn't realize how much I'd missed that in my life. Women smell good, do you know that? Even when they sweat, it's a sweet aroma."

"Sir," Jessica said, poking her nose in the air, "women do not sweat. We glow with dew." She laughed. "Or some such nonsense I read somewhere."

Daniel smiled. "I like you, Jessica MacAllister.

That must come across as a strange thing to say, but I sincerely mean it.''

''I like you, too, Daniel Quinn,'' Jessica said, matching his smile, ''and I don't think it's strange at all. It's very, very nice.''

Smiles faded as they continued to look directly into each other's eyes. The now familiar heat began to gain force from the embers within them that were not fully extinguished. Hotter. Hearts began to beat in a wild tempo.

Without realizing they were moving they began to lean toward each other, wanting, needing, the flames of desire licking throughout them and—

''No,'' Jessica said, nearly jumping to her feet. She placed one hand on her racing heart. ''There must be a law written somewhere declaring what you do to me illegal.''

''If there is,'' Daniel said, rising to stand next to her, ''then you're guilty of the same charge. You turn me inside out, Jessica. I want you. Again. Now. Right now.''

''And I want you. However, sensibility shall prevail. I've got an early court date and I must get to bed. Alone.''

''Yeah, okay,'' Daniel said, frowning.

''You know, Daniel, I've been spending every spare minute I've had on the grant application and it's ready to be submitted except for your addition of the request for money for armed guards at The Peaceful Dove. You'll be in my neighborhood when you pick up Tessa from Patty's tomorrow evening. Why don't you come from there to my place and we'll wrap things up?''

Daniel nodded. ''Sounds good.''

''I'll fix us some dinner,'' Jessica said, starting toward the door. ''Don't expect a gourmet meal, though. I'm a whiz with a microwave. Fancy dining it will not be.''

As Jessica gripped the doorknob, Daniel's hand shot out to lie flat on the door next to her head.

''Aren't you going to kiss me good-night?'' he said.

Jessica laughed as she turned toward him. ''Do you want me to tuck you into bed, too?''

Daniel snagged her around the waist and pulled her close. ''Now there's an enticing thought.''

''I...''

''Shh.''

''Yes,'' Jessica whispered.

Daniel kissed her. He kissed her good-night with an intensity that shouted the fact that he didn't want the night to end. He kissed her until she was certain her bones were going to dissolve and her legs would refuse to hold her for another second. He kissed her and she kissed him back in total abandon.

Jessica pushed gently on Daniel's chest and he broke the kiss slowly, very slowly.

''I...'' She cleared her throat when she heard the thread of breathlessness in her voice. ''Must go. Bye.''

''Bye,'' Daniel said, then took a step backward.

Jessica scooted out the door and closed it behind

her with a click. Daniel shoved his hands into the back pockets of his jeans and stared at the door, not moving, hardly breathing.

"What in the hell are you doing, Quinn?" he finally said aloud.

With a shake of his head he turned and walked over to the playpen where the pretty tree stood, seeing in his mind's eye how the multitude of colors had looked as they'd danced over Jessica's bare skin.

He wasn't *doing* anything wrong by becoming involved with Jessica MacAllister, he argued with himself. They'd addressed the...the rules of their relationship, for lack of a better word, like mature adults, laid it all out on the table and accepted it as it stood. No ties. No promises. No commitments. Neither of them would be hurt by participating in their...their affair.

Damn, he wished there was a better way to put it. Affair. He'd had a few of those in the past, always knowing they were temporary flings, fun and games. And a good time was had by all.

He just didn't want what he had with Jessica to be lumped into that pile of old news. What he was sharing with her was richer, more meaningful, honest and real. And right. He...

"Ah, hell, Quinn, give it a rest," he said, then unplugged the tree. "Don't analyze it to death, just enjoy it while it lasts and..."

While it lasts, his mind echoed as he made his way down the hall in the dark. Well, yeah, that's how it was. Temporary. That's what affairs were. Temporary. They ended. Both people went their separate ways and usually didn't see each other again. So be it.

Daniel prepared for bed, then lay staring up at a ceiling he couldn't see.

He was a big boy, he mentally rambled on. He knew the score, understood the rules. So, why did the mere thought of never seeing Jessica MacAllister again cause a cold fist to tighten in his gut?

"Forget it," he said.

Daniel forced himself to relax and drifted off to sleep, only to toss and turn through the long hours of the night in a restless slumber.

The next afternoon, Jessica entered the office and plunked her briefcase on the floor. Esther, the secretary Jessica and Mary-Clair had been able to hire at long last, looked at her questioningly. Esther was in her fifties, was plump and pleasant, and loved to bake. She'd brought a red tin filled with goodies for Jessica and a blue tin brimming with sugar-free cookies for Mary-Clair, and kept both tins well supplied with treats. Jessica snatched up her red tin, pried off the top, gobbled up a chocolate chip cookie, then another.

"You are not a happy camper," Esther said.

"Not even close," Jessica said, reaching for another cookie. "The judge was a jerk. The kids told the dad that Mom is taking them to live by Grandma, who happens to reside in Cleveland. So, what happens? The judge rules that my client, said Mom, has to pay half of the travel expenses that will be incurred by Dad when he visits his sons.''

''Oops,'' Esther said.

''I'm thinking of a stronger word than that,'' Jessica said, ''but I'm too ladylike to say it out loud. Oh, sure, Dad is paying child support in accordance with his income, but when he flies to Cleveland? Oh-h-h, I'm so angry I could chew nails.''

''Chew on another cookie, instead,'' Esther said. ''Nails could be detrimental to your pearly white teeth.''

''Thank you, I will,'' Jessica said, reaching in the tin again. ''Well, darn it, I ate them all.'' She glanced quickly toward Mary-Clair's office.

''You eat Mary-Clair's goodies in her blue tin,'' Esther said, shaking her head, ''she's liable to murder you on the spot.'' She sighed. ''What can I say? I'll have no choice but to tell the cops that it was justifiable homicide.'' She smiled sweetly. ''Speaking of homicides and what have you, how is the yummy Lieutenant Quinn? Mary-Clair and I were chatting about him.''

Vivid images of the previous night with Daniel took up instant residency front row center in Jessica's mind and a warm flush stained her cheeks.

''Who?'' she asked, batting her eyelashes.

''That good, huh?'' Esther said, wiggling her eyebrows. ''I'm delighted for you, my dear.''

Jessica placed the empty red tin back on Esther's desk with a thud.

''Whatever are you talking about, Esther?'' she

said, an expression of pure innocence on her face. "I didn't say one word."

"You didn't have to. Your pretty pink cheeks tell me everything I need to know."

"Who has pretty pink cheeks?" Mary-Clair said, coming through the front door. "Oh, you do, Jessica. I can see them. Are we by any chance discussing Lieutenant Hunk-of-Stuff?"

"No," Jessica said.

"Yes," Esther said at the same time.

"Would you two cut it out?" Jessica said, planting her hands on her hips. "I've had a rough day due to a judge who must have had an argument with his wife this morning, and I still have to go to the grocery store to buy whatever it is I'm going to cook for dinner, which I have no clue as to what it is, but I suppose there had better be plenty of it because Daniel is...a...big...man...oh, crumb, I have such a big mouth."

"Daniel Quinn is the answer to the age-old question of guess who's coming to dinner?" Mary-Clair said. "Dynamite." She frowned. "Except for the fact that you're a lousy cook, Jessica. Do we want him to know that already? Men place a lot of importance on food, you realize. This is *not* good, not good at all."

"Well, there's a place across town called Mother's Cupboard that will take your order for dinner and you just zoom by and pick it up on the way home," Esther said. "It's expensive to do that, though. How's your budget, Jessica? No, forget that. There are times when money just can't be allowed to be a factor, and this is one of them. Mash potatoes. Fill him up with mash potatoes.''

''And steak,'' Mary-Clair said. ''Or roast beef. Something that will really stick to those gorgeous ribs of his. Whatever you do, don't serve him a casserole. My brothers have informed me that casseroles have nipped many a relationship in the bud. For some dumb reason men don't like their food all smushed together on the plate and—''

''Aakk,'' Jessica screamed, pressing her hands against her cheeks. ''You two are driving me crazy.''

Esther placed fingertips on her ears. ''I think you broke something in my head.''

''Listen…to…me,'' Jessica said. ''Daniel is coming to dinner because we have to finish the grant application for The Peaceful Dove. He's picking up Tessa from Patty's house, which is close to where I live, and it was the most efficient manner in which to complete the necessary paperwork. That's it. End of story.''

''Oh,'' Mary-Clair said. ''That sounds reasonable except for the fact that grant applications usually don't cause people to blush a pretty pink as far as I know.''

''Mary-Clair,'' Jessica said, a warning tone to her voice.

''Okay, okay,'' Mary-Clair said, raising both hands. ''I'll change the subject. What did you do yesterday?''

''Yesterday? Yesterday,'' Jessica said. ''Sunday. That was yesterday. Well! I…'' She threw up her hands in defeat. "Phooey, I give up. So, okay, Daniel and I went shopping for Christmas presents for Tessa, then bought a tree, put it in the playpen and decorated it so he could take pictures to show her her first tree, first Christmas."

She picked up the blue tin and shoved it at Mary-Clair. "Have a cookie, or I'll eat them myself to relieve my stress." She spun around and marched into her office.

Mary-Clair opened the tin and popped a cookie into her mouth as she nodded. "Things are lookin' good, Esther," she said, reaching for another treat. "Jessica is definitely shook, and pretty pink cheeks don't lie."

"I certainly hope she remembers to order gravy for the mash potatoes," Esther said, tapping a fingertip against her chin.

Jessica stepped back to survey the table she'd set for dinner in the small dining alcove next to the kitchen. She yawned, then sank onto one of the chairs. Plunking one elbow on the table, she rested her chin in her palm and closed her eyes.

She was exhausted, she thought. She'd been running at full-steam-ahead all day, following a night when she'd gotten very little sleep.

"Hmmm," she said, wiggling her shoulders in an attempt to relax the tightness.

She'd still been in a rosy glow when she'd arrived home last night from Daniel's and had anticipated falling asleep the moment her head touched the pillow.

But that, she thought wearily, was not how it had gone. Not even close. She had had no regrets about making love with Daniel, none at all. What they had shared was special, rare, incredibly beautiful. Such lovely remembrances she had to tuck away in the treasure chest in her heart.

And, no, she wasn't becoming edgy, nervous, about agreeing to have a no-strings-attached affair with Daniel because they had been completely honest with each other. Daniel was right…neither of them could get hurt because they knew exactly where they stood.

What had swept over her in the darkness of her bedroom were the haunting and painful memories of what had happened with William so many years before.

She'd buried all that deeply within her where it was hidden, unable to torture her except on the occasions, usually at The Peaceful Dove, when something triggered the ugly scenes and gave them a seat front row center in her mind.

But telling Daniel about William, reliving it all with the hope that it would help him rid himself of his guilt about Karen, had brought it all back into her reality, and it was chilling and frightening.

When she had managed to doze, she'd dreamt of William, who had appeared nearly as tall as a building, looming over her with tight fists, threatening to hit her. She'd wakened once with tears on her cheeks, hearing the echo of her shouted words of "No, please, no."

At 3:00 a.m. she'd left the bed, unable to remain

there a moment longer. On impulse she decided to decorate her Christmas tree which had, thankfully, quieted her mind and pushed William and what he had done back into the dusty corner of her mind where it belonged.

She'd suffered through the agony of remembering for Daniel. If she had to do it over, would she keep silent rather than endure what she had once she'd returned home?

Jessica opened her eyes and stared at the far wall.

No. If she could turn back the clock to last night, she'd do it all again. She'd tell Daniel her innermost secret, give it to him as a gift that might ease his own pain. Even knowing the consequences, what it would cost her once alone, she would do it...for Daniel.

A knock sounded at the door and Jessica jerked in her chair at the sudden noise. She got to her feet, smoothed her bright blue sweater over the waistband of her jeans, and started across the room.

With each step she took, she realized, the lingering chill within her from the memories of William and what he had done was replaced by a growing warmth that had consumed her by the time she opened the door with a genuine smile on her face.

Daniel matched her smile as he greeted her. Jessica stepped back so he could enter, then closed the door behind him and the baby he was holding.

''Okay, Tessa,'' Daniel said, ''do your thing.''

Tessa was nestled in the crook of Daniel's arm and in one tiny hand she was squeezing the daylights out of the stems of three pink carnations.

"A token for our hostess," Daniel said.

"Are those for me, Tessa?" Jessica said, extending one hand.

The baby leaned forward and dropped the flowers, which Jessica managed to catch before they landed on the floor. She gathered them together and inhaled their lovely aroma.

"These are the most beautiful flowers I've ever received," she said, aware of a funny little flutter in her heart. "Thank you so much."

"You're welcome," Daniel said. "Tessa and I talked it over and decided that three was the number of flowers we wanted for tonight. They represent us, the party of three, who are going to dine together tonight. How's that?"

"That," Jessica said, smiling at him warmly and feeling tears sting at the back of her eyes, "is absolutely perfect."

Chapter 11

While Jessica placed the dinner she'd prepared of baked chicken, mash potatoes and gravy, corn and a tossed salad on the table, Daniel attempted to entertain Tessa and keep her away from the Christmas tree in Jessica's living room that was *not* protected from busy little fingers by a playpen. Daniel dug into the diaper bag and produced the toys he'd stuffed inside to bring along to Patty's.

"Here," he said, dropping the selection on the floor. "Chew on these, Tessa. Hey, toys, kiddo. Not the tree. Whoa."

He swept the baby up into his arms as she crawled as fast as she could toward the pretty, beckoning lights. Tessa patted him on the cheek, then began to wiggle, wanting to get down.

"Nope, nope, nope," Daniel said, nuzzling her

neck. "I'm the evil king and I'm holding you captive in my castle." Tessa squealed in delight as he continued to tickle her neck. "You smell good. Like powder, or something. Your magic perfume is casting a spell over me and your wish is my command. That does not include letting you demolish Jessica's tree."

"Dinner is ready," Jessica said, stepping into the room, "King Quinn and Magic Tessa."

"Great, I'm a starving man," Daniel said. "But what am I going to do with this bundle of trouble-waiting-to-happen while we eat?"

"I stopped by my parents' house and borrowed one of those seats that clip on to the edge of the table," Jessica said. "They have all kinds of equipment at their place for when the family visits. I also got my mother's recipe for baked chicken." Jessica laughed. "So, the way I figure it, if it tastes terrible, it's all her fault. When in doubt, blame it on your mother."

Daniel chuckled as he crossed the room. "That sounds about right. Patty fed Tessa her dinner so all she needs is something to entertain her."

"Cheerios," Jessica said, opening a cupboard. "I've seen many a MacAllister baby occupied with a pile of these little gems."

Daniel shrugged as he slipped Tessa into the seat. "You're the expert."

"Me?" Jessica said, as they sat down. "Not even close. I've helped out with the kiddies at family gatherings, but I was always following instructions. I don't know if I have any natural maternal instincts or not." She paused. "Please, fill your plate, Daniel."

"It looks great," he said.

And Jessica had looked more than great, he thought, when she'd opened the door and greeted him. It was a good thing he'd had an armload of baby at that moment or he probably would have pulled Jessica into his arms and kissed her before he'd even said hello.

"See?" Jessica said. "That cereal is doing the trick. One in the mouth. One on the floor. Tessa is happy as a clam." She frowned. "Did you ever think about that description, Daniel? I mean, what did they do? Go around interviewing a zillion clams, found they are extremely well-adjusted and decided to use them as an example of happy to the max?"

Daniel chuckled as he took a big bite of the crispy chicken.

Man, he thought, he liked this woman. He really did. She was extremely intelligent, yet had a whimsical side that was enchanting. Who else would dither over where the phrase "happy as a clam" came from? Oh, she was something, this Jessica MacAllister. Something very, very special.

This night was about coming together at the end of a long work day to relax and enjoy hot, nourishing food. It was about sharing events that had transpired since they'd been together the previous night. It was a sweet, happy baby making them laugh as she suddenly flung a Cheerio into the mash potatoes.

It was Jessica and Daniel and Tessa...together. As the time ticked by, Jessica became very aware that a scene like this had never before taken place in her home. It was creating warm fuzzy feelings within her that were rather unsettling and, she decided, best ignored because they really didn't mean anything of importance, or anything permanent.

"Can you appeal the judge's decision to have the ex-wife pay the ex-husband's traveling expenses to Cleveland to see the kids?" Daniel asked, bringing Jessica from her rambling thoughts.

"What? Oh, no, we agreed to the terms, because the husband's attorney was going for full reimbursement and I was arguing for zip. When the judge ruled on half the cost I grabbed it. Fuming inwardly, you understand, but I kept my mouth shut. Dad has a new girlfriend so I'm hoping she won't like him winging off to Cleveland too often, which would result in draining my client financially dry."

"Those kids won't really know their father after a while, will they?" Daniel said quietly. "He'll just be a guy who shows up once in a while, probably with an armload of presents to make up for not being around."

"He was rarely home when that couple was married," Jessica said. "Some men in this world just aren't cut out to be fathers."

Daniel glanced over at a babbling Tessa.

"I think I'm eligible to be president of that club," he said, frowning as he looked at Jessica again. "I'm *not* father material, never planned on having kids because I can't be counted on to be there when I should because of my career choice.

"My ex-wife and I agreed. No kids. Then *she* got

tired of my unpredictable schedule and wanted me to quit the force. That was that.'' He shook his head. ''Tessa is liable to look back on her childhood and remember nothing more than a string of promises I made, then broke, because I was called out on a case. Man, that little kid got dealt a lousy hand all the way around the block.''

Jessica leaned forward slightly. ''Tessa will know and remember how much you loved her and that you did the very best you could as her father. Don't stretch the future out like a gloomy dark road, Daniel. Concentrate on now, on bonding with her, loving her to pieces, just taking one step, one day at a time.'' She smiled. ''End of speech. Would you like some ice cream?''

''Sure. Thanks,'' Daniel said. ''I'll help you clear the table.''

''No, I'll do it. It will be faster because I know where everything needs to go. Shall we give Tessa a little bit of ice cream?''

Daniel shrugged. ''I don't know. Are babies' stomachs ready for cold stuff like that? Hell, I don't have a clue.''

Jessica stared into space, obviously deep in thought.

''What?'' Daniel said.

''I'm thinking,'' Jessica said. ''You know, doing reruns in my mind of MacAllister outings and... bingo...there's my cousin, Sarah, holding a Popsicle for her baby at about the age Tessa is now. Sarah has three kids, so she's close to being a pro about this stuff. Good news, Tessa, you get some ice cream.''

Daniel smiled. ''I wish I could solve my cases at work that easily.''

''I'll ditto that in regard to my caseload,'' Jessica said, getting to her feet. ''Hey, maybe this parenting business is easier than we think.''

''Somehow,'' Daniel said, then sighed, ''I seriously doubt that.''

Jessica heard Cheerios crunch under her feet as she walked away from the table.

''I seriously believe you,'' she said. ''I was going to pick that cereal up before it got ground into the carpet and I forgot it was there. Well, okay, being a parent is not a breeze, but it's worth it if you really want that role in your life.''

''And if it's suddenly thrust on you?'' Daniel said. ''What then, Jessica? How do I keep from messing up this kid's head? How do I even begin to be for Tessa what Karen would have wanted me to be?''

Jessica returned to the table and handed Daniel a big bowl of ice cream and also a small one. She went back for her own dessert, then took her seat.

''Just love your daughter,'' she said softly, looking directly into Daniel's eyes. ''And give her a chance to stake a claim on your heart. Just love her, Daniel.''

Daniel nodded slowly as he continued to hold Jessica's gaze. The heat of desire began to hum and glow within them and Daniel tore his gaze from Jessica's and spooned some ice cream into Tessa's mouth.

''Right,'' he said, his voice slightly husky. ''Just

love her. It should be so easy to do that. Tessa is a sweet, innocent baby, who smiles at me when I walk into the room, for Pete's sake. But...I don't know. I feel as though something just shut down inside of me when Karen died, like a part of me is...is dead, too. I'm not certain I can ever love anyone again."

Daniel looked at Jessica again.

"I'm sorry," he said. "I didn't intend to put a damper on this evening. You're very easy to talk to, but that's no excuse for my dumping on you all the time and it's really out of character for me. I apologize, Jessica."

Jessica reached across the table and covered one of Daniel's hands with one of hers.

"Oh, please, don't apologize," she said. "I'm honored that you feel you can share your feelings with me, especially since you say it's not something that you usually do with anyone."

"No, I don't." Daniel shrugged. "I talk to Mick sometimes, but...he's the only one, besides you, who knows what really happened to Karen. I just didn't feel like getting into it with anybody else. The guys at work know my sister was killed and assumed it was an automobile accident. I just left it at that.

"Mick says I need to give this whole thing time. You know, accepting Karen's death, coming to grips with it, not blaming myself, being comfortable in my role of instant father."

"He's right," Jessica said, removing her hand from Daniel's.

Tessa slapped her tiny hands on the table.

"Madam would like more ice cream, Daddy," Jessica said, smiling. "You're flunking spoon-in-the-mouth."

"Here you go," Daniel said, popping the spoon in Tessa's mouth. "I sure don't see how Patty tended to two of these little creatures all day."

"Patty loves being a mommy," Jessica said, then ate some of her own ice cream.

"Did you ever notice how good babies smell?" Daniel laughed. "Well, most of the time."

"That magic perfume you were telling Tessa about," Jessica said, nodding. "Yes, I'm aware of it. We should figure out a way to bottle it and make a million dollars."

"There you go," Daniel said. "Okay, we're rich. What would you buy with all your bucks?"

The lighthearted mood was restored and they finished their dessert by listing outrageous purchases they would make with their newfound wealth.

While Jessica cleaned the kitchen, Daniel gave Tessa a quick bath, then zipped the baby into her fuzzy pink sleeper, which he said he got points for remembering to pack in the diaper bag. They played with the baby, who was soon rubbing her eyes and sucking on her fingers.

"I guess her first busy day in a new place is catching up with her," Daniel said. "I'll give her a bottle, then we can put her down on your bed, if that's all right."

"Sure," Jessica said.

Tessa was soon sleeping peacefully in the center of

Jessica's double bed, a pillow fortress surrounding her. Jessica spread out the paperwork for the grant application on the dining room table and Daniel scanned what she had already done.

"Nice work," he said, nodding. "Excellent."

Jessica opened a laptop computer and sat down at the table. "You can dictate what you want to say about money for armed guards, I'll print it out at work tomorrow, and get this thing in the mail." Jessica wiggled her fingers. "Okay, Lieutenant, speak. I'm ready."

Jessica's fingers flew over the keys as Daniel paced back and forth behind her chair, making his pitch for the extra funds. She marveled at how articulate he was, how he was able to put his thoughts into concise, powerful sentences that were extremely persuasive.

"That's it," he said finally.

"I'm truly amazed," Jessica said, pressing the button to save what she had typed. "I thought you would want to do a rough draft, then we'd shape it up. It's perfect as it stands."

"That comes from many years of writing police reports," Daniel said, smiling. "I hate doing them, so I just jump in and get them done."

Jessica repacked her briefcase, snapped it closed and gave it a pat.

"One application for grant money for The Peaceful Dove ready to go," she said, getting to her feet. "Oh, Daniel, they just have to approve this. The shelter was originally the rental property of a wealthy couple who donated it, along with a sizable sum to run it, but that money is almost gone. The service group donations we receive just aren't enough. We have to get this grant.''

Daniel wrapped his arms around Jessica and pulled her close. She encircled his waist with her arms and looked up at him.

''If they don't approve the application, I'll arrest them for stupidity,'' he said. ''How's that?''

''Whatever works. The Peaceful Dove has to have that money so it can stay open and have the repairs done that are needed so badly and—''

''Guaranteed,'' Daniel interrupted, then lowered his head and kissed her.

Desire exploded within them like fireworks on the Fourth of July. Daniel deepened the kiss and Jessica slid her hands upward to splay on his back, savoring the feel of his tight muscles.

He'd been waiting all day for this moment, Daniel thought hazily. He was only now realizing that, but it was true. He broke the kiss and drew a ragged breath.

''Thanks,'' he said, chuckling, ''I needed that.''

''Me, too,'' Jessica said, willing her racing heart to quiet.

''I want to make love with you, Jessica,'' he said, not releasing his hold on her. ''But Goldilocks is sleeping in your bed.''

''But, sir,'' Jessica said smiling, ''we have a lovely tradition of making love in the glow of Christmas tree lights. I just happen to have a Christmas tree that is calling our name.'' Her smile faded. ''I want you, too, Daniel. I truly do.''

Daniel nodded. With his arm across her shoulders they left the kitchen, turning off the light as they went. Just as Daniel snapped off the lamp on the end table next to the sofa, the pager clipped to his belt buzzed.

''Damn,'' he said, turning the light back on. He glanced at the pager to see the number on the tiny screen. ''I have to call in. Hopefully it's just someone reporting to me while I'm the acting captain for a few weeks.'' He dropped a quick kiss on Jessica's lips. ''Wish that this is not a case that Mick and I have to respond to. We're next up on the roster.''

''Wishing,'' Jessica said.

As Daniel went into the kitchen to use the telephone on the wall, Jessica turned to stare at the lovely Christmas tree, a delicious shiver of anticipation coursing through her as she envisioned making love with Daniel in the glow of the multicolored lights.

The perfect ending, she thought dreamily, to a perfect evening. Oh, my…yes.

Daniel strode back into the room, bringing Jessica from her sensuous musings.

''I have to go,'' he said gruffly. ''There's been a homicide and…damn it, Jessica, I'm sorry. I sure as hell don't want to leave but…'' He shook his head. ''Maybe I'll become a bus driver.''

Jessica smiled and closed the distance between them, stepping into Daniel's embrace when she reached him. "You and your bus would probably be assigned the night shift."

"The way my luck is going, you're right." Daniel framed Jessica's face in his hands. "Man, oh, man, I really do not want to go out that door."

"Duty calls, Lieutenant," she said. "I do understand, you know. I grew up with my uncle Ryan and Uncle Ted being called away time and again in the middle of some family celebration. And my aunt Kara is a doctor and she was always zooming out the door and...I want you to stay, believe me, but I'm not angry because you can't."

"Thank you for that," Daniel said, then kissed her deeply.

When he finally released her, he stared up at the ceiling for a long moment to regain control.

"Whew," he said. "You are one very potent lady, Ms. MacAllister."

"You're not too shabby yourself," she said, then took a much-needed breath.

"Well, I'm outta here," Daniel said, starting toward the door. He stopped and threw up his hands. "Look at this." He spun around to face Jessica again. "Would you look at this? Oh, yeah, I'm great. I deserve the Father of the Year Award. My kid is asleep down the hall and I forgot all about her." He dragged one hand through his hair. "Hell."

"Daniel, leave Tessa here," Jessica said. "In the first place, you have nowhere to take her. In the second place, she's sound asleep and there's no sense in dragging her out into the cold night air. In the third place, I don't mind having her stay over.''

''Are you sure?''

''Positive. If you wrap things up on your case in the middle of the night, just go home and get some sleep yourself. You can pick Tessa up in the morning. If you're not here by—'' she narrowed her eyes as she envisioned her schedule for the next day ''—by nine-thirty tomorrow morning, I'll take Tessa to Patty's.''

''Okay,'' Daniel said, nodding. ''I really appreciate this and...I've got to hustle. Mick is going to wonder where in the hell I am.''

''Go,'' Jessica said, flapping her hands at him.

''Right,'' Daniel said, then left the apartment.

Jessica stood statue still after hearing the lock clicking into place on the door. She wrapped her hands around her elbows as the sudden silence in the room pressed against her with an oppressive, chilling weight.

She missed him, she thought incredulously. Daniel had been gone about fifteen seconds and she already missed him. That was absurd. Well, no, maybe not. She was a healthy woman who had been about to share fantastically beautiful lovemaking with a very special man and then...poof...he was gone. It stood to reason that she wished he was still there with her.

Jessica sighed and wandered down the hall and into her bedroom. She turned on the bathroom light to cast a soft glow over Tessa where she slept peacefully in the center of the bed. Jessica sat down, shifted the pillows nearest her to the floor, then stretched out next to the baby.

"Hello, pretty girl," she whispered, as she sifted her fingers through Tessa's silky hair. "Your daddy had to go to work so I'm going to take care of you. I'm winging it so be patient with me, okay?"

What a precious baby, Jessica thought, her gaze riveted on Tessa. She looked so much like Daniel with her dark hair and eyes, and tawny skin.

When the three of them had been Christmas shopping in the mall, she remembered thinking that there was probably no doubt in anyone's mind that Tessa was Daniel's daughter and...and what? She, Jessica MacAllister, was the wife and mother in the picture-perfect trio?

No, she'd known then just as she knew now that she would never have those roles. Not with Daniel, or anyone. She'd made that choice, and she was comfortable with it.

Tessa stirred, found her thumb she'd been seeking even in sleep, popped it into her mouth, and stilled, sleeping the sleep of the innocent.

But tonight, Jessica thought, smiling at the exquisite infant, she was going to indulge in a fantasy for no other reason than that she felt like doing it. Besides, fantasy wasn't always based on secret dreams and yearnings. Her fantasy wasn't what she really wanted from life, and it was hard to resist indulging in as she lay next to this little miracle. There was no harm in it.

Tessa was Daniel's daughter. Daniel was Daddy.

She was Daniel's wife. She was Mommy. Tessa was Baby. And there should be a kitten, or a puppy, to complete the family. Yes, that was good.

In a few years there would be a...mmm...okay, a brother for Tessa. Yes, a boy came next. Daniel Quinn, Junior? No, that got too confusing when you were calling people to the telephone or...no, they'd think of a strong, masculine name for their son and use Daniel as a middle name. Much better. Something Daniel Quinn.

They'd need a big house, of course, but that was no problem. Her family was overflowing with architects, was even connected through Aunt Kara and Uncle Andrew to Malone Construction. The house was a given.

What else? What was missing?

Love.

She was painting a picture on a blank canvas that didn't have a foundation of love. Even in a fantasy she couldn't evoke emotions in Daniel that would never be there, directed toward her. And her feelings for Daniel?

"Oh, enough of this nonsense," she said, slipping off the bed.

Jessica replaced the pillows securely next to Tessa, then hurried from the room, having the irrational thought that if she rushed away she could leave that ridiculous fantasy behind and forget she'd ever indulged in something so out of character for her.

But the picture she'd painted in her mind followed

her into the living room, causing her to pace restlessly around the room.

Why had she done that? she thought frantically. She didn't even *want* what was in her fantasy, yet she'd been filled with a strange and foreign warmth as she'd added more details to the scenario.

"Oh, Jessica, get a grip," she said, stopping her trek and planting her hands on her hips. "You went nuts, that's all, because there's a baby staying the night in your home for the first time." She paused. "Daniel Quinn's baby girl.

"Stop it," she said, spinning around and heading for the kitchen. "It was a silly thing to do and it won't happen again. I'm going to have another bowl of ice cream and forget the whole dumb thing."

But several hours later, with Tessa tucked next to her in the bed, Jessica dreamt about the fantasy, saw herself holding Tessa with Daniel's arms encircling them both. A kitten and a puppy tumbled in play at their feet as they all stood in the grassy backyard of a large home. They were smiling and warm sunshine poured over them as their mingled laughter danced through the air.

Jessica woke with a start in the middle of the night, shaken by the dream and unsettled further when she realized that tears had dampened her cheeks.

Chapter 12

At seven-thirty the next morning, Jessica sat at the kitchen table with a mug of coffee, a container of yogurt and two pieces of toast. She was wearing a full-length, coral-colored satin robe she'd received for Christmas the previous year from her parents, and her hair was still damp from her shower and shampoo.

Tessa had wakened at five, eagerly received the bottle Jessica offered her, then had fallen back to sleep and was still snoozing in Jessica's bed.

As Jessica took a bite of toast a quiet knock sounded at the door.

Daniel, she thought, swallowing the toast and getting to her feet. He was the only one who would have any reason to be knocking on her door so early. Daniel was here.

Jessica rushed across the living room, knowing

there was a bright smile on her face and making no attempt to curb it. She peered through the peephole and her smile disappeared as she looked at Daniel. When she opened the door, concern was etched on her face.

"Come in, come in," she said, stepping back to make room for him to enter. "Oh, Daniel, you've been up all night, haven't you?" She swept her gaze over him, noticing his stubbly beard, tousled hair, the tie that was pulled to the center of his chest, and the fatigue radiating from the depths of his dark eyes. "You look done in. Would you like some coffee?"

"Sounds great," he said, yanking off his tie and stuffing it into his pocket. "I thought I should come by and get Tessa and deliver her to Patty's before I go home and get some sleep."

"You didn't have to do that," Jessica said, leading the way to the kitchen. "I would have taken Tessa to Patty's house."

"Tessa is *my* responsibility," he said, a sharp edge to his voice. "She's *my* daughter." He sank onto a chair at the table.

"I realize that, Daniel," Jessica said, placing a mug of coffee in front of him. "I was just trying to be helpful, that's all."

"Oh, cripe," he said, leaning back in the chair and dragging both hands down his face. "I'm sorry. I didn't mean to bark at you. I'm just so damn tired, but that's no excuse. It was a long night."

"Are you hungry?"

"No. Thanks, but no." Daniel picked up the mug

and took a swallow of the hot coffee. "This is all I need. I interrupted your breakfast and...where's Tessa?"

"She went back to sleep after an early bottle," Jessica said, sitting opposite him at the table.

"I like that...that robe thing you're wearing," Daniel said. "So, this is how you look in the morning, huh? You're very beautiful, Jessica. After last night it's good to see someone who is alive and happy and..." His voice trailed off and he took another swallow of coffee.

"Would you like to talk about the case you're on?" Jessica said, looking at him intently. "I'd listen, you know."

Daniel frowned and stared into the mug as he ran one fingertip slowly around the top edge. A long, silent minute ticked by and Jessica was hardly breathing when he spoke again.

"She killed him," he said, lifting his head to meet her gaze. "The guy had been beating up on her and the kids for years and last night she'd had enough. She picked up a knife in the kitchen and stuck it in his heart. Yep, she killed him dead as a post."

"Dear heaven," Jessica whispered.

"I talked to her, Jessica," Daniel said, fatigue producing a gritty quality to his voice. "I asked her why she'd stayed so long, why she hadn't left the scum years ago. She said he was always so sorry after he'd hit her or the kids that he cried and begged for forgiveness, swore he'd never do it again. And every time...every damn time, she believed him.

"Why? I asked her that. Why?" Daniel laughed, the sound rough and sharp, holding no hint of true humor. "Know what she said? Because she loved him. Can you believe that, Jessica?"

"Yes," she said softly, feeling the color drain from her face as a shiver coursed through her. "She had picked him as the one to give her heart to and she couldn't bear the thought of having been so terribly wrong. In her case, he was the father of her children, too.

"He couldn't be all bad, she'd say to herself. Oh, please, don't let him have a soul as dark as night. Not the man she'd chosen. Not the man she loved. He'd change. He would. Of course, he would."

"Oh, yes, Daniel, I believe every word you're saying."

"She always took him back," Daniel said, making a fist and slamming it onto the table. "She made that conscious decision on her own. Just...just like Karen did."

"Yes," Jessica said, her voice quivering. "And... and just like...just like I did, Daniel."

"What?"

"I didn't tell you because I was so ashamed," Jessica said, her eyes filling with tears. "But you need to know now, because I think you're finally coming to understand that nothing you could have said or done would have convinced Karen to do anything other than what she did."

"Go on," Daniel said, narrowing his eyes.

"When...when William...hit me, I screamed at

him to leave, never to come near me again.'' Jessica
drew a shuddering breath. ''The next night he showed
up at the apartment where I was living then…with a
bouquet of roses and…I told him to go away. He
stood in the hallway outside my door where anyone
passing could see him and he cried, he begged me to
forgive him, promised me he would never strike me
in anger again. And, Daniel?'' Tears spilled onto Jessica's pale cheeks. ''I believed him. And I allowed
him back into my heart, my home and…and my
bed.''

''Damn it, Jessica, why?'' Daniel said, leaning toward her.

Jessica dashed the tears from her cheeks, got to her
feet and planted her hands flat on the table.

''Because I didn't know how to deal with the dev-
astating emptiness, of feeling as though I'd lost myself when my esteem and confidence were shattered.
I loved William, had made love with William, had
daydreamed about having William's babies. *And he
wasn't even close to being who I believed him to be*.
Do you have any idea what facing that does to a
woman, Daniel? What it did to me? What it did to
Karen?

''It's shattering. It diminishes your self-worth and
makes you question your ability to make the simplest
decision regarding your life. Should I buy this pair of
shoes or that pair? This pair. But what if I'm wrong?
What if they don't look right with the dress I'm planning on wearing them with? Then everyone who sees

me with those shoes on my feet will know I lack the wisdom to make intelligent, womanly choices.

"So, no, God, no, I can't have been wrong about this man I was so certain was my soul mate. No, said battered Jessica, but of course William hit me again and *then* I threatened to press charges against him.

"No, said abused Karen, but every promise her husband made was a lie waiting in the shadows to erupt in anger and be delivered with painful blows that further destroyed her self-confidence.''

"Jessica…" Daniel said, getting to his feet.

"No one could have kept me from taking William back, Daniel," Jessica said, nearly choking on a sob. Tears streamed down her face and along her neck, and she swiped her hands across her cheeks. "I made my own decision and paid the consequences. Do you understand yet? Do you realize that you could not have stopped what happened to Karen? No matter how much you loved her, wanted to protect her, keep her from harm, *the final choice was hers to make.* Do…you…understand…that, Daniel?"

"Yes, I…" Tears shimmered in Daniel's eyes. "Yes, I do. I understand, Jessica, and it's time I allowed Karen to…to rest in peace."

He shook his head. "I don't deserve you, what you've put yourself through by reliving those horrible memories in an attempt to help me be free of the crushing guilt I've been carrying on my back. How do I thank you, Jessica? What do I say?"

"Thanks really aren't necessary, Daniel," she said, managing to produce a small smile. "I'll be able to put the memories of what happened with William back where they belong, away from me, soon. I'm sure I will. This has been…yes, like a refresher course in remembering that I have a definite flaw to deciphering the true colors of men.''

"Do you think you might be wrong about *me?*" Daniel said, splaying one hand on his chest. "You and I are lovers, you've given yourself to me and…but you're not certain I'm who I present myself to be?"

Jessica wrapped her hands around her elbows. "What we're sharing is temporary, Daniel. We're not planning a future together, a forever. Yes, we make love but we're not in the process of *falling* in love. You said yourself that neither of us can be hurt by our…our relationship, and you're right."

"I see," he said, dragging a restless hand through his hair. "I just don't like the idea that you could have even a fleeting thought that I might have a side to me that I'm not revealing and…never mind. I'm so tired I can't think straight. What you said probably made perfect sense."

"Daniel, if…if the woman admitted that she killed her husband and, I presume, you arrested her, why were you up all night?"

"Do you mind if I finish my coffee?" Daniel said. "You should eat that breakfast you've got there, too."

They sat back down opposite each other and Daniel drained his mug.

"Would you like more?" Jessica said.

"No, thanks." Daniel paused. "You know, it just hit me that when Tessa grows up and the time comes when I have to explain what happened to her mother, I'm not going to be telling Tessa that it's my fault that Karen died. I'll be focusing on choices we make and how far-reaching they can be, I guess."

"Yes," Jessica said, poking holes in her cold toast with a fingertip.

"Maybe I've got a fighting chance of Tessa not hating me."

"But first you must come to love her, Daniel," Jessica said quietly.

Daniel took a deep breath, then let it out slowly, puffing his cheeks. "My brain is on circuit overload. I'll deal with some of this stuff after I've had some rest. You asked why I was up all night. I didn't need to be. Mick was long gone because there was no reason to hang around. Social Services sent a woman to pick up the kids and the uniforms took the wife downtown. We had a confession so Mick and I were done with our part."

Jessica cocked her head slightly to one side. "So where have you been all these hours?"

"Gathering evidence that will help the attorney with the woman's defense. I want her to be united with her kids and start a new life. A *real* existence where she won't live in fear all the time.

"I was way out of line doing what I did," Daniel went on. "I flashed my badge as I woke up neighbors and took statements from them, spoke with the emergency room personnel at the closest hospital to where the woman lived and hit pay dirt, even got the principal of the school where the kids go out of bed. I handed everything over to the woman's public defender and she's out on bail.''

Jessica smiled. ''That was wonderful of you, Daniel. I wish all the women at The Peaceful Dove had a crusader like you in their corner. I'm sure that woman will be very grateful when she comes to realize what you did.''

''Oh, I don't know,'' he said, sighing. ''She still has to deal with the fact that she killed a human being. I shot a man in the line of duty years ago, a drug addict who was determined to waste me. I was justified in what I did, but it's still not an easy road to go.''

''There are counselors available to help her through that,'' Jessica said. ''She just has to make the decision to seek them out.''

''Decisions,'' Daniel said. ''Choices. It all seems to boil down to choices, doesn't it? Life? It's all about the choices we make and where we end up because of them.''

''Yes, I suppose you're right.''

''Well, at least a choice I settled on recently is one of the best I've ever made.'' Daniel got to his feet, rotated the stiff muscles in his neck, then looked at Jessica again. ''You...being with you, spending time with you, laughing, talking, sharing, making love with you...you're a million-dollar *choice,* Jessica Mac-Allister, and I owe you so damn much for so many things.''

Jessica smiled as she got up from the table and went to Daniel, wrapping her arms around his neck.

"A million-dollar choice? Me?" she said, smiling up at him. "Well, fancy that. My goodness, don't I feel special?"

"You are special," he said, lowering his head slowly toward hers. "Very rare, very wonderful and very, *very* special."

Daniel kissed Jessica and they both instantly knew that the kiss, too, was very, *very* special.

It was a kiss that conveyed messages of being grateful for secrets shared and the heartfelt willingness for having done so.

It was a kiss that spoke of a greater trust between them, of understanding and caring taken to a depth greater than before.

It was a kiss shared by a man and a woman who had witnessed each other's tears and thought more, not less, of the person because of them.

It was Jessica and Daniel's kiss and they savored every heart-stopping moment of it.

When Daniel finally raised his head, he looked directly into Jessica's eyes, drinking in the sight of who she was, etching indelibly in his mind what she had done for him.

"Go home and get some sleep, Lieutenant," Jessica whispered. "I'll deliver your daughter safely to Patty."

Daniel nodded, kissed her gently on the forehead, then turned and strode from the room. As he closed the apartment door behind him, Jessica smiled.

"And now, Daniel, *you* can sleep the sleep of the innocent just like Tessa," she said.

Before Daniel went to his beckoning bed, he drove to the cemetery and hunkered down in front of Karen's grave that was next to where their parents were buried.

"It's all about choices, Karen," he said, his voice husky with emotion. "God knows I wish yours would have been different, but...well, they were yours to make." He nodded as he swallowed heavily. "Rest in peace, baby girl."

Then Daniel lowered his chin to his chest and gave way to cleansing tears.

Chapter 13

The remainder of the week and on into the next one represented the countdown to Christmas and the seemingly endless string of parties that went along with the holiday season.

Jessica and Mary-Clair divided up the invitations to the gatherings that came under the heading of "we really should put in an appearance, even though we don't want to." Mary-Clair fussed and fumed, declaring she was using up a year's supply of willpower by not indulging in the scrumptious goodies being offered at the festive events.

Despite the hectic pace, Jessica managed to finish her Christmas shopping, then stayed up until 2:00 a.m. one night getting all the gifts wrapped.

She bought Tessa a soft, fuzzy white lamb that played a lullaby when its tummy was pressed. Even though Daniel seemed to feel less responsible for his sister's death, Jessica didn't want to risk evoking haunting memories of Karen by presenting Tessa with a teddy bear.

Jessica dithered over whether or not she should buy Daniel a present.

No, a gift for Tessa was enough. She and Daniel hadn't been together long enough to do something as sentimental and romantic as exchanging gifts on the special holiday. Besides, if she got something for him and he didn't reciprocate, he'd be embarrassed. So... no.

But then again...

Yes, of course, she should have a gift for Daniel under her tree. He was her...her lover, and it would be remiss of her not to remember him along with all the others on her shopping list.

But then again...

"Going nuts here," Jessica said, as she wandered through a mall one evening.

She stopped in front of a shop window and swept her gaze over the display, her heart suddenly quickening.

There it is, she thought. Daniel's gift.

It was a carving that stood about seven inches high and was done in a warm shade of wood that had been polished to a lustrous sheen. The detail was exquisite. It was a man's hand gently cupped around the tiny hand of a child that was splayed in the larger palm.

"Oh, my," she whispered.

A short time later Jessica emerged from the store

with the carving gift wrapped and nestled in a bag. When she returned home, she placed it beneath her tree, staring at the gift for a long moment with a soft smile on her lips.

On the day before Christmas Eve, Daniel sat at his desk at the station reading a report. Mick settled into his chair at the desk next to him.

"Mick," Daniel said, "what are you getting Rosemary for Christmas?"

"I got her a sweater that has this stuff around the neck. You know, pearls and glittery things that make it look fancy."

"Oh." Daniel nodded.

"And…um…I also bought her a…" Mick cleared his throat. "A little baby doll wrapped in a blanket."

"Huh?" Daniel said, turning to look at his partner. "A what?"

Mick swiveled his chair so he could meet Daniel's confused gaze.

"Rosemary wants another baby," he said. "She hit me with that news flash about a month ago and I told her there was no way we could afford to raise three kids on my salary. I told her the subject was closed. But then…"

"Then?" Daniel prompted. "Then…what? You won the lottery?"

"No, I started remembering how incredibly beautiful Rosemary was when she was pregnant, how she glowed with happiness. And I remembered watching my son and daughter being born and holding them for the first time, then later seeing their first smile, taking their first steps, how I felt ten feet tall when their faces lit up...still do...when I come home.''

Mick laughed. ''What can I say? I want another baby as much as Rosemary does. So, rather than just say 'hey, yeah, let's go for it,' I thought it would be corny but sort of special to let her know how I feel by giving her the baby doll.''

''I'll be damned,'' Daniel said, smiling. ''Ten bucks says she cries when she opens that gift.''

''That's a given,'' Mick said, chuckling. ''Hell, we *can't* afford to raise three kids, but the thought of having a baby in the house again...well, we'll manage somehow. Whatever sacrifices we have to make will be worth it.''

''Yeah, but your kids are six and eight years old. They're people,'' Daniel said. ''You want to do bottles and diapers and *teething* again?''

''Yep,'' Mick said, nodding. ''I really do. They grow up so fast, Danny. One minute you're holding this tiny bundle that looks like a wrinkled prune and the next thing you know, they're heading out the door to play with their friends and you practically have to make an appointment to have a conversation with them. I'm telling you, buddy, enjoy every second of Tessa while she's tiny because she won't stay that way for long.''

Daniel frowned. ''I feed her, change her diapers, give her a bath, walk the floor with her when her teeth go nuts, but...enjoy her? There's never enough time to…besides, how do you *enjoy* a kid who can't talk, or really play, or…I don't get it, Mick.''

"Make time, Danny," Mick said. "Put Tessa on your lap after her bath and read her a story.''

"She can't understand a story.''

"That's not the point," Mick said. "Cripe, you're dense. It's quality time, don't you see? You and your daughter, together. Tonight, no matter what, read Tessa a story.'' He paused. "Back up here a minute. Why did you ask me what I was getting Rosemary for Christmas?''

"Oh. Well.'' Daniel directed his attention to lining up three pencils in perfect order on his desk. "I thought I might get…what I mean is, it seems appropriate that I should buy a gift for…Jessica.''

Mick's eyes widened. "Jessica MacAllister?''

"How many Jessicas do you think I know?'' Daniel said, shooting a glare at Mick. "Yes, Jessica MacAllister. Okay? We're seeing each other when schedules allow and…what I mean is, she and I…ah, hell, forget it.''

"Interesting, very interesting,'' Mick said, leaning back in his chair and linking his fingers behind his head. "Rosemary has been worried that you and Tessa would be alone on Christmas because we're going to San Diego. Can I assure my sweet wife that you'll be with the lovely Jessica on the big day?''

"Well, yeah, Tessa and I are going to have Christmas dinner at Jessica's parents' house. It's a potluck number, you know? I'm taking a pumpkin pie from the bakery and...well, I haven't figured out if I should buy Jessica a gift.''

"Tomorrow is Christmas Eve, Danny,'' Mick said. "You're kind of letting this go down to the wire. You'd better head out on your lunch hour and buy Jessica something special. You can't shop tonight because you'll be busy reading Tessa a story.''

"You're a nag,'' Daniel said. "I never noticed that about you before. It's a pain in the butt.''

"Yeah, well,'' Mick said, shrugging, "you've never been in a situation where you didn't have a clue as to what you're doing. You're a father now and you need my expertise. You're also involved with a very classy lady. This is not your usual love 'em and leave 'em scenario, partner. For those you didn't need my advice, that's for sure.''

"Don't get crazy here, Mick,'' Daniel said, frowning. "Jessica and I have an understanding. No commitments. No promises. No strings. This is no different from the relationships I've had in the past.'' He paused. "Well, that's not entirely true, I guess. Jessica is very special, very rare and...she's beautiful, intelligent, has a great sense of humor and...well, she cares very deeply about...things.''

Daniel picked up one of the pencils and began to tap the eraser on the top of the desk.

"Because of Jessica,'' he went on quietly, "I've come to realize that I couldn't have prevented what happened to Karen. My sister made her own choices, and paid the ultimate price for them. Jessica helped me understand that because of...well, I won't get into details because it's her private business, but it cost her a lot, emotionally, to share what she did with me and I'm very grateful to her for that.''

"Like I said," Mick said, "she is a classy woman. I'm glad you've moved past the guilt you were carrying around about Karen's death, Danny. It wasn't your fault."

"No, it wasn't," he said. "I know that now, thanks to Jessica."

"Good. That's good," Mick said. "You definitely need to buy that lady a Christmas present. Do you have any idea what you might get her?''

"Nope," Daniel said, tossing the pencil aside. "Not a clue."

"Well, forget eating lunch," Mick said decisively. "You're going shopping."

"Because I'll be busy reading a story to Tessa tonight," Daniel said, frowning.

"Got it in one. There were some books in that stuff that Rosemary gave you that our kids had outgrown. You're all set."

"I'm all set to feel like an idiot while I'm reading a book to a baby who can't understand one word of what I'm saying."

"Just shut up and do it," Mick said.

"Right."

That evening Daniel leaned over the playpen and placed the prettily wrapped gift he'd gotten for Jessica beneath the Christmas tree.

He sure hoped she liked it, he thought, staring

down at the present. Maybe it was dumb, really corny. It was a small, hand-painted ceramic house with a removable roof that allowed a candle to be placed in the holder inside. When the candle was lit, the glow would shine through the windows representing a warm, welcoming home.

Oh, yeah, no doubt about it…it was corny.

Well, damn. He'd really liked it when he'd seen it in the store in the mall. It had reminded him of Jessica, of the way she seemed to fill a room, his home, with sunshine and laughter and…hell, this was getting cornier by the minute.

"Okay, forget it," he said, scooping a pajama-clad Tessa off the floor. "Are you ready for this nonsense, kid? I'm going to read you a story. Is that ridiculous or what? Don't answer that because I already know the answer."

Daniel settled onto the sofa with Tessa on his lap and opened the book.

"Okay," Daniel said, "here we go. The lesson to be learned from this one, Tessa, is never talk to strangers. Got that? This little girl in the red coat is taking some dessert or something to her grandmother, which her mother should never have allowed her to do alone, and there's this wolf guy who…never mind, I'll just read it. Pay attention. There will be a test on this later. Ready? Once upon a time…"

As Daniel read, Tessa leaned her head back against his chest and stuck her thumb in her mouth. She sat perfectly still, her gaze riveted on the book. Daniel tilted his head as he turned each page to see if Tessa had fallen asleep because she was so quiet, but she was awake and seemingly hanging on every word.

At one point Daniel dipped his head and buried his nose in Tessa's silky hair, inhaling the mystical fragrance of baby. He began to put more effort into his reading, giving the wolf a gravelly voice, the grandmother a squeaky one, and Little Red Riding Hood a southern drawl, just for the heck of it.

He was, he realized, as he neared the end of the book, really enjoying this. There was no reason why story time couldn't be incorporated into Tessa's going-to-bed ritual. He'd buy her some more books, too, but check them over very carefully because this one had a tad too much violence for his daughter to hear just before nodding off to sleep. She might have nightmares.

"The end," Daniel said finally, closing the book.

He looked sideways at Tessa again and discovered that she was sound asleep. He set the book on the end table, then didn't move. He just sat there, liking the feel of the solid little bundle on his lap.

"Your Uncle Mick is a smart man, Tessa," Daniel said quietly. "I think maybe this is the stuff of which memories are made."

The next morning Daniel once again stared at the present for Jessica beneath the tree.

There was no way, he decided, that he was going to sit there like an idiot at Jessica's parents' house on Christmas day and have the whole MacAllister clan see what a corny gift he'd bought Jessica. No way.

He picked up the telephone receiver and punched in Jessica's number, hoping to catch her at home before she left for the office. The ringing began on the other end of the line.

"Hello?"

"Hey," Daniel said.

"Hi, Daniel," Jessica said. "How nice to hear from you. It seems like...well, forever, since I've seen you."

"Ditto," he said, knowing he was smiling at the sound of her voice. "Listen, I...that is, Tessa has a Christmas present for you and I was wondering if we could get together tonight so I...she could give it to you."

"That would be perfect," Jessica said. "We'll have a private little gift exchange instead of getting caught up in the bedlam tomorrow at my folks'. Their living room will end up looking like a wrapping paper factory exploded right there on the spot."

Daniel chuckled. "Interesting image. Why don't I order in Chinese and you can come here after work?"

"I'll be there." Jessica paused. "I'll be looking forward to it, Daniel."

"Yeah, me, too. See ya."

"Goodbye."

Jessica replaced the receiver, but didn't remove her hand. She'd missed Daniel, she thought, still staring at the telephone. A quick call each day just hadn't been enough. She wanted to see him, drink in the sight of him, feel his arms around her and his lips on hers.

Jessica snatched her hand away from the receiver

as though it had suddenly become too hot to touch. She returned to her chair at the table and took a bite of toast, followed by a sip of coffee. She sighed and stared into space.

Daniel Quinn, she mused, was occupying her thoughts far too often. Even her subconscious was working overtime, had produced sensuous dreams of her and Daniel together night after night.

"I've got to get a grip," Jessica said aloud.

She could not, would not, lose control of her emotions in regard to Daniel. *She would not fall in love with Daniel Quinn.*

"Got that, Jessica?" She nodded decisively. "I certainly hope so."

Of course, now that she really thought about it, her relationship with Daniel had been taken to a greater depth of caring than she'd anticipated. She had, after all, shared her innermost secrets with him, and he had told her his.

Together they had rescued Daniel from his prison of guilt regarding his sister's death. She'd relived her pain and shame in regard to William so that Daniel could understand that what had happened to Karen wasn't his fault. Karen had made her own choices.

Daniel had also bared his soul, told her he was having difficulty bonding with Tessa, wasn't certain he could love the baby or anyone else, for that matter. She could only hope for both Tessa and Daniel's sake that he would be able to move past that wall and give Tessa the fatherly love she deserved to have.

As for Daniel becoming capable of loving a woman,

falling in love, that had nothing to do with her. Nope, not a thing. Somewhere down the road he might very well lose his heart to a woman, marry, produce brothers and sisters for Tessa and—

Jessica frowned.

Daniel holding some faceless woman in his arms? Kissing her? Caressing her? Taking her to his bed and—

"That's the most depressing thought I've ever had in my entire life," Jessica said, then pressed one hand to her forehead. "And to top it off, I'm losing my mind."

Shaking her head in self-disgust, Jessica got to her feet. She cleaned the kitchen and headed for her bedroom to get dressed for work.

Temporary, temporary, temporary, she repeated in her mind like a mantra. What she had with Daniel Quinn was, by mutual agreement, temporary. Which was exactly the way she wanted it. What they had together would be over, would end, be finished. Kaput. Done.

She knew that.

"I know that," she repeated aloud, as she slipped on the jacket to the suit she'd chosen to wear. "And that's fine. No problem. But for now, Daniel is mine."

The day was a study in frustration for Jessica. She went to the courthouse to file some papers for one of her clients only to find that the offices were closed for Christmas Eve, something she'd forgotten to check beforehand.

She waited for Mary-Clair to arrive at the office so she could brainstorm with her partner on a particularly complicated custody battle Jessica was facing. She was finally told by Esther that Mary-Clair had informed them both a week ago that she was taking Christmas Eve off to help her mother prepare food for the next day's festivities.

"Oh. Right. I forgot," Jessica said, opening her red tin and finding it empty.

"Jessica," Esther said, as Jessica turned the tin upside down and patted the bottom to catch the few remaining crumbs in her hand. "I told you that I'm baking this week for my church because they're serving Christmas dinner to the homeless. That's why your goodie tin and Mary-Clair's are empty."

"Oh. Right. I forgot," Jessica said.

Esther narrowed her eyes and squinted at Jessica.

"You're a tad preoccupied, aren't you, dear?" the secretary said.

"Well, it's a busy time of year, Esther," Jessica said, smiling brightly. "Busy, busy, busy. I mean, my stars, if it wasn't for my Day-Timer telling me where I'm supposed to be when, I'd never show up at... where I'm supposed to be...when. Or whatever. Yes, very busy."

"How's Daniel?" Esther said.

"Oh, he's wonderful," Jessica said dreamily. "I'm seeing him tonight...finally, because we've both been dashing to the obligatory holiday parties and…and I can't believe I just said that.''

"Why not?" Esther said. "If Daniel is wonderful, then there's nothing wrong with saying so, which you just did. Mary-Clair and I think it's fabulous that you and Daniel are an…item, for lack of a better word.''

"There is a better word," Jessica said, plunking her red tin onto Esther's desk. "Temporary. That's what Daniel and I are, Esther. He and I are seeing each other, spending time together, enjoying ourselves, but it's…temporary.

"Neither of us is interested in a long-term, serious relationship. At some point, we'll just end things and that will be that. It will be…over and…why don't you go home early? There's certainly nothing going on around here. Have a lovely Christmas, Esther.''

"The same to you and Daniel," Esther said. "And Tessa, too, of course. Are you having problems with the baby grabbing the Christmas tree?''

"No, Daniel and I put it in the playpen and outfoxed the little cutie. By next Christmas Tessa will be able to understand the concept of 'no, don't touch' in regard to the tree so this is the only year we had to get tricky.''

"You won't be around next Christmas to witness Tessa's comprehension of the word 'no.'''

"Pardon me?" Jessica said, frowning.

"Well, you just said that what you have with Daniel is temporary," Esther said. "Surely you two will have gone your separate ways by the time the holidays roll around again. Unless, of course, you have a different definition of temporary than I do.'' She paused. ''Just how long *is* temporary, Jessica?''

''Oh, it's…'' Jessica started. ''What I mean is, it's… Well, phooey, I don't know. Don't have a clue. Maybe I should discuss that with Daniel. Esther, are you intentionally trying to scramble my brain?''

''Would *I* do that?''

''In a New York minute,'' Jessica said, nodding. ''Go home.''

''Merry Christmas,'' Esther said, laughing as she got to her feet.

''Merry Christmas, Esther,'' Jessica said.

Jessica and Daniel arrived in the parking lot of his apartment building at the same time. Jessica juggled the shopping bag containing her gifts and a babbling Tessa. Daniel toted the diaper bag and a big white sack that was filled to the brim with little boxes that were sending delicious aromas wafting through the air.

''We three are the image of the modern-day family,'' Daniel said, as they rode up in the elevator.

Jessica's head snapped around and she stared at Daniel with wide eyes.

''Pardon me?'' she said.

''Take-out food for dinner,'' Daniel said, nodding toward the sack. ''The majority of the time both parents work these days and an average family eats a lot of fast food. I'm not passing judgment on that, I'm just stating a fact.''

''Oh,'' Jessica said, nodding. ''I couldn't imagine

what you were referring to when you said...but you're right, at the moment we represent the way it is. Mom and Dad have put in long days at work, baby has been with a caregiver, and someone else has prepared dinner.''

The elevator bumped to a stop, the doors swished open, and they started down the hallway to Daniel's door.

Daniel had thrown her for a loop when he'd suddenly announced what he had, Jessica thought. Her heart had done a funny little two-step, then had been consumed by a strange tingling warmth as he described the three of them as being the image of a modern-day family. What a silly reaction she'd had to a just-making-conversation remark. But she was fine now, just fine.

In Daniel's living room, he headed for the kitchen while Jessica took Tessa into the nursery for a fresh diaper. They met in the kitchen and Jessica slipped the baby into the high chair. Jessica unpacked the sack while Daniel began to feed Tessa. He'd placed plates, serving spoons, forks and napkins on the table, and Jessica fixed them drinks of cola.

"All set," she said, sitting down opposite him.

"We're a good team," Daniel said, looking over at her. "Don't you think so? We've only been home about ten minutes and we're ready to eat. If you hadn't been here, I'd probably still be struggling to get Tessa's jacket off."

Jessica began to fill her plate. "Well, once the agency finds you a nanny you won't have to worry about things like that. Tessa will be here waiting for you when you get home.''

''Mmm,'' Daniel said, nodding.

That was true, he thought, and would certainly simplify his life again. But why did that picture look so bleak? The nanny would disappear into her room within minutes after he arrived, he'd spend time with Tessa, including reading her a story, then bathe the baby and put her to bed. After that? There he'd sit. All alone. With the hours of the evening stretching before him like a blank blackboard and—

''Daniel,'' Jessica said.

''What?'' he said, snapping back to attention.

''Tessa is leaning toward that spoon in your hand,'' Jessica said, ''but she can't reach it.''

''Oh. Sorry, kid,'' he said, popping the spoon into her mouth. ''That should hold you for now. I'm a starving man and the way you're going at those boxes, Jessica, I'd better get my share while there's some left.''

''You'd better believe it,'' Jessica said, laughing. ''This is delicious food and I'm hungry.''

They ate in silence for several minutes with Tessa occupied by a pile of crisp noodles that Daniel put on the high-chair tray.

''Mick's wife told him that she wants another baby,'' Daniel said suddenly.

''Oh?'' Jessica said. ''And Mick's reaction to that news flash?''

''At first he said no because they can't afford to raise three kids,'' Daniel said. ''But when he thought about it he realized he really wanted another baby, too. Instead of just telling Rosemary that, he's giving her a baby doll in a blanket as part of her Christmas present. Mick said the present was corny but kind of special, and we both figure she'll cry when she opens it.''

"That is so-o-o sweet," Jessica said. "Oh, that is just...oh-h-h." She sniffled.

Daniel chuckled. "Rosemary is *definitely* going to cry if you're getting all misty just hearing about it. Women are amazing creatures. You never know what is going to turn on the waterworks." He frowned. "My gift...that is, Tessa's gift to you, won't do that, though. The more I think about it, it's dumb. At the time I bought it it represented...but then when I really thought about it later it...corny to the max."

"What is it?" Jessica said, leaning toward him. "I can't stand the suspense."

"Then finish your dinner so you can open it," Daniel said. "That's the rule."

"I'm full. Where's my present?"

They both burst into laughter and Tessa joined them as the happy sound lilted through the air. They consumed the majority of the food, placed the remainder in the refrigerator and after cleaning up, headed for the living room. Daniel plugged in the tree and turned off the other lights. They settled onto the floor, and Jessica gave Tessa the brightly wrapped musical lamb.

"That's cute," Daniel said, after helping Tessa tear away the paper. He pressed the toy's tummy and the soft music began to play. Tessa lay back on the carpet and held the lamb. "She really loves it and she says thank you, Jessica."

"This is for you, Daniel," Jessica said, handing him the gift.

"You didn't have to…"

"I wanted to. I hope you like it."

Jessica was hardly breathing as Daniel unwrapped the present, then opened the box beneath the paper and swept back the tissue. He lifted out the wooden sculpture of the man's hand cradling the child's and stared at it, no readable expression on his face.

Jessica took a much-needed breath and waited for a reaction from Daniel. And waited…and waited…

"You hate it," Jessica said, her shoulders slumping. "Well, stick it on a closet shelf and forget it's there."

"Geez, Jessica," Daniel said, "I don't hate it. I'm sitting here scrambling for the words to express how much I like it, how much it means to me. It's… beautiful. I just hope that someday…" he traced one fingertip over the tiny wooden hand nestled in the larger one "…that I will have earned this kind of love and trust from Tessa."

"You will," Jessica said softly. "I'm glad you like it, Daniel."

"'Like' isn't a big enough word, but I can't express…thank you. That isn't big enough, either, but it's all I can come up with."

"You're welcome."

Daniel got to his feet to place the carving carefully

on an end table, then lifted Jessica's gift from beneath the tree. He settled back onto the floor and handed the present to Jessica.

"Just open it and put me out of my misery," he said, frowning. "My defense is that I haven't had much practice at buying my lady a Christmas present."

"Is that what I am? Your lady?" Jessica said, looking at him intently.

"Well, yeah, sure." Daniel paused. "Aren't you?"

"Yes, I guess I am. For now."

"Let's not get into all the rules and regulations of our relationship," Daniel said. "Open the damn present. Oops. You didn't hear that, Tessa. Tessa? Hey, she went to sleep and she's hugging her lamb. I think we're witnessing a Kodak moment here. I, however, forgot to buy a camera."

He lifted Tessa and the lamb into his arms and got to his feet.

"Open your gift while I put her to bed," he whispered, so as not to wake the sleeping baby. "That will shorten the duration of my suffering."

When Daniel returned to the living room, he saw that Jessica had placed the little ceramic house on the end table next to the wooden sculpture of the hands. She'd apparently gone into the kitchen, found some matches and lit the candle in the base of the house because a warm glow was shining from the minuscule windows. When she looked up at him, there were tears shimmering in her eyes.

"You're crying?" he said. "Is that good? Does

that mean I hit a home run on sentimental and romantic like Mick and his baby doll in the blanket? Do you understand the message the house is conveying? When you're in my home, Jessica, you turn a gloomy day to sunshine and fill up the place, and...it's like that house. See? Because you lit the candle it looks warm and inviting and...that's what *you* do for me, for this home and...and I'm blithering like an idiot here.''

Jessica got to her feet and smiled at him through her tears.

"I understood the message of the house, Daniel, and how you could have thought for one second that it was corny, I'll never know. I'll cherish my gift forever. Thank you so very much.''

"I'll be damned," he said, smiling. "You like it.''

"I love it.''

Daniel opened his arms. "Come here. I've missed you, Jessica.''

Jessica nearly ran into Daniel's embrace, the distance separating them suddenly far too great. He wrapped his arms around her and pulled her close to him, capturing her lips in a searing kiss at the same moment as she encircled his neck with her hands.

The kiss was heaven and heat, desire bursting into raging flames and consuming them instantly. Too many days and lonely nights had gone by since they had experienced this ecstasy and they savored it, the kiss deepening as tongues met in the sweet darkness of Jessica's mouth.

Daniel raised his head finally only far enough to be able to speak.

"I want you, Jessica," he said, his voice gritty with passion.

"Yes."

"We're going to make love in my bed, not on the floor," Daniel said. "We'll take that little house into the bedroom and make love in the glow of the candlelight, the sunshine, that you create here."

"You're going to make me cry again," Jessica said, then sniffled.

Daniel chuckled, then released her so he could pick up the house. They went down the hallway to his room and he set the house on the top of his dresser. A soft aura of golden light was cast over the bed. Daniel swept back the blankets and with no motions wasted, they shed their clothes, reached for each other and tumbled onto the bed.

They had been waiting an eternity to be together again, to share the intimate act that was so rich and real, so exquisitely beautiful. They kissed and touched, stroked and caressed, rediscovered the wondrous mysteries of each other, and murmured the name of the only other person who existed in their world.

When Daniel finally entered Jessica's heated body, she gasped at the pure pleasure of receiving him, all of him. He groaned deep in his chest as she tightened around him, then he began to move within her, building the tempo to a thundering cadence.

Jessica held tightly to Daniel's shoulders as she

matched him beat for beat, raising her hips to bring him closer yet.

Only seconds apart they reached the sought-after climax and were flung into glorious oblivion... together. They tumbled amidst brightly colored lights like those on the Christmas tree in the living room, then floated slowly back to rest with heads on the same pillow in the glow of the sunshine radiating from the little house.

The candle in the house flickered, then went out, casting the room into a cocoon of darkness.

And they slept.

They slept with Jessica's hand nestled in Daniel's, just like the trusting hands of the wooden statue.

Chapter 14

A MacAllister Christmas was definitely a day to remember, Daniel decided, as the festivities began to draw to a late-evening close. He swept his gaze over the large room where everyone was gathered, singing carols while Margaret MacAllister played the piano.

Jessica had laughed and told him that she and her sisters had all been subjected to piano lessons when they were little girls and the triplets had proven to be fumble-fingers, unable to successfully play even the simplest tune. To their delight the hated lessons ended, but the piano was kept so their grandmother could play for them whenever she visited.

Triplets, Daniel mused. Identical triplets, yet the three were very different. He'd met Emily at the tree-trimming party and his detective instincts had kicked in as he watched her go through the event with an almost continual smile on her face.

It was a facade, he'd thought at the time. He'd seen Emily tug at the dress she wore that was too snug over her extra pounds and had caught a glimpse of sadness that had flickered in her eyes and across her face before she'd put the false smile back into place. Emily MacAllister was *not* a happy woman.

Today he'd met the third sister, Alice, who was called Trip. Jessica had quietly explained that when Alice was ten or eleven she had made it clear that she detested being part of a matched set and the world might as well just call her Trip, one of the triplets, because no one bothered to view her as an individual.

She'd left home as soon as she'd graduated from high school and had kept a definite emotional and physical distance between herself and her large extended family ever since. No one even knew what Trip did for a living, or where she might be living at any given time.

The MacAllister triplets, Daniel thought. They were all very unique, complicated, and interesting ladies. And one of them was his.

Daniel glanced quickly at Jessica where she sat next to him on the sofa, singing as she held Tessa on her lap.

One of them was his? he mentally repeated. For a second he'd had the irrational thought that Jessica might have read his mind, and would be ready to do battle. She wasn't his, for Pete's sake.

Well, yes, she was. Sort of. She was his lover,

his…lady, his significant other. For now. Until they ended the relationship by mutual agreement and went their separate ways.

Don't go there, Quinn, he ordered himself. Not today. Just…enjoy.

Daniel slid his arm across Jessica's shoulders and she looked up at him in surprise. He smiled at her, aware that while the MacAllisters appeared to be totally engrossed in singing their little hearts out, they would not have missed the rather possessive, she's-with-me message his action was telegraphing.

When Jessica returned his smile, he relaxed and left his arm where it was.

"You're not singing, Daniel," Jessica said. "Don't tell me that you've run out of Christmas spirit."

"Not at all, but I'd scare every baby in the room if I sang," he said, chuckling. "You do remember my rendition of the multitude of beer bottles, don't you?"

Jessica laughed. "Who could forget it? Grim. Very grim. But I was no better when I sang to Tessa that night. The nice part about having a big family is that no one can really hear me when we do our traditional carol singing."

"There are a lot of nice things about being part of a family this size," Daniel said, then paused. "I really like your cousin, Ryan. We had an interesting discussion about law and order in Korea. He's very intelligent, very perceptive. Yeah, Ryan is a sharp guy."

"Is that a pun?" Jessica said. "His name is Ryan Sharpe."

"I forgot that was his last name," Daniel said. "It's a bit tricky keeping straight who's who in this..."

"Zoo," Jessica finished for him, then frowned in the next instant. "Ryan and I have always been very close. It just breaks my heart to see him so...oh, I don't know...so lost at times. He just returned from Korea where he went seeking a sense of belonging, because his biological mother was Korean. But having an American biological father made him taller than the average person over there and his hair is lighter and wavy and...he told me he didn't feel as though he fit in in Korea any more than he did here in this country. I hope he'll find an inner peace about his mixed heritage. I really do."

Daniel nodded as he looked across the room at Ryan, who was standing next to his grandfather... well, everyone considered Robert MacAllister to be his grandfather. Yep, Sharpe had a lot going for him. Intelligence, a solid career with the MacAllister architects, good looks, which probably had women flocking to his door.

Too bad he was fighting inner demons. That heavy internal load could rip a guy up. He knew that only too well because of the misplaced guilt he'd carried within him about Karen.

But he was free of all that. Thanks to Jessica. Now he had to tackle connecting emotionally with Tessa, to figure out how to be a real and loving father for

Karen's...for *his* daughter. He had to move past the chilling feeling that something had died within him with Karen's death.

He had to learn how to love again.

Now that, Daniel thought, could be dangerous. What if, while emerging from the dark shadows, he fell in love with Jessica? What if learning to love again resulted in him losing his heart to her?

Not good. That would not be good. Jessica had total control of her emotions, would never let down her defenses and trust her instincts in choosing a man to love. She was adamant about that.

If he fell in love with Jessica MacAllister, he would end up alone and lonely, and nursing a broken heart. But if he didn't allow his heart to heal, he would never be a proper father for Tessa.

Well, hell, what a mess.

"Happy New Year, Daniel," someone said, snapping Daniel back to attention. "Happy New Year, Jessica. Happy New Year, Tessa. There, I've officially covered your lovely little trio."

"Maggie MacAllister," Jessica said, "are you extending those wishes a week early because you've volunteered to work a double shift on New Year's Eve in the E.R. at the hospital again this year? So we won't see you at Grandma and Grandpa's annual New Year's Day open house?"

"Hold it," Daniel said, as a loud rendition of "Santa Claus Is Coming To Town" was being sung. "This is a test. Maggie MacAllister. E.R. nurse. Single. Daughter of Michael and Jenny. One brother,

Bobby, who is married and has a baby on the way. How am I doing?''

Maggie laughed. "Excellent, Daniel. There are people who have known this gang for years who can't get us all straight when we're together."

Daniel tapped his temple with a fingertip. "Genius mind at work here."

"Oh, please," Jessica said, rolling her eyes heavenward. "Back to my question, Maggie. Why did you volunteer to work New Year's Eve again? It's that old wives' tale of yours, isn't it? The belief that a kiss at midnight on New Year's Eve should be shared with someone very special, not just a casual date."

"Yep," Maggie said. "And since there is no one special in my life, I'm going to work and let someone else party. Makes sense to me."

"I don't think you're going to find your prince in the E.R. that night, cousin of mine," Jessica said.

"What prince?" Daniel said.

"Oh, it's a silly family joke," Maggie said. "When I was small, I blew out the candles on my birthday cake and said I had wished that I would marry a prince when I grew up. This family, weird that it is, jumped on that and didn't forget it. So, just for fun I've wished the same wish every year in what has become a nonsensical tradition. I, supposedly, am waiting for a true-blue Prince Charming to come charging into my life and sweep me romantically off my feet."

"A real prince? In Ventura?" Daniel said. "Somehow I don't see that happening."

"I know, I know," Maggie said, laughing. "I must continue on my rounds with my New Year's message. Bye for now."

"Bye." Jessica shook her head. "I've lost count of how many years Maggie has volunteered to work on—"

"May I have your attention, please?" Robert MacAllister said, standing by his wife at the piano.

The room fell silent and everyone directed their attention to the senior MacAllister.

"It's been a fantastic day," Robert said, "but I see little ones growing sleepy and I know some of you are getting ready to leave. Therefore, I'm making my announcement now while you're all still here.

"The gifts you received from Margaret and me today were traditional presents in the Christmas spirit. However, over the next weeks I'm going to be meeting privately with each of my grandchildren and giving you a gift I have selected especially for you."

Robert laughed. "I'm allowed to do that because I'm old and eccentric. I'll telephone you when it's your turn and we'll set a date to get together in my study at home. That's it. Merry Christmas to you all."

The room exploded with questions directed at Robert, who just smiled, raised both hands and shook his head.

"I'll go crazy," Jessica said, looking at Daniel. "How can he do this to me? A special present, and I have to wait for an appointment before I can have it?"

Daniel laughed. "I don't think you'll survive this, Jessica."

"I know I won't," Jessica said. "I wonder if Grandpa could be bribed?" She frowned. "Nope, he can't. I tried that once when I was about twelve. I told him I'd bake his favorite cookies once a month for a year if he'd help me convince my parents that I should be allowed to stay up later on school nights. He turned me down flat. Oh, this is going to be agony."

Tessa suddenly began to cry as she tugged on one ear and rubbed her eyes with her other hand.

"Uh-oh," Daniel said. "Somebody is all partied out. I'd better get her home before she does her air raid siren thing."

"Are you a sleepy girl, Tessa?" Jessica said, jiggling the baby, who cried louder. "Never mind answering that. We get the message."

Daniel lifted Tessa into the crook of one arm, got to his feet and extended his other hand to Jessica. She placed her hand in his and he pulled her up to stand next to him. Margaret MacAllister approached where they stood.

"Grandma," Jessica said, "give me a teeny tiny hint about my special present from Grandpa. Please?"

"I can't," Margaret said, smiling, "because your grandfather hasn't told *me* what the gifts are. He has been going off alone to shop and I know as much as you do on the subject...nothing."

"Well, phooey," Jessica said.

"Pouting won't help, Jessica," Margaret said.

"You've been the very worst one about waiting for gifts since you were a little girl. We all learned years ago to ignore you, dear."

"Darn it," Jessica said.

"Daniel," Margaret said, "I want to extend a personal invitation to you and Tessa to come to Robert's and my open house on New Year's Day."

"Thank you," Daniel said. "That's very nice of you. I'll try to drop by, but I'm scheduled to work New Year's Eve and the next day because I had Christmas off." He frowned. "I'd better start looking for a day-care center that will be open on the holiday."

"Well, stop in and have some eggnog if you get the opportunity," Margaret said, then walked away to say goodbye to others who were preparing to leave.

"I'll take care of Tessa on New Year's Eve and the next day, Daniel," Jessica said. "She and I will attend the open house, too."

"You don't already have plans for New Year's Eve?" Daniel said.

"You just said you had to work," Jessica said, frowning in confusion.

"Yes, but..." Daniel leaned down to speak quietly. "I thought we had a no-commitments relationship here."

Jessica glanced quickly around the room to be certain that no one was close enough to hear her.

"That's true," she said, her voice hushed, "but I certainly don't intend to date anyone else while you and I are...are...you know...lovers." Her eyes widened. "Would you have asked another woman out on New Year's Eve if you weren't on duty?"

"No, of course not," Daniel said indignantly. "What kind of a guy do you think I am? I wouldn't socialize with another woman while I'm...you know... forget it. We obviously agree that we aren't dating other people while we're...involved with each other." He shook his head. "Nothing like attempting to have this conversation in the middle of Grand Central Station."

How long is temporary? Jessica thought, suddenly remembering Esther's query. Oh, well, in for a penny and all that good stuff.

"Which leads to the next question," she said. "We haven't discussed just how long this arrangement should go on. In other words, how long is temporary, Daniel?"

Daniel shrugged. "I have no idea. We'll wing it, I guess. How's that?"

"That's fine. For now," Jessica said, smiling. "So! Shall I baby-sit Tessa on New Year's Eve and take her to the open house the next day?"

"Sure."

"Good. Now then, that bundle who has fallen asleep on your shoulder needs to get home and be tucked into her crib, Lieutenant."

"Why did I think that coming in separate vehicles was a good idea?" he said.

"Because of that sleepy person in your arms, remember?" Jessica said.

"But that means our evening, yours and mine, ends

in the driveway,'' Daniel said. ''I don't want you coming to my place, then driving home alone later when the heavy holiday drinkers are on the road. And if I follow you home and we put Tessa down on your bed, I'll have to take her back out into the cold later and...we're back to saying good-night in the driveway.''

''That's what we agreed was the best plan,'' Jessica said.

''That was then. Now I hate it. What I really want is to...'' Daniel looked around, then chuckled. ''Never mind. We're pushing our luck about not being overheard as it is. I guess I'll just have to settle for saying phooey.''

''Well, do know that what you want to do is what I want to do, too,'' Jessica said.

Daniel groaned. ''Oh, Ms. MacAllister, you are wicked. You're turning me inside out even as we speak.''

''Hold the thought,'' Jessica said, smiling at him warmly. ''Tomorrow is another day.''

Two hours later, Jessica lay in bed, gazing at the little house that Daniel had given her. She'd lit the candle and set the gift on her dresser, drinking in the sight of the welcoming glow in the tiny windows.

A home...not just a house...filled with sunshine, warmth, laughter and...and love, she thought sleepily. She would cherish that present forever...because Daniel had given it to her. Oh, my, what a wonderful Christmas this had been, just absolutely perfect.

She yawned and closed her eyes.

A Christmas to always remember...because she'd shared it...with Daniel.

Jessica slept and a short time later, the candle flickered and went out. Left unattended, the little house became dark and cold.

Chapter 15

In a repeat of what had taken place the year before, Jessica and Mary-Clair were extremely busy seeing new clients the week between Christmas and New Year's Eve.

The women who sought their help said basically the same thing—as the new year approached they'd made up their mind not to remain in a marriage that was bringing them nothing but heartache. They were taking steps to start the new year with the hope for a happier future.

Daniel, too, was in the midst of a rerun of a year ago as he and Mick were called out to investigate three homicides, all of which were determined to be suicides, a grim statistic that increased in number during the holidays.

Four days after Christmas, Daniel was able to hire

a teenager in his building to baby-sit Tessa so he and Jessica could celebrate an early New Year's Eve. They dressed in their finest and Daniel made reservations at an exclusive restaurant, which also offered dancing.

She was Cinderella at the ball, Jessica thought dreamily, as she and Daniel swayed to the dreamy music. When they returned to Jessica's apartment, they made sweet, slow love for hours in the glow of the candle they replaced several times in the little house on top of the dresser.

"Happy New Year, Daniel," Jessica said, as she lay nestled close to his side.

He kissed her on the forehead. "Happy New Year, Jessica."

During the remainder of the days until New Year's Eve, they managed to speak briefly on the telephone. On the big night, Daniel arrived at Jessica's with Tessa, a car seat and a diaper bag packed to overflowing.

Before Jessica could say more than hello, Daniel dropped a quick kiss on her lips, told her he'd just been called out on another case and said goodbye. He set the car seat on the floor, loaded Jessica's arms with a squirming baby and the rest of her paraphernalia and left the apartment, leaving a rather stunned Jessica staring at the door.

Jessica blinked, then smiled at Tessa.

"Well, cutie," she said to the baby, "are you ready to rock and roll? Watch the big ball come down in Times Square? Have popcorn and pretzels and..."

Tessa began to cry. "Guess not. What you're ready for is bed." Jessica laughed. "I think you and I just set a record for the shortest party ever held by two people."

Having fully intended to watch the festivities in Times Square on television, midnight found Jessica sound asleep on the sofa. She woke with a start shortly after one, wished for Daniel's safe return to her, then shuffled down the hall to curl up next to Tessa in the bed.

The New Year's Day open house at the senior MacAllisters was well attended, with great quantities of Margaret's homemade eggnog and delicious pastries being consumed. Just as some partygoers left, more arrived, and Jessica had a marvelous time chatting with people, some of whom she hadn't seen since the traditional party the year before.

But while she was having a lovely time, her eyes kept darting to the front door whenever one of her grandparents opened it to welcome new guests. She was watching, waiting, hoping to see Daniel come striding into the living room and seek her out amid the crowd.

She wanted him there, with her. She wanted to talk to him, laugh with him, share the very first day of a brand-new year with him.

In the middle of the afternoon, Jessica put a fussing Tessa down for a nap in the crib in the fully equipped nursery her grandparents kept set up in one of the bedrooms. The baby was asleep before Jessica even left the room.

When she reentered the living room, Robert MacAllister opened the front door.

"My goodness," Robert said, "what in heaven's name happened to you, Daniel? Or maybe I should ask what the other guy looks like. Come in, come in."

As Daniel and Mick entered the house, Mick introduced himself to Robert, who closed the door behind the two men. Jessica hurried forward, then halted so abruptly that she teetered for a second, her eyes widening in horror as she swept her gaze over Daniel.

He was listing slightly, his eyes were half-shut, and he had a rather dopey smile on his face. There was a nasty-looking scrape on one cheek and his right arm was encased in a cast that was cradled in a sling. His clothes were dirty and there was a rip across one knee of his slacks.

"Daniel?" Jessica said. "You're hurt. Oh, this is terrible. Dear heaven, what happened? Are you in pain? Why are you smiling that weird smile? Why aren't you answering my questions?"

"Because you're using all the air space, sweetheart," Robert said, chuckling. "Give the poor man a chance to get a word in." He frowned. "First, though, I do believe we'd best get Daniel into a chair before he goes over on his nose."

"Good idea," Mick said. "They pumped him full of painkiller at the hospital and, quite frankly, the mighty lieutenant is stoned."

Daniel was eased into a comfortable chair as Jessica hovered close, wringing her hands. Ryan MacAllister and Ted and Ryan Sharpe wandered over to see what was going on. Margaret MacAllister, as well as Jessica's parents arrived seconds later.

"Hi. Happy New Year," Daniel said, his speech slurred. "Where am I? Oh, there's Jessica. Beautiful Jessica. Hello, my lady, I'm here."

"Relatively speaking," Robert said, laughing. "This boy is high as a kite."

"Mick," Jessica said, her voice trembling slightly, "would you please tell me what happened to Daniel?"

"Sure," Mick said. "We answered a call about a possible body in an alley behind a restaurant in one of the big malls. The body turned out to be a pile of old rags, but when we got there, a guy ran from the shadows...obviously not wanting to chat with us after we identified ourselves as cops...and Danny took off after him. Danny tackled the guy at the top of the stairs leading to the basement and...blam...the two of them rolled all the way down the steps."

"Oh, God," Jessica whispered.

"Anyway," Mick went on, "to cut this short...the guy is in jail because his pockets were loaded with packets of drugs ready for sale, I took Danny to the hospital and he insisted that I bring him here. The doc told me to take him home and put him to bed, but Danny wasn't having any of that. He said that Jessica was waiting for him to drop by this party and that's exactly what he intended to do."

"Happy New Year!" Daniel yelled.

"What a hoot," Ryan MacAllister said, with a burst of laughter. "Bring back memories, Ted? Remember the time that fruitcake whopped you with the beer keg? You sure saw stars that time, buddy."

"Oh, let's not forget your moment of glory, MacAllister," Ted said, grinning. "I do believe it was an eighty-year-old lady who stood about five feet tall who leveled you with the frying pan. You spent the night in the hospital with an economy-size headache, if I recall. Then there was the kid who—"

"What's wrong with you people?" Jessica said, nearly shrieking. "Daniel is injured, he's in pain, and you're standing around reminiscing about the bad old days?"

Ted frowned. "Daniel is just a cop who got banged up a little in the line of duty, Jessica honey. Don't get so upset. He's right-handed, though, isn't he? Mmm. He's going to have a heck of a time shaving in the morning with that cast on. Now *that* could be a bloody crime scene. Oh, man, that reminds me of the time—"

"Don't you say another word, Uncle Ted," Jessica said, narrowing her eyes. "It may be machismo to the max to recount war wounds, or cop wounds, or whatever it is you're doing, but that's enough." She pointed at Daniel. "That is a man who fell down a flight of stairs. Understand? A...flight...of...stairs! Where is your compassion, your human kindness, your..."

"Jessica," her mother said, smiling, "we're all

very sorry that Daniel was hurt while performing his civil duty.'' She poked Forrest in the ribs with her elbow. ''Aren't we? Very sorry.''

''Oh!'' Forrest said quickly. ''You bet. Very sorry. You are overreacting a tad, baby girl, but what the heck. I remember, though, that Ted looked a lot worse when he got clocked with the beer keg. He had a broken nose, two black eyes and—''

''That's it,'' Jessica said, slicing one hand through the air. ''This family is heartless, totally heartless. Shame on you, all of you. Well, I'm not about to just stand here and do nothing. I certainly am not. I'm going to…um…''

Jessica's voice trailed off as she realized that everyone, except Daniel who was staring into space, was looking at her intently, including a dozen more people who had joined the group to see what was creating all the commotion.

''Just what is it you're going to do about this situation, Jessica?'' Jillian MacAllister said pleasantly. ''We're all waiting breathlessly to hear what you have to say.''

Jessica lifted her chin and silently hoped that no one noticed the flush she could feel warming her cheeks.

''I'm going to move into Daniel's apartment,'' she said, ''and take care of Tessa until Daniel is capable of resuming the tasks befitting a father. A person can't change a diaper, or give a baby a bath, with only one hand. It's the least I can do as I owe Daniel a tremendous debt of gratitude for his invaluable assistance in helping me fill out the grant application for The Peaceful Dove.''

"Sounds like a plan," Ryan Sharpe said, nodding.

"This may be upsetting you, Dad," Jessica went on, "but my mind is made up so there's no point in launching into one of your sermonettes about ladylike behavior.''

"It sounds like the perfect solution to the problem," Forrest said, shrugging.

"It does?" Jessica said, frowning. "Did you really hear what I said? I'm moving in with a man. Daniel Quinn, to be precise. We'll be living under the same roof…without benefit of marriage and—''

"Yep," Forrest said. "You know, if you wrap a plastic trash bag around that cast of Daniel's, he'll be able to take a shower.''

"That's true," Jillian said.

"I could stop by and shave him," Ryan Sharpe said. "Men are very reluctant to allow a woman to do that. It's a guy thing." He paused. "Maybe I'd better follow you over to your place to get your things, Jessica, then on to Daniel's so I can haul him out of your car.''

"Oh, what a nice thing to do, Ryan," Margaret said. "Why don't you wait until Tessa wakes up from her nap, though, Jessica? Daniel won't know the difference and it might eliminate the possibility of having a crabby baby to deal with in addition to tending Daniel's needs. There, family, I do believe we've covered all the details.''

"Except for the fact that you're all cuckoo," Jessica said, throwing up her hands. "Don't ever let it be said that MacAllisters are predictable. I really don't understand why you aren't pitching a fit about this, Dad."

"You'll figure it out one of these days," Forrest said, smiling.

"I certainly hope so," Jillian said.

"Happy New Year!" Daniel shouted.

Late that night, Jessica slipped into bed next to Daniel, who was sleeping and had been ever since Ryan had put him to bed hours before.

Well, she thought, lying stiff as a pencil, here she was, Florence Jessica Nightingale MacAllister.

When her eyes adjusted to the darkness, she rolled to her side and stared at the silhouette of Daniel as he slept peacefully and deeply. A soft smile formed on her lips as gradually she was able to see Daniel more clearly.

The white cast on his arm that ran from below his elbow to the tips of his fingers seemed to glow with brightness. His chest was bare and rose and fell in the steady rhythm of sleep.

Yes, Jessica thought, here she was, next to Daniel, close to him, drinking in the sight and aroma of him and knowing there was nowhere else she wished to be.

For now.

How long is temporary?

Oh, she wasn't going to address that question. Not tonight. And not tomorrow.

Shifting onto her back, Jessica couldn't help but

think about the man lying beside her. There was no reason to believe that Daniel wasn't exactly who he presented himself to be. He was a dedicated police officer, had been a loving brother to his sister, was attempting to adapt to his new title of father. He was kind and thoughtful, funny and fun, and she would rather, given the choice, be with him, sharing and caring, than going about her business alone.

Daniel Quinn was chipping away at her protective wall, inch by emotional inch, and she could not allow that to continue. Because she didn't suddenly possess the wisdom necessary to accurately judge a man. No, her flaw was in place forever.

Jessica slid her hand across the bed to cover Daniel's left hand where it lay splayed on the blanket.

Oh, how could she be wrong about this man? she thought. There wasn't a dark side to him that might surface at any moment. No, not within Daniel. He was everything and more that she believed him to be.

She'd been convinced the same was true about William.

Jessica sighed. Facts were facts. They couldn't be changed. She was who she was, and nothing could convince her to trust herself where a man was concerned.

Jessica closed her eyes and soon drifted off to sleep, her hand still covering Daniel's.

"Oh-h-h," Daniel said, "what size was the truck that hit me? Oh, my head, my arm, my entire body is screaming for mercy."

He was propped up against the pillows on the bed, having taken one sip from the mug of coffee Jessica had brought him. She was dressed for work and Tessa was in the playpen, now free of the Christmas tree, her diaper bag packed and ready to go to Patty's.

"How much do you remember about what happened?" Jessica said, sitting down on the edge of the bed.

"Bits and pieces," Daniel said, then took another swallow of coffee. "I broke myself rolling down the stairs at the mall, and Mick put the cuffs on the guy. The hospital bit is a blur, then we were at your grandparents', I think, and this morning I woke up to see you emerging from the shower wrapped in a towel. This confusing maze in my mind is not all bad, believe me."

"Well, thank you," Jessica said, smiling. "I'll be staying here with you until you can tend to Tessa on your own, or the agency finds you a nanny, whichever comes first. You're to rest today, so says Mick, and he'll come by later and see how you're doing. He said someone else is filling in for the captain for the next couple of days. Then he'll be back on duty. I'm taking Tessa to Patty's in about five minutes, then heading to the office."

"I really appreciate your help, Jessica," Daniel said, "but I don't want to be the cause of a problem between you and your family. Your father is a very protective daddy. He can't be thrilled with this plan."

Jessica frowned. "My parents, grandparents, everyone for that matter, thought this was a perfect solution to your problem. It was very strange. I kept waiting for my dad to go ballistic but it didn't happen."

"Why not?"

"I don't have a clue." Jessica got to her feet. "I've got to go. Tessa and I will be back by early evening. Is there anything else you need now?"

"A kiss."

"You're pouting," Jessica said, laughing.

"Damn straight I am," Daniel said, frowning. He set the coffee mug on the nightstand. "Look at this arm. There's enough plaster on here to sink a ship. Every bone in my body hurts and...oh, yes, I definitely need a kiss to make it better."

"I live to serve," Jessica said, then leaned down and captured Daniel's lips with hers.

Daniel whipped his left arm around Jessica's waist and pulled her across his lap, causing her to break the kiss and gasp in shock. In the next instant, Daniel's mouth melted over hers in a searing kiss.

Jessica wrapped one arm around Daniel's neck and returned the breath-stealing kiss, surrendering totally. She welcomed the familiar heat of desire that consumed her, and a murmur of pure feminine pleasure caught in her throat.

In the distance Tessa began to cry.

"Oh!" Jessica said, then moved out of Daniel's embrace. "I've got to get to work." She drew a steadying breath and got to her feet again. "Gracious, for an injured man you certainly are...erase that. I don't think it's a good idea to discuss it.''

Daniel chuckled. "There are parts of me that aren't injured, Ms. MacAllister."

"I'm well aware of that, Lieutenant Quinn," she said, smiling. "I'll see you this evening. Bye for now. Have a nice day."

Daniel watched as Jessica hurried from the room, calling to Tessa that she was coming as commanded. A few minutes later he heard the door of the apartment close and a heavy silence descended. He picked up the coffee mug, drained it, then slammed it back onto the nightstand.

"Have a nice day?" he said. "Hell. What am I supposed to do? Watch soap operas?"

Daniel slid back down in the bed, moaning loudly in the process just because he felt like it. He glared at the heavy cast on his arm, then slid his free hand beneath his head and stared at the ceiling.

What a crazy turn of events, he thought. It had been years since he'd gotten banged up on the job. He felt like a little kid who had fallen off his bike and broken his dumb arm. Ridiculous. This whole situation was really—

A slow smile began to form on Daniel's lips and grew into a big grin.

Fantastic, his mind rushed on. No more long nights tossing and turning in that bed, aching for Jessica, wanting her with an intensity that defied description. No more of those crummy nights because Jessica would be right there next to him. Unbelievable. And fantastic.

But why wasn't Jessica's father flipping out over Jessica moving in with him? That didn't make sense. Jessica was the daughter of a very protective Forrest MacAllister. She was his baby girl. Both of her parents, the whole family, in fact, thought this was the best solution to his problem? Weird.

Well, *he* sure wasn't going to complain. Jessica would return after work with Tessa in tow, they'd have dinner, share the evening, put the baby to bed, just like…well, just like a real family. The three of them…together. Mom and Dad and baby. Man, the image of all that in his mind looked so good, so warm and welcoming and—

"Whoa, Quinn," Daniel said.

It was temporary, and he'd better remember that. Oh, yes, indeed, he'd enjoy every moment of it, soak it up like a thirsty sponge, but there would be no erasing the fact that it wasn't what it appeared to be.

He had to concentrate on his mission of somehow bonding with Tessa, somehow learning to love his daughter the way she deserved to be loved. If and when he was able to do that, he would have earned the right to be called father, to hold Tessa's hand safely in his like the beautiful wooden statue Jessica had given him for Christmas.

And the vision of him as a husband?

"Forget it," Daniel said.

Even if he broke free of the demons within him and came to love not only Tessa but was capable of giving his heart to a soul mate as well, Jessica was the wrong woman. She had no intention of ever loving again, of trusting a man enough to make a commitment to forever.

No matter what happened, he must *not* fall in love with Jessica.

The following days and nights were close to perfection. Jessica returned to the apartment at the end of each work day with Tessa in her arms and Daniel was at the door to greet them. While Jessica made dinner Daniel read Tessa a story, having carefully chosen the book during the day. The baby snuggled on his lap and he came to realize how much he looked forward to their special time together.

After dinner, Daniel watched as Jessica gave Tessa her bath and zipped her into her fuzzy sleeper. Then the three of them played with toys until it was time for Tessa to be put to bed. Daniel often stood next to the crib after Jessica left the room and watched the baby drift off to sleep.

Four days after the scuffle, Mick drove Daniel to the doctor, who cleared him for limited duty, which translated into being stuck behind a desk at the station after being picked up by Mick and delivered back home again by his partner.

On the fifth night, Jessica and Daniel arrived home at nearly the same time and their pattern for the evening fell easily into place. Daniel read to Tessa while Jessica prepared dinner.

In the kitchen Jessica smiled as she heard Daniel

creating voices for the various characters in the book he was reading to the baby.

Didn't Daniel realize what was happening? Jessica mused as she stirred spaghetti sauce on the stove. He was bonding with his daughter. His face just lit up when he saw Tessa each night and the baby reached out her arms, wanting to be held by her daddy. Daniel was doing it. Slowly but surely, he was becoming a true and loving father and it was glorious to watch.

Jessica sighed in contentment as she drained the spaghetti.

Everything about this time they were all sharing was glorious, she thought. She felt so...so fulfilled, so complete. She was busy during the day with her career, but she eagerly anticipated the moment she would walk through Daniel's door and put on her wife and mother hats.

A warm flush stained Jessica's cheeks as she embraced the memories of the exquisite lovemaking she and Daniel had shared each night since she'd moved in. The bulky cast on Daniel's arm did nothing to diminish the ecstasy waiting for them as they reached for each other in his bed.

Jessica blinked and sharply brought herself back to reality and the fact that the garlic bread she had prepared was ready to be removed from the oven. As she placed the food on the table and called to Daniel that dinner was ready, the telephone rang. She snatched up the receiver on the wall phone in the kitchen.

"Hello?"

"Jessica? It's Ryan. I bet I caught you at dinner time, didn't I?"

"Just putting it on the table, sweet cousin," she said. "Talk fast or we'll be eating soggy spaghetti."

"Could I stop by later and see you and Daniel?" Ryan said. "There's something I want to show you."

"Hang on a sec," she said, then relayed Ryan's request to Daniel as he slipped Tessa into her high chair. Daniel shrugged and nodded. "That's fine, Ryan," he called out, "but give us a chance to get Tessa down for the night. How about eight o'clock?"

"I'll be there," Ryan said.

"Hey, don't you dare hang up without giving me a hint about what you want to show us, Ryan Sharpe," Jessica said. "You know I get crazy if there's a secret in the works."

Ryan laughed. "No joke. Well, here's your hint. I had my private appointment with Grandpa and received my gift he spoke about on Christmas. He's always considered me a grandchild and I love him as I would if he was really my grandfather and, well, I was summoned to his study and...I want to share this with you and Daniel."

"Oh, my gosh," Jessica said, her eyes widening. "What did Grandpa give you, Ryan?"

"See you at eight," Ryan said, then hung up.

"Ryan?" Jessica said to the dial tone. "Well, darn it." She replaced the receiver, settled onto her chair at the table, then told Daniel what Ryan had said. "I wonder what Ryan received from our grandfather?"

Daniel chuckled. "You'll never make it to eight

o'clock without going nuts." He managed to shovel a spoonful of food into Tessa's mouth with his left hand. "That a girl, Tessa. Gobble that right up. You sure enjoy good food, don't you, kiddo?"

"Just like her Daddy does," Jessica said, looking at Daniel intently.

Daniel snapped his head around to meet Jessica's gaze, an instant frown on his face. As Jessica continued to look directly at him, a smile began to form on his lips.

"Yeah," he said finally, "just like...like her Daddy. That's me."

"Yes, Daniel," Jessica said softly, struggling against threatening tears, "that's you. You're Tessa's father. Tessa is your daughter. You're beautiful together. It's all falling into place, don't you see? The bond, the trust, the love. You didn't think it could happen, but it is. I'm here, witnessing it, and it's wonderful."

Daniel nodded, unable to speak past the lump in his throat. He shifted his attention to his plate, took a bite of spaghetti, chewed and swallowed.

"I...I stand by Tessa's crib at night, watching her sleep," he said quietly, slowly meeting Jessica's gaze again, "and I know...*I know*...I would lay my life on the line for her. I would, Jessica."

"Because you love her," she whispered.

Daniel turned his head to stare at Tessa, who was busily smearing her high-chair tray with several pieces of spaghetti, babbling happily as she decorated.

"Yes, I do," Daniel said, awe echoing in his voice.

"I truly do love her. She's mine. She's my daughter. She's my...my baby girl. God, when did this happen? How did it happen? Forget it. That's not important." He looked at Jessica again. "Ah, man, look at you. You've got tears on your cheeks."

"I'm just very happy for the two of you," Jessica said, dabbing at her nose with her napkin. "You're a real family now. Father and daughter."

Daniel frowned. "You left yourself out of that picture."

"I'm only here...temporarily, Daniel. You and Tessa are forever."

"I don't care. You *are* here now, so for *now*, you're part of this family. Got that?"

Jessica smiled through her tears. "Yes, sir. Whatever you say, sir. Now, let's eat our dinner or we'll still be sitting here with you becoming grumpier and grumpier when Ryan arrives. Oh, I can't stand it. I wonder what Ryan received as his special gift from Grandpa?"

It was an exquisite antique globe on a carved, wooden stand, the entire delicate creation standing about seven inches tall. Ryan removed it from a tissue-filled box and set it carefully on the coffee table in front of the sofa in Daniel's living room.

"Oh, Ryan," Jessica said, "it's beautiful, absolutely lovely."

Daniel nodded. "Yeah, it's nice, really something, Ryan."

"I wanted you two to see it," Ryan said quietly,

"and to hear what Grandpa said when he gave it to me. You and I have always been close friends, Jessica, and you, Daniel, well, I feel as though I've known you for a long time."

"Ditto," Daniel said. "So Robert had some kind of message to go along with the globe?"

"Yes," Ryan said, then drew a deep, steadying breath. "He said that I shouldn't be so driven to find my place in the world, to feel that I have to choose between my two cultures. If I would accept who I am, as I am, I would be bigger than the world and its prejudices. I should feel blessed to have two unique and different cultures to call my own and..." Emotions closed Ryan's throat and he shook his head, unable to continue.

"Whew," Daniel said. "That's heavy stuff, but right on the mark. You two have a very wise grandfather."

"Yes, we do," Jessica said, then hugged her cousin. "Oh, Ryan, I hope you can do what Grandpa said and find the inner peace you deserve to have."

"Amen to that," Daniel said.

"This globe," Ryan said, his voice gritty, "makes me realize that I've been feeling sorry for myself because I didn't seem to fit in here, or in Korea. Look how small and unthreatening that world is. I've got some personal homework to do, but I'm determined to settle this war within myself and get on with my life."

"I'm going to cry," Jessica said, sniffling. "I'm definitely going to cry."

Tessa wailed in the distance.

"Her highness beat you to it," Daniel said, getting to his feet. "I'll go see what her problem is."

As Daniel left the room, Jessica hugged Ryan again.

"I just know you'll find your inner peace, Ryan," she said. "Oh, thank you so much for sharing this with me and with Daniel, too."

"Well, you two are special to me," Ryan said, "and since you're obviously in love with each other, it seemed appropriate to come here where you're together to show you the globe and tell you what Grandpa—"

"Wait a minute," Jessica interrupted. "Back up. Daniel and I aren't in love with each other, Ryan."

"Hey, come on, Jessica," Ryan said, smiling. "This is me…your buddy Ryan. You don't have to deny it. It won't do you any good anyway. The whole family knows how you and Daniel feel about each other. Why do you think your dad and everyone else was so laid-back about you moving in here with him?"

"What?" Jessica said, her eyes widening.

"Well, we're not stupid people." Ryan laughed. "The MacAllister women are rubbing their hands together, waiting for the moment when you make the announcement and they can start helping you plan the wedding."

Jessica jumped to her feet just as Daniel returned to the living room.

"The family is wrong," Jessica said, feeling the

color drain from her face. "Tell him, Daniel. You and I are *not* in love with each other. There is *not* going to be a wedding."

"Huh?" Daniel said. "How did we get from a globe to a wedding?"

"Never mind," Jessica said, wrapping her hands around her elbows. "It's not worth discussing. Ryan, what Daniel and I are…are sharing here is temporary. Understand? You can inform the family that I don't want to hear one word about love, and weddings, and forever and ever and…not one word. I'll be leaving here just as soon as Daniel can tend Tessa, or the agency finds him a nanny. This…is…temporary. Right, Daniel?"

Daniel stared at Jessica for a long moment. "Yeah, right," he said quietly. "It's all…it's all temporary."

Chapter 16

The next afternoon, Jessica sat behind the desk in her office, attempting for the third time to read a settlement proposal from the lawyer representing the husband of one of her clients. And for the third time she was unable to concentrate on the offer being made.

With a sigh of defeat she tossed the document aside, then leaned her head on the top of the chair and stared at the ceiling.

Her relationship with Daniel was unraveling like a skein of yarn, she thought miserably. It wasn't ending in a dramatic explosion like a balloon suddenly pricked by a pin, but was coming apart slowly, painfully, the tension between them building by the hour.

She had been deeply shaken by Ryan Sharpe's announcement that everyone in the family was convinced she and Daniel were in love with each other, she admitted to herself. She wasn't certain why that declaration had thrown her so off-kilter, but it had. After Ryan had left the apartment, she'd apologized to Daniel for her family's false assumption, not quite meeting his gaze as she spoke. Daniel had simply said, "No problem."

Jessica lifted her head and smacked the arms of the chair with her palms. Darn it, it *was* a problem, she thought. She should be laughing off what Ryan had said, chalking it up to the overly romantic Mac-Allisters getting carried away, but she hadn't been able to do that, not even close.

She'd been edgy and restless the remainder of the evening after Ryan's departure and had finally told Daniel she was especially tired and needed to get some extra hours of sleep. When he'd offered to come to bed early with her, she'd said there was no reason for him to cut his evening short, then had hurried from the room without even kissing him good-night. When Daniel had slipped into bed hours later, he'd spoken her name softly several times but she'd pretended to be asleep.

And if that performance wasn't immature enough, she'd topped it off this morning by bustling around, chattering to Tessa and not really speaking to Daniel before whisking the baby out the door.

Oh, yes, what she had shared with Daniel was unraveling because she, herself, was coming unglued.

Because she was unable to ignore what her cousin had announced, she was being forced to examine her true feelings for Daniel, and she absolutely, positively refused to do that. It was too frightening, too dangerous, and she was *not* going to do it.

Besides, she thought, it would serve no purpose. What if she discovered that she'd fallen in love with Daniel Quinn? God, what a disaster. She didn't trust her own judgment, not one iota. Plus there was the fact that Daniel was not, nor did he ever intend to be, in love with her. Dear heaven, if she was in love with Daniel, she didn't want to know.

"Oh, damn," Jessica said, sinking back in the chair again. It was Friday and the weekend officially began when she left the office in a few hours. She couldn't face the prospect of two whole days with Daniel and Tessa. Every time she looked at Daniel she'd hear Ryan's words echoing in her beleaguered brain.

But she couldn't tell Daniel a bald-faced lie, saying she had oodles of work to catch up on and had to put in some hours at the office, because Daniel wasn't capable of tending Tessa on his own.

Oh, why was this happening? Jessica asked herself for the umpteenth time. Why, why, why was she falling apart over something that wasn't even true?

The telephone on the desk rang and Jessica jerked in her chair, shaking her head at the further evidence of her jangled nerves. A few moments later Esther appeared in the doorway.

"Handsome hunk Lieutenant Quinn is on the line," Esther said, smiling. "Maybe he wants to know if he should pick up some milk or something on the way home. Wouldn't that be sweet?"

"Just too sweet for words," Jessica said, staring at the blinking light on the base of the telephone.

Esther laughed. "I'll close the door and give you two some privacy."

When the door had been closed behind Esther, Jessica slowly and reluctantly picked up the receiver.

"Hello, Daniel," she said, knowing she sounded as gloomy as a cloudy day.

"Hi," he said quietly. "I just wanted you to know that I had a checkup at the doctor's early today and they put a smaller soft cast on my arm. I'd clocked out at work for the day and I picked up Tessa and came on home, so you won't have to go get her. I can drive now, change a diaper, the whole bit."

Jessica sat straight up in the chair and a chill swept through her. She tightened her hold on the receiver to the point that her knuckles were white.

"I see," she said, her voice trembling slightly. "Well, that's good news, isn't it? You'll be able to shave yourself and...yes, well, you...you won't need me to be there any longer, will you? No, you and Tessa will be just fine on your own until the agency finds you a nanny and...you must be so pleased that you can—"

"Jessica," Daniel interrupted, "talk to me. What's going on? You've been acting strangely ever since Ryan left the apartment last night. I've gone over everything that happened while he was here and I just don't get it. So he told you some nutso thing about your family thinking we're about to get married or whatever, but that's crazy and no big deal and...did

I do something to upset you like this? Come on, Jessica, I'm going out of my mind here trying to figure out what's wrong.''

Jessica propped the elbow of her free arm on the desk and rested her forehead in her palm.

"No, no, you haven't done anything to distress me," she said. "I'm just loaded with work here and I'm very tired and..." She paused. "No, forget that. I won't lie to you, Daniel. What Ryan said about us has really thrown me for a loop. It's made me realize that I was very foolish to believe that I could exist in a...a fantasy world, even for a short time, and not have to pay the piper. Everything is suddenly so complicated and there are so many people I'll have to explain the truth to that it has overwhelmed me."

"I'm sorry your being here has caused you so many problems," Daniel said. "I guess what Ryan said explains why your father didn't object to your coming here in the first place. He, and all the MacAllisters apparently, believed that you and I...whew. What a mess."

"Yes. Yes, it is." Jessica lifted her head. "But at least now it's over...the fantasy."

"What do you mean?"

"Well, you can tend Tessa on your own," Jessica said. "I'll come by and collect my things after work and go back to my own apartment. Like I said, you don't need me anymore, Daniel." She paused for a moment. "I have another call waiting and I must go. I'll see you when I've finished up here. Bye."

Jessica replaced the receiver, then pressed trembling fingers against her lips, stifling the sob that was threatening to escape from her throat.

After the disturbing telephone conversation with Jessica ended, Daniel began to pace the living room, a deep frown on his face as a string of expletives zinged through his mind. He glanced quickly at Tessa to be certain she hadn't read his naughty thoughts, only to see that the baby had fallen asleep in the play-pen.

He slouched onto the sofa, then got to his feet again in the next instant, as he mentally replayed what Jessica had said.

Jessica MacAllister, he thought incredulously, was about to walk out of his life. Yeah, sure, she'd said she was just moving back to her own apartment because he could now tend to Tessa on his own, but he'd gotten the message loud and clear. She was leaving him. Ending their relationship. It was over.

Damn it, this was crazy. Jessica was very upset, obviously, because her family had gone nuts and decided that he and Jessica were in love and a wedding would be scheduled in the near future.

How had she put it? Something about what Ryan had said making it impossible to continue living in the fantasy world that she and Daniel had created and being jerked back to reality as it really stood, or some such thing.

Because her family had gotten carried away, Jessica was going to stop seeing him, end their...their affair? No, she hadn't said that in so many words, but he could feel it in the cold chill in his bones. Damn.

Why didn't she just straighten the MacAllisters out on the subject? Tell her huge clan that, no, she and Daniel weren't in love, were *not* getting married, but would be continuing to be a couple, per se, whenever their schedules allowed. That would solve the rather sticky problem, wouldn't it? Yes, it would.

Daniel stopped his trek, narrowed his eyes, and stared at the wall.

Okay, he was getting it now. Jessica wanted out. She'd had enough of being involved with a man with an unpredictable work schedule. A man who came with a baby in tow. She'd had enough of him, of being his lady, his lover.

She was using her family's wrong assumption as an excuse to exit stage left from his life. She'd even thrown in the pop in the chops about his not needing her anymore because he could take care of Tessa, as though she'd been little more than a resident nurse-maid for his daughter.

Yes, what Ryan had said had ended the fantasy, but Jessica was upset because the sudden reality she was now facing was that she really didn't care very deeply for Daniel Quinn. So, what they had was over.

"Well, hell," Daniel said, then took a shuddering breath. "I obviously don't get a say in this decision. It sure doesn't matter how *I* might feel about all of this, does it?"

Daniel sank onto the sofa again.

Just *how* did he really feel? he asked himself. Bottom line? He didn't want Jessica to leave him. He cared for her a great deal and...well, no, he wasn't in love with her. Was he? No, of course, he wasn't. But he didn't like the idea of what they had together being over, of never seeing her again, never laughing with her, sharing, making love. Never again? Damn it, he was really hating this.

"You're getting dumped, Quinn," he said. "The most fantastic woman you have ever known is rejecting you. Big time."

The knot in his gut was matched by a cold fist in his chest that caused his heart to hurt.

He did not want Jessica to leave him.

But there wasn't a damn thing he could do about it.

When Jessica arrived at Daniel's that evening, he was feeding Tessa her dinner. He answered the knock at the door, then had to greet Jessica over his shoulder as he hurried back into the kitchen where Tessa was already objecting loudly to his failure to deliver the next spoonful of food. He'd registered the facts that Jessica hadn't smiled when she'd seen him and that she was very pale.

"I'll...I'll just collect my things," Jessica said, starting across the living room.

"Yeah, okay, but..." Daniel gave Tessa a big bite of applesauce, then shifted in the chair to look toward the living room. "Can't we talk about this? I'm not stupid, Jessica. You're ending the whole thing, aren't you? You're not just moving back to your apartment, you're calling it quits. Our relationship, affair, whatever, is over. Right?''

Jessica sighed and walked slowly into the kitchen. Daniel placed some Cheerios on Tessa's tray and got to his feet, turning to face Jessica. The ten feet that separated them seemed like a mile to him as he stared at her.

"Yes, I..." Jessica said, her voice trembling. "I think it would be best if we didn't see each other again, Daniel. I don't understand myself right now. I'm so confused, and I can't get a handle on why I feel as I do. I guess maybe I'm not cut out to have an affair."

"But you don't want anything more than that," Daniel said, his voice rising. "You've made that clear. No commitments, no promises, no...damn it, Jessica, this doesn't make sense."

"I know that," she said, nearly yelling. "I need to go home where I belong and attempt to figure out what's wrong with me."

"Ah, come on," Daniel said. "Why don't you just say it? Put it right on the table, Jessica. You've had enough of me, of my kid, of what we were sharing together. What are you going to lay on me next? That you need to get in touch with your inner child? Give me a break. You want out of this relationship? Fine. It's over, finished, done. It was great while it lasted but, hey, see you around."

"It's that easy for you?" Jessica said, feeling the sting of tears at the back of her eyes. "Hey, see you around?"

"You're the one pulling the plug on us here, not me," Daniel said, none too quietly. "You didn't ask for my input on the subject. Because of what Ryan told you, you did a reality check, and I didn't measure up. It's a tad tough on the ego, but I'll survive. Have a...have a nice life, Ms. MacAllister."

Jessica's eyes brimmed with tears. "I intend to, Lieutenant Quinn."

She spun around and left the room, nearly running as the unwelcomed tears spilled onto her cheeks. Daniel started after her, but he'd only taken two steps when Tessa began to wail as she stiffened in the high chair. Daniel looked at the baby, the direction Jessica had gone, then sighed in defeat as he sat back down in front of Tessa.

"Did we scare you with all that yelling, baby girl?" he said gently. "I'm sorry, sweetheart. I'm sorry. Here. Have some applesauce."

The baby drew a sob-laden breath, then leaned forward and opened her mouth to receive the spoon. A few minutes later Jessica reappeared in the kitchen doorway.

"Goodbye, Daniel," she said quietly.

Daniel got to his feet. "Jessica, please, wait a minute." He ran a hand through his hair. "It can't end...*we* can't end like this...not like this. It's crazy. One minute we were fine. We were happy together...you, me, Tessa. Next thing, we're yelling at each other and..." He sighed. "Forget it. There's nothing I can say that will make you stay with me, is there?"

Jessica shook her head, unable to speak past the tears closing her throat. She turned and hurried across the living room and out the door, closing it behind her with a click that seemed to hammer against Daniel like a painful, physical blow.

He lifted Tessa from the high chair and held her close, aware of an achy sensation in his throat as he tightened his arms around his daughter.

Jessica hardly remembered driving home. She set her suitcase on the floor just inside the door and went directly to her bedroom, feeling so exhausted she had to tell herself to put one foot in front of the other.

She got ready for bed even though it was early and she'd had no dinner.

She just wanted to sleep, she thought miserably. Not think. Just escape from her heartache and confusion in the oblivion of a deep slumber that would hopefully hold no haunting dreams of Daniel.

As she reached automatically for the matches next to the little house on the top of the dresser, her hand stilled and fresh tears filled her eyes.

No, she thought. She wouldn't light the candle that would create the warm, welcoming glow that would shine through the windows of the exquisite, tiny home.

The house would remain dark.

And empty.

Just like her heart.

Chapter 17

A week later, Mary-Clair entered Jessica's office, tossed an envelope onto the top of the desk, then sat down in one of the chairs.

"This just came by special messenger," Mary-Clair said, nodding toward the envelope.

"Hmm?" Jessica said, her attention on the computer screen in front of her.

"The return address indicates that it just might be the response to your application for a grant for The Peaceful Dove."

"Hmm?" Jessica said, then her head snapped up and she spun around and picked up the envelope. "Oh, my gosh, you're right." She held the envelope above her head and narrowed her eyes. "Darn, I can't see a thing."

"Well, open it, Jessica," Mary-Clair said.

"What if they turned us down?" Jessica said. "The entire future of the shelter will be determined by what is inside this envelope." She extended it toward Mary-Clair. "You open it."

Mary-Clair did as instructed, then unfolded the letter that was in the envelope and read it quickly.

"Well, my, my," she said. "Yep. I see. Isn't that fascinating? They use as much legal jargon in their stuff as we do in ours. Interesting."

"What does it say?" Jessica said, leaning forward. "I'm going crazy here, Mary-Clair. Tell me."

"Ms. MacAllister," Mary-Clair said, smiling, "your application for grant money for The Peaceful Dove has...drumroll, please...been approved. Including, I might add, the additional funds requested to hire armed guards to be on duty at the shelter twenty-four hours a day."

"Yes!" Jessica said, jumping to her feet. "Oh, that's wonderful!"

"Wait. There's more," Mary-Clair said. "The funds will be disbursed in approximately thirty days to the board of directors of the shelter, said board being required to furnish receipts for all monies spent in the future from such funds and blah, blah, blah. Congratulations, Jessica."

"Oh, I'm so relieved and so grateful," Jessica said, sinking back onto her chair with a big smile on her face. "I'm going to call the president of the board of directors right now and share the great news. Do you realize what this means, Mary-Clair?"

"Well, for one thing," Mary-Clair said, "it means

you also need to tell Daniel that his part in applying for this money was rewarded with a victory. He has the right to know, don't you think?'' She paused. ''As an editorial note, I might add that the smile that was just on your face for about three seconds was the first one I've seen from you in a week. It disappeared, however, as soon as I said Daniel's name.

''Jessica, what on earth happened between you and Daniel? I saw you two together. You were happy, had a...a glow about you, both of you, and then...what? I didn't want to pry after you said you weren't seeing Daniel anymore, but you have been one gloomy Gus all week. Can't you...I don't know...fix whatever went wrong and get back to the we're-so-happy-together bit? I mean, cripe, what crummy thing did the guy do that you can't forgive him for it?''

''Daniel didn't do anything wrong,'' Jessica said quietly, tracing a pattern with her fingertip on the top of the desk. ''I was the one who ended things because...because my family got all carried away with what they believed was happening between Daniel and me, and that made me realize that one can't live in a fantasy world without paying the piper at some point, and I became totally overwhelmed by everything, and I'm so confused, and I really hate having such inner turmoil, not being able to get in touch with myself and get the answers I so desperately need, and I miss Daniel so much, but I can't see him because—''

''Jessica! Stop a second and take a breath of air,''

Mary-Clair said, "before you faint dead on your nose from lack of oxygen."

Jessica took a sharp breath and blinked several times. "There. That's better. Anyway, now do you understand why I ended things with Daniel?"

"I don't have a clue," Mary-Clair said, frowning. "Just what exactly are you confused about?"

"I don't know," Jessica said, nearly wailing.

Esther whizzed into the office and handed Jessica her red tin.

"Have a cookie," the secretary said. "They're good for what ails you."

"I don't know what ails me," Jessica said, popping the lid off the tin and selecting a cookie. "I've never experienced anything like this before in my life and it's awful, just terrible." She sniffled, then ate the cookie, following it with another. "I'm so miserable."

Esther and Mary-Clair exchanged smug, knowing glances, then Mary-Clair got to her feet.

"Love is a confusing number at times," she said. "Or so I'm told. I have yet to discover that for myself. If you'd calm down a tad, Jessica, things just might become clear to you. I mean, gracious, you've muddied your emotional waters to the point that you couldn't see the truth that you're in love with Daniel Quinn if it bit you on the nose."

"I am not in love with Daniel Quinn," Jessica said, none too quietly.

"Could have fooled me," Esther said, shaking her head as she turned and left the office.

"No joke," Mary-Clair said. "Well, I'm off to court. Jessica, that cookie you just ate was number six. You'd better quit stuffing yourself before you get sick. You need all your energy to concentrate on your dilemma because your entire future happiness is at stake here. My goodness, what are you afraid of? Why is the very thought of being in love with Daniel so terrifying? Oh, cripe, look at the time. I'm gone. Bye."

"Bye," Jessica said, sniffling again, then shoved another cookie in her mouth.

What are you afraid of? Why is the very thought of being in love with Daniel so terrifying?

Jessica stared into space, nibbling on another cookie, as Mary-Clair's words echoed over and over in her mind.

Forget it, she thought. She didn't have to address Mary-Clair's questions because she was *not* in love with Daniel Quinn. No, of course, she wasn't.

Jessica's hand stilled halfway to her mouth and her eyes widened.

Was she?

Esther appeared in the doorway. "Your grandfather is on the phone for you, Jessica."

"What?" Jessica said. "I didn't hear the telephone ring."

"That's because you have a very important matter occupying your thoughts, dear," Esther said. "Love may only be a four-letter word, but it's an enormous entity when it arrives in all its splendor." She paused and smiled. "Well, wasn't that just the most profound thing you've ever heard? Not bad. Oh, talk to your grandfather.''

Jessica glared at a retreating Esther, then picked up the receiver. A few minutes later she hung up and stared at the telephone.

Bless her grandpa's heart, she thought. She now had something exciting to focus on. When she left work, she was to go directly to her grandparents' house and have her private meeting with Robert MacAllister to receive her special gift.

Oh, she couldn't stand the suspense. What had her grandpa selected especially for her?

A welcoming fire crackled in the hearth in Robert MacAllister's study. He and Jessica sat in matching high-back chairs facing the leaping flames, a small table between them. Jessica finished removing the wrapping from her gift, then gasped as she saw what she had received.

It was an exquisite, hand-carved ivory chess set, with black bases on one group of the pieces to distinguish them from the white ones. It came in a butter-soft, dark leather case large enough to hold the board as well.

"Oh, Grandpa," Jessica said, "it's beautiful, absolutely lovely. Thank you so much."

"Set up the pieces on the board, Jessica," Robert MacAllister said. "You can do it right there on that table next to you."

"Goodness, it has been years since I've had the time to play chess," Jessica said, starting to put the pieces on the board. "You and I had some great matches while I was growing up once you finished teaching me how to play this intricate game, but you'd have me at a definite disadvantage tonight from plain old lack of practice."

"I don't intend for us to play a game of chess, Jessica," Robert said. "Just finish placing the pieces in their proper places on the board."

"Okay," Jessica said, with a little shrug. A few moments later she frowned as she stared at the board. "The white queen isn't here." She glanced at the carpet surrounding the chair where she was sitting. "Do you see it? Did it fall to the floor?"

Robert leaned back in his chair and produced the missing queen from the pocket of the gray cardigan sweater he was wearing.

"Here it is," he said. "The white queen. But you can't have it, Jessica. Not now. Not yet."

"I don't understand, Grandpa," Jessica said, confusion evident on her face and in her voice. "This set is incomplete without that piece. Why...why are you keeping such an important part of this gift? Not allowing me to have it?"

"Because, my darling Jessica," Robert said, "the white queen represents you."

"Pardon me?"

"The other pieces of the set," Robert went on, "are your blessings...your family, career, your beauty and intelligence, your good health, and on the list goes. But the queen? The queen is you, and you've removed yourself from what you should be holding dear.''

"I..."

"Let me finish," Robert said, slipping the queen back into the pocket of his sweater. "You have focused so totally on your career that life is passing you by, Jessica. You have turned your back on what might already be on that chessboard...true love, a special man with whom you would have endless happiness, children born of the union with that man. This chess set will remain useless until you open your heart to love, and embrace *all* that life brings you."

Tears filled Jessica's eyes as she listened to her grandfather speak.

"I'm scared, Grandpa," she whispered. "I'm so afraid of...of myself, of my inability to truly know who a man might be beneath the surface and..." She shook her head as a sob caught in her throat.

"Because of what happened with William?" Robert said gently.

Jessica dashed two tears from her cheeks. "Oh, God, you know about...but how—"

"It's not important how I know," Robert said. "What matters is that you're allowing ghosts from the past to determine your present and future. That's wrong, Jessica, and terribly sad. Believe in yourself, my darling child, and move forward with your life. Look carefully at the chess pieces already in place and see if maybe, just maybe, the special man, your soul mate, is already here, waiting for you."

"But..."

"Shh," Robert said, reaching over and patting Jessica's knee. "Pack up your gift, go home, and think about what I've said tonight. You'll know when the time is right to come to me and get the missing queen."

Jessica looked at Robert for a long moment, then nodded slowly.

"I love you, Grandpa," she said. "And thank you. Thank you so very, very much."

Through the long hours of the night Jessica lay in bed, slowly and carefully examining her life. Reaching deep within herself for courage, she flung the ghost of William into dark oblivion, then rejoiced in the wondrous sense of freedom and peace that consumed her.

Drawing a steadying breath, she opened her mind... and her heart...to the image of Daniel.

And she knew.

There in the private darkness while others slept, Jessica MacAllister knew that she was deeply and irrevocably in love with Daniel Quinn.

He was everything she believed him to be. He was Daniel. And she loved him with all that she was. Love wasn't frightening, not any longer. Her confusion had been born of past hurt and fears, and her refusal to acknowledge her true feelings for Daniel.

She wanted to spend the rest of her life with him, be his wife and Tessa's mother, have more babies that she and Daniel would create together.

"Oh, Grandpa," she whispered, as fresh tears filled

her eyes. "You are so wise, so wonderful. How well you know me, even better than I know myself. Thank you, thank you, thank you. But..."

Jessica frowned.

What if...oh, dear heaven...what if Daniel didn't love *her* as she did him? He had, she knew, freed himself of *his* ghosts, allowed his sister, Karen, to rest in peace, enabling him to truly love Tessa as a father should. He had opened his heart to love and allowed that precious baby to stake a claim.

But had Daniel then closed the door on his heart again before his growing feelings for her could enter? Had he already put her out of sight out of mind since she'd ended their relationship? Dismissed any lingering memories of what they'd shared together as unimportant and not worth dwelling on?

How was she to know how Daniel felt about her? If Daniel loved her?

"You swallow your pride, Ms. MacAllister," she said, hearing the shaky quality of her voice. "You go to him, declare your love honestly and openly, then you accept with womanly dignity whatever his heart answers."

Jessica sighed as exhaustion began to creep over her senses. But before she succumbed to blissful slumber, she left the bed and lit the candle in the little house on the dresser.

Back in bed, her lashes drifted down as she gazed at the warm, welcoming glow in the windows of the tiny house that was, to her, the home she wished to share with Daniel, Tessa and the babies yet to come.

Chapter 18

Jessica slept until nearly noon the next day and felt fully rested for the first time since the last, heartbreaking scene with Daniel. She hummed as she showered and shampooed her hair, then dressed in jeans and a peach-colored sweater. She ate a late lunch of a BLT on whole-wheat toast.

And through it all she thought of Daniel.

She cleaned the kitchen after her meal, then went into her bedroom and sank onto the side of the bed, staring at the telephone on the nightstand.

This was it, she thought, pressing one hand against her stomach as a flurry of butterflies arrived. She was going to call Daniel and ask if she could meet with him to discuss something important.

"Oh, good grief," she said, patting her cheeks.

"I'm a wreck. Something important? Yes, I'd say that the rest of my life is rather important."

What if Daniel said he was very flattered by her declaration of love for him, but sorry, toots, he just didn't feel that way about *her?* What if...

No, Jessica thought, lifting her chin. She refused to sit there and allow her imagination to produce one grim scenario after another.

Yes, there was a very real chance that Daniel might not be in love with her. By going to him and revealing her true feelings she was running the risk of having her heart and pride shattered.

But being in love meant that sometimes it was necessary to run those kinds of risks, to lay it all on the line. It was the only way to discover the depth of Daniel's caring for her. It was the only way she would be worthy of receiving the queen to the chess set.

"Fine," she said, with a decisive nod.

Just as Jessica reached for the receiver, the telephone rang, causing her to jerk in surprise at the sudden noise. The call was quick, just a reminder that Jessica was scheduled to be on duty at The Peaceful Dove that night and that the spreading news about the grant was fantastic.

"But..." Jessica said to the dial tone, then dropped the receiver back into place.

So, okay, she'd forgotten to check her calendar that morning. Well, she'd go to Plan B, which she was inventing right now. She'd call Daniel, tell him about the approval of the grant application, then ask if she might meet with him tomorrow. Yes, that would work.

A few minutes later Jessica hung up the receiver again and stared at it with wide eyes.

Daniel had a new nanny for Tessa. The woman sounded as if she was in her fifties or sixties and had a delightful English accent. She and Daniel had been introduced at the agency the previous evening, the nanny said. She'd spent the morning with Tessa and Daniel, then settled in, allowing Lieutenant Quinn to leave for work after lunch. Did she wish to leave a message?

Jessica rolled her eyes heavenward.

She'd been so stunned when a woman who sounded like Mary Poppins answered the telephone at Daniel's apartment that the request for a message had caused her to chatter like a magpie. Please tell Daniel, she'd said, that the grant application was approved, including the money for armed guards. And please tell Daniel, she'd rattled on, that she'd really like the opportunity to speak with him about a private matter. And please also tell Daniel that since she had to work at The Peaceful Dove that night, she'd phone him tomorrow with the hope that they could arrange a time to get together.

The nanny had assured her that all those details would be relayed to the lieutenant without fail except, love, would she care to leave her name as well?

"What a performance," Jessica said, with a shake of her head. "How am I ever going to survive until tomorrow?"

* * *

Several hours later Daniel frowned as he dropped the telephone receiver back into place on the corner of his desk at the police station.

"You don't look too happy," Mick said, glancing over at him. "Aren't things going well with Tessa and the new nanny?"

"What?" Daniel said. "Oh, yeah, they're doing fine, just great."

"Just as they were an hour ago?" Mick said, smiling. "Give the poor woman a break, Danny. She's going to get a complex the way you keep checking up on her."

"She's taking care of my daughter, Mick."

"Okay, okay," Mick said quickly. "Don't get hostile." He paused. "If everything is dandy at home, why the frown when you got off the phone?"

"Jessica called the apartment," Daniel said quietly, staring into space. "The application for the grant money was approved, including funds for armed guards for The Peaceful Dove."

"Oh," Mick said. "Well, that was decent of her to let you know, but I was hoping she had wanted something more...personal, shall we say."

"She left the message that she would like to meet with me tomorrow," Daniel said. "She can't do it tonight because she's on duty at the shelter. So... tomorrow."

"Now, that's more like it," Mick said. "You two will finally have a meaningful dialogue about what went wrong between you, determine a way to fix it, then I won't have to strangle you for being impossible to be around since you and Jessica split.''

Daniel glared at his partner. "I don't know what she wants to see me about. Maybe she misses Tessa and will ask if she can take her to the park or something.''

"Maybe she misses *you,* buddy," Mick said.

"In the movies, or one of those romance novels, that's how it would be," Daniel said, fiddling with a pencil, "but this is real life."

"But *you* miss *her,*" Mick said.

Daniel didn't speak for several long moments, then finally sighed and nodded.

"Yeah, I do," he said, turning to meet Mick's gaze. "I really do. She brought so much into my life, Mick. It's hard to explain but...hey, you know, I'm enjoying Tessa and we're having a great time together but when Jessica was there, too, it felt so...so right, so complete, so...ah, hell, forget it. I'm not making any sense."

"Wrong," Mick said. "You're coming across loud and clear. You're in love with Jessica MacAllister."

"Oh, whoa," Daniel said, raising one hand palm out. "Don't go any further down that road, because you're way off track. I am *not* in love with Jessica MacAllister."

Mick shrugged. "Okay."

"That's it?" Daniel said, leaning slightly toward him. "You're giving up that easily on your nutso theory?"

"What more can I say?" Mick said. "When I'm

right, I'm right. If you're too dense to figure it out, then it's your loss. But remember this, Danny. I am a man who is deeply in love. I know the signs, the symptoms, whatever the hell you want to call them. You, Quinn, are down for the count. You can deny that fact from now until forever, but it isn't going to change how you feel about Jessica. I am now going into the coffee room to see if there are any doughnuts left.''

''Stop off and see a shrink on the way back,'' Daniel shouted after him, ''because you are certifiably insane, Smith.'' He shook his head as Mick disappeared from view. ''Really cuckoo.''

He was *not* in love with Jessica, Daniel fumed. Yeah, sure, he missed her. Ached for her. Hadn't had a decent night's sleep since she'd walked out of his life.

So, okay, it seemed like something really wonderful had been packed into Jessica's suitcase and left with her. But that didn't mean that he was in love with the woman, for crying out loud.

Was he?

When Jessica entered The Peaceful Dove shortly after six o'clock that evening, she stopped just inside the door she'd closed and locked behind her and frowned.

It was so quiet in here, she thought. Some of the women were usually watching television and poked their heads out to greet whoever had come in, and many times a baby was fussing in the distance. But for some reason the door leading to the living room was closed.

She couldn't ever remember such total...silence at the shelter.

A shiver coursed through her and Jessica shook her head in self-disgust. She was being silly. Everyone was occupied elsewhere at the moment, that was all. And all the kiddies were happy at the same time for a change.

She'd better get herself into the office and ready to answer the telephone because she was late due to the heavy traffic. The volunteer on duty before her had no doubt gone home a half hour earlier, leaving only women living there to listen for the telephone.

As Jessica turned and started toward the office, the door to the living room opened and slammed against the wall, causing her to spin around in shock at the sudden noise, her heart racing.

Then everything seemed to stop. Jessica was frozen in place by chilling fear and her briefcase slipped from her fingers and landed on the floor with a thud. She could hear her own rough breathing echoing in her ears and tiny black dots flitted across her vision as she swayed unsteadily on her feet.

It was Sonny, she thought foggily. Sonny, Chrissy's husband. She recognized him from the night he'd tried to break into the shelter and the police had arrested him. It was Sonny.

And he had a gun gripped in both hands, pointing the terrifying weapon directly at her.

She was hot, so unbearably hot, that the heat was

stealing the breath from her body, making it nearly impossible for her to breathe. No, no, she was cold, shivering, and her legs were trembling and—

"Pay dirt," Sonny said gruffly. "I saw you in the doorway after the cops grabbed me the night I came here to get my wife and son. You were the one I was hoping to find and I did. What's your name?"

"I..." Jessica started, then took a shuddering breath of much-needed air.

"Name!"

"Jessica," she whispered.

"Well, Jessica," Sonny said, "come right in here and join the party. You're the one I've been waiting for and here you are. This is meant to be. This is the night I get my family back because you were the one who took them away from me. Get in here. Now."

Jessica moved forward, telling herself to put one foot in front of the other. At the doorway to the living room she inched around Sonny and entered the room. Her heart sank as she saw that Sonny had gathered all the women and children staying at the shelter into the room. They were huddled together, terror evident on their faces.

Don't faint, Jessica ordered herself. Don't cry. Don't do anything stupid. This wasn't a nightmare she would wake from, this was horrifyingly real and she had to gather courage from deep within herself. Somehow.

"Sonny," she said, praying her voice wasn't as shaky as it sounded to her, "you're making a terrible mistake by doing this, but it's not too late to realize that. Put the gun down and leave. Chrissy and your son are *not* here. You know that, Sonny, because you have everyone who lives here in this room. Chrissy and the baby aren't here. Please, put down the gun.''

''Not a chance, lady,'' Sonny said. ''You're going to tell me where Chrissy and my boy are. You sent them away where I couldn't find them, but we're going to fix that, you and me. I'll leave as soon as you tell me what I want to know.''

Jessica wrapped her hands around her elbows. ''I'm not telling you anything until you let the others go. They have nothing to do with this, Sonny. They have no idea where Chrissy and the baby are. This is between the two of us, just you and me.''

''Let them go?'' Sonny said, with a bark of harsh laughter. ''Yeah, right. The minute they're out the door they'll call the cops.''

''So? What can the police do?'' Jessica said. ''You're the one with the gun and a hostage. You have the power. They'll have no choice but to stand around outside and try to figure out what to do. You're in control. They can't make one move toward this house because it would put my life in jeopardy. You can't keep track of all of us at the same time, Sonny. Let the others leave. I won't tell you one thing about Chrissy unless you do.''

Sonny swung the gun around to point it at the group of women and children, then whipped it back in the next instant toward Jessica.

''See?'' Jessica said. ''There's too many of us, and like I said, they don't know where Chrissy is.''

"Yeah, yeah," Sonny said, nodding. "It'll be just you and me and…wait, wait, I have to think. I don't want some rookie cop doing something dumb out there. There were big shots here that night. I saw them. Suits. Detectives. They came in here. Two of them. Who were they? What were their names? I want to talk to one of them, tell them they'd better not come close to this building or you're dead. You got that, Jessica? Dead. What were their names?"

Lieutenant Daniel Quinn, Jessica's mind screamed. *Please, Daniel, help me. Come to me. I'm so scared and…Daniel!*

No, she thought in the next instant. She wasn't going to divulge Daniel's name. She wasn't going to do anything to put the man she loved in potential danger. No. But, oh God, what choice did she have? If she made up a name and Sonny realized what she had done…oh, Daniel.

"Names!" Sonny yelled, causing Jessica to jerk.

"Yes, all right." She looked at the women. "Kathy, you make the call to the Ventura police station when you leave the shelter."

"But, Jessica," Kathy said, "you can't stay here with—"

"Listen to me carefully," Jessica said. "Call the station and ask to speak to either Daniel Quinn or Mick Smith. Have you got that? If neither of them are there, tell them to find them. Tell them that Sonny has a gun and I'm a hostage here. Tell them he's not going to release me until I tell him where Chrissy and his son are. Understand?"

"Yes," Kathy said, nodding. "Daniel Quinn or Mick Smith. Okay."

"Good. That's good," Sonny said. "And tell those jerks that if they make one move toward this house that Jessica is as good as dead. Go. All of you. Get out of here before I change my mind."

The women hurried from the room, Kathy looking helplessly at Jessica as she left. Jessica's legs refused to hold her for another second and she sank onto the sofa. She heard the front door close behind the fleeing group and looked up at Sonny.

He wasn't making any move to lock the door, she realized. She had to divert his attention before he thought of it.

"There," she said. "You're very smart, Sonny. Now you don't have to worry about keeping control over a whole group of people. Oh, yes, you're clever, one step ahead of the police."

"Damn straight," Sonny said, sitting down in a chair opposite the sofa and pointing the gun at Jessica. "I'm calling all the shots here. You tell me where Chrissy and my boy are and we leave together. The cops won't be able to do a damn thing about it. In fact, we'll be long gone before they can even get here. Yeah, that's the ticket. We'll go now. They'll show up and find this place empty. Ha! This is great. Okay, Jessica, tell me where Chrissy is. Right now."

Jessica lifted her chin. "I...I don't know."

Daniel leaned back in his chair at his desk at the station and raised his arms over his head in a stretch, yawning at the same time.

"I'm all caught up on my paperwork, Mick," he said. "Can you believe that? I think that happened once before, about five or six years ago." He paused. "Sure is a quiet night."

The telephone on Daniel's desk rang.

"See what you did, big mouth?" Mick said. "You just had to say out loud that nothing is happening. You are such a dope."

Daniel chuckled and picked up the receiver halfway through the third ring. "Quinn."

The chill that swept through Daniel was so intense it caused a throbbing ache in his head and chest as he gripped the receiver tighter and tighter.

He listened intently, getting to his feet without realizing he was doing it. "Okay, I understand," he said finally. "All of you stay right there by the convenience store. We'll meet you there. We're on our way." He dropped the receiver onto the base of the telephone. "Let's roll, Mick. I'll radio on the way for backup and SWAT."

Daniel grabbed his jacket from the chair and sprinted across the room with Mick right behind him.

"Where are we going?" Mick yelled.

"The Peaceful Dove," Daniel said. "That scum Sonny has a gun and is holding Jessica hostage so he can find out where his wife and kid are."

"Oh...hell," Mick said under his breath.

"He's got Jessica," Daniel said, picking up speed as he ran. "Damn it to hell, he's got my Jessica."

* * *

Sonny narrowed his eyes and gripped the gun with both hands as he pointed it at Jessica.

"Don't play games with me, lady," he said. "I'm going to ask you one more time and you'd better give me an answer. Where are Chrissy and my boy?"

"I...don't...know," Jessica said, flinging out her arms. "When a woman wishes to relocate, only one of us becomes involved in the process for the sake of secrecy. Chrissy wasn't assigned to me, Sonny. I have no idea where she and the baby are."

"You're dead," Sonny said. "I swear I'm going to shoot you dead as a post."

"And then what?" Jessica said. "You'll never find your wife and son if you kill me. The only way to discover where your family went is for me to determine who was in charge of setting them up in a different town. I'll have to telephone those who do that, call them all until I get the right person."

"How many people are you talking about?" Sonny said.

Four. And she was one of them. That was only three calls maximum, providing she didn't find the right volunteer on the first try. That wasn't enough time for Daniel to put together a plan to—

"How many?" Sonny shouted.

"Fourteen," Jessica said quickly.

"Damn it," Sonny said, getting to his feet. "Okay, up. We're going into the office and you're going to start making those phone calls. Don't try anything tricky, Jessica, or I'll kill you. Understand?"

Jessica got to her feet. "Yes, Sonny, I understand. I...um...I have to find the list with all those names and phone numbers, though. The filing system here is really a mess and...but, believe me, I know you'll shoot me if...please don't hurt me, Sonny."

And, oh, dear God, please don't hurt my Daniel, she thought. She couldn't bear it if anything happened to Daniel. She loved him so much, so very much.

"Okay," Daniel said, hanging up the radio receiver in the vehicle. "SWAT will meet us at the convenience store as well as every patrol car in the area, coming in with no lights, no sirens. Drive faster, Mick."

Mick pressed harder on the gas pedal. "Listen to me, Danny. You've got to tell the SWAT leader that you don't know how Jessica might handle being terrified like this. That's important info for the squad leader to have. She could be falling apart, making Sonny even more wired."

"No, you're wrong," Daniel said. "Jessica is hanging in there, scared but steady, until I can come and get her out of that place."

"How in the hell do you know *that?*" Mick said.

"I know Jessica," Daniel said quietly. "It's as though...as though I can hear her speaking to me. I guess that sounds crazy, but it's true, Mick."

Mick nodded slowly. "Okay. I can relate to that. Rosemary and I are that in tune with each other, too, because we're..."

"In love with each other," Daniel finished for him. "This is a helluva time for me to figure it out, isn't it? But...but, yeah, I'm in love with Jessica Mac-Allister. I love her, Mick, and it feels so...right. I couldn't save Karen from herself, from her own choices. But this time? Nothing is going to happen to my Jessica.'' He drew a breath that seemed to come from his very soul. ''Please, God, let me make the right decisions when we get there. I can't lose her, Mick. I love Jessica so damn much.''

''Hurry up,'' Sonny yelled, as Jessica took another file from the cabinet and flipped through it.

''I can't find the list,'' Jessica said. ''You're watching every move I make. You know I'm trying. We've been meaning to get this filing system in proper order, but there's never enough time and—''

''Shut up and keep looking,'' Sonny said. ''You better not be playing games with...'' Bright light suddenly flooded the room through the window in the small office. ''What's that?''

''Sonny!'' a voice bellowed in the distance, amplified over a speaker. ''Sonny, this is Daniel... Quinn. I'm here, just like you wanted me to be. Let Jessica go and come out with your hands up.''

''Okay, okay,'' Sonny said. ''So we didn't leave before the cops got here, but the big shot is running the show. Good. That's good. He won't do anything stupid. He'll know I'll kill you unless he does exactly what I say. Yeah. Everything is going just fine.''

''Sonny...'' Jessica said.

''Quiet. Don't say another word.'' Sonny crossed the room and Jessica gasped as he wrapped one arm around her neck and pulled her back against his body. "Walk. Over to the window. You're a tall one, aren't you? I'm totally covered by you. They can't take a shot at me without hitting you. Ha! I'm running this show. Big time."

At the window Sonny tore the curtain rod off the wall and flung the bottom pane of glass up. He centered Jessica in front of the window, the bright spotlights causing her to narrow her eyes. It was impossible to see beyond the glare. He pressed the end of the gun against Jessica's temple.

"Let her go," Daniel said, using a bullhorn. Dear God, Sonny had a gun to Jessica's head. He could see her so clearly in the bright light, wanted to run to her, to grab her out of that scum's hands and— "Give it up, Sonny. The entire building is surrounded and you can't win this one. Toss the gun out the window before someone gets hurt."

"Not a chance, Quinn," Sonny yelled. "The someone who's going to get hurt is this lady if you don't do exactly what I tell you. I want to know where my wife and boy are. Understand? You have sources. You can get what I want. That's the deal, Quinn. Tell me where my family is or this woman dies."

Daniel looked heavenward for a long moment.

This was it, he thought, feeling the cold fist in his gut tighten to the point of pain. *Please, Jessica, understand what I'm saying to you. Please.*

He lowered the bullhorn and looked at the leader of the SWAT team.

"Okay," Daniel said. "You know the plan. If Jessica gets the meaning of my message, you should have a clean shot. Don't shoot to kill unless you have to.''

"Got it, Lieutenant," the man said. "But what if she doesn't understand what you're asking her to do?"

"One step at a time here," Daniel said, not wishing to consider the ramifications of the man's question. "Here we go." He raised the bullhorn to his mouth. "Sonny, the women you released earlier told me you wanted to know where Chrissy and your son are. I have that information. Let Jessica go, Sonny, and we'll talk."

"You think I'm stupid, cop?" Sonny yelled. "I let her go and you'll blow me away. You tell me where my family is, then Jessica and I are walking out of here together. We'll get in my car and drive away. If anyone follows me, or is waiting where Chrissy is, Jessica dies. When I have Chrissy and my boy, I'll let Jessica go."

"Okay, Sonny," Daniel said. "You win. Regulations say I have to put the safety of the hostage first. I'll tell you what you want to know."

"You're being smart, Quinn," Sonny said.

"The woman I talked to didn't have the exact address," Daniel went on, "but she said Jessica would be able to give you directions once I told you the general location of where Chrissy and your son were taken."

"Yeah, yeah, okay, hurry up," Sonny yelled.

Please, Jessica, Daniel mentally pleaded. *Please understand this, my love.*

"Sonny," Daniel said into the bullhorn. "Chrissy and your son are down where Tessa lives. Got that? That's where they are. Down...where...Tessa...hangs out."

What? Jessica thought. Tessa? Baby Tessa? What on earth was Daniel— Wait! Yes, of course. Tessa spends her time on the floor because she can't walk yet and...I hear you, Daniel. I hear you, my love.

"I can't take anymore," Jessica said. "I feel faint. Black dots are...oh-h-h."

She went limp, her entire weight pulling against Sonny's arm around her neck as she crumbled. Sonny was so startled by the sudden motion that he released his hold on her and she landed with a thump on the floor.

In the next instant a shot rang out and Sonny fell backward, blood spreading on his left shoulder. He hit the floor, dropped the gun and clutched the wound, moaning in pain.

Jessica didn't move. She stayed huddled on the floor and heard shouting in the distance, then what sounded like an army converging on the house. A moment later Daniel swept her up into his arms and carried her across the hallway to the living room. Jessica wrapped her arms around his neck and buried her face in his shoulder.

In the living room, Daniel stood statue still, his hold on Jessica tightening.

"You understood what I was saying," he said, his voice gritty with emotion. "About Tessa. About Tessa's world being the floor right now and...you were wonderful, so damn brave and...oh, God, if anything would have happened to you, I don't know what I...ah, Jessica, I love you. I love you so much. I want to marry you, spend the rest of my life with you. I know you don't want those things, marriage, commitment and...but I had to tell you how I feel and..."

Jessica raised her head. "You love me?"

"Yeah," Daniel said, looking directly into her eyes. "I do. I guess that's not what you want to hear but..." His voice trailed off.

"You love me," Jessica said, an incredulous tone to her voice. "You're honest to goodness in love with me. I... Daniel, put me down, please. You have a broken arm, remember? I'm a little shaky, but I'm really all right, I think."

Daniel set her on her feet and she took a steadying breath before meeting his gaze again.

"Thank you for saving my life," she said.

"We did it together," he said, "because we heard what we were saying to each other and—"

"You love me?" Jessica interrupted.

Daniel frowned. "Don't beat it to death. I know you don't want any part of love and the forever and ever thing and...leave me a little pride here."

"Oh, Daniel," Jessica said, her eyes filling with tears as she smiled at him. She framed his face in her hands. "I love you with all that I am as a woman. I have chosen you to give my heart to and this time, oh, yes, this time, I have chosen well. I want to be your wife and Tessa's mother. I want to create beautiful babies with you and...oh, Daniel, I do want forever...with you.''

''You love me?'' he said.

''Let's not start that again,'' she said. ''Just kiss me, Lieutenant.''

And he did.

Daniel kissed Jessica with such tenderness that fresh tears misted her eyes. Then the kiss intensified as it spoke of their love, the commitment they were making, the future they would share. It was a forever kiss that would become one of their precious memories.

''Danny, we're wrapping it up here and...oops,'' Mick said, coming into the room.

Daniel broke the kiss and he and Jessica turned to look at Mick who was grinning from ear to ear.

''Mick, I'm getting married,'' Daniel said.

''Oh?'' Mick said. ''Anyone I know?''

''Me,'' Jessica said, laughing.

''It's about time you two came out of the ether,'' Mick said, ''although this isn't a very romantic spot to settle on such a momentous thing.''

''It'll be a great story to tell our grandchildren,'' Danny said.

''True,'' Mick said. ''Best wishes to you both. I'd tell you to be happy but that's a given. Take your bride-to-be out of here, Danny. We're bringing the women and kids back, Sonny is on his way to the hospital then jail, and we got uniforms lined up to spend the rest of the night on duty here. Go.''

''We're gone,'' Daniel said.

"Hey, when is the big day?" Mick said. "The wedding? I gotta get my good suit cleaned."

"Soon," Jessica said, smiling up at Daniel with love shining in her eyes. "Very soon. Oh, and we're going to have very unusual decorations on the top of our cake."

"We are?" Daniel said.

"I'll explain it all to you," Jessica said, "and then you'll understand why the top of our wedding cake will hold the king and the queen from a beautiful chess set. Oh, my darling Daniel, let's go home."

*   *   *   *   *

Find out what happens when
Maggie MacAllister meets
an actual prince in

A WISH AND A PRINCE,

coming only to Silhouette Books
in December 2001.
And now for a sneak preview of this
short story, published in the

CROWNED HEARTS

3-in-1 collection,
please turn the page.

Chapter 1

Maggie MacAllister plunked one elbow on the desk and cupped her chin in her palm, sighing as she stared into space.

It was a typical New Year's Eve in the Emergency Room of the Ventura Hospital, she mused. At shortly before midnight it was quiet, the lull before the storm that would keep her and the other nurses, plus the doctors on duty, running at full speed once the party-goers really got into the holiday spirit.

She was feeling a tad blue, she realized, because this was exactly where she'd been one year ago, the year before that and several more, having volunteered to work so that others could attend festivities with their special someone.

She was here by choice, having refused three... count them...three invitations from very nice men to be their date on this couple-oriented night. She'd politely refused...three times...because, well, yes, it was admittedly rather silly of her, a romantic notion she'd had for as long as she could remember, but she believed that the kiss at midnight on New Year's Eve should never be shared with a casual date.

According to MacAllister nonsense, of course, she thought, laughing softly, that special someone had to be a prince, the one she'd wished for on her birthday since she was a little girl. Yes, he was supposed to be an honest-to-goodness member of a royal family.

That was just a long-standing, silly MacAllister joke as far as her family of countless numbers was concerned, Maggie thought. What they didn't know was that she really was waiting for a prince.

Oh, not a real one, not a titled member of royalty, but a man with princely charms, one who was thoughtful, caring, tender and kind, and who believed in old-fashioned romance. A man, she was beginning to gloomily believe, who didn't exist, at least not for her.

The wail of a rapidly approaching ambulance jerked Maggie from her whimsical, romantic thoughts, and she rushed to the double doors as a stretcher was pushed through and two attendants and a uniformed police officer entered.

The officer stopped Maggie before she could approach the patient.

"I gotta get back out into the jungle, Maggie," the officer said, then chuckled. "This guy wasn't mugged. He was knocked over on a sidewalk by a

rollerblader who is convinced he's going to jail for
life.'' He frowned. ''The thing is, the guy who's out
cold there had no wallet, no identification of any kind
on him. Weird. You've got a John Doe, but not because he was ripped off as far as I can tell, and I saw
the whole thing happen. Well, whatever. Happy New
Year.''

''Same to you,'' Maggie said, smiling as the officer
strode away.

Maggie stared at the man known for the moment
as John Doe. ''Oh, my,'' she said, feeling her heart
do a funny little two-step.

He was, without a doubt, the most incredibly handsome man she had ever seen.

He had light brown hair, that was tousled from his
tumble, and long, dark lashes fanned against tan skin
on a face that was ruggedly masculine, yet possessed
sensuous, oh-so-kissable appearing lips. He was
around thirty years old and...

He had wide shoulders that were clearly defined in
an obviously expensive blue sweater, and long, muscular legs that were covered by dusty black, perfectly
tailored slacks. The black shoes he wore probably
cost more than she made in a week.

Maybe he was a wealthy, absentminded genius, or
a...

What color were his eyes? Maggie mused on. What
would he look like when he smiled and...

''Maggie, for heaven's sake.'' She shook her head
slightly to dispel the eerie, sensual mist that had

seemed to swirl around her and the man, encasing them in a private cocoon. "Get a grip. Be a nurse."

She lifted her hands, hesitated, then sank her fingers into the man's hair, marveling at its silky thickness as she gently probed, then found, an egg-sized bump on the back of his head.

"Okay, John Doe, it's time to wake up," she said, patting one of his cheeks. "That's enough snoozing. Come on. Open your eyes. Can you hear me? Say, are you my prince? The one I've been waiting a lifetime for? And now you've been delivered right to me, like a special New Year's Eve present?"

"Fifteen seconds until midnight," a man yelled from the outer area. "And here we go, folks...ten seconds and counting."

A chorus of voices from people Maggie couldn't see began the countdown until the big moment. Then a shout went up and honking horns outside the building could be heard along with firecrackers.

Before she even realized she was moving, Maggie bent over and kissed the unconscious man, discovering that his lips were, indeed, every bit as soft and kissable as they appeared.

"Happy New Year, my prince," she whispered.

#1 *New York Times* Bestselling Author

NORA ROBERTS

**Will enchant readers with two
remarkable tales of timeless love.**

Coming in September 2001

TIME AND AGAIN

Two brothers from the future cross centuries to
find a love more powerful than time itself in the
arms of two beguiling sisters.

Available at your favorite retail outlet.

Silhouette®

™ *Where love comes alive*™

Visit Silhouette at www.eHarlequin.com   PSTA

In August look for

AN IDEAL MARRIAGE?

by *New York Times* bestselling author

DEBBIE MACOMBER

A special 3-in-1 collector's edition containing
three full-length novels from America's favorite
storyteller, Debbie Macomber—each ending
with a delightful walk down the aisle.

Father's Day
First Comes Marriage
Here Comes Trouble

Evoking all the emotion and warmth
that you've come to expect from
Debbie, AN IDEAL MARRIAGE?
will definitely satisfy!

Visit us at www.eHarlequin.com
PHIDEAL

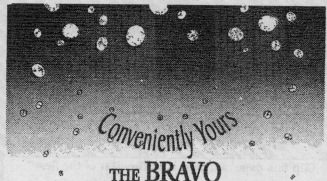

Conveniently Yours

THE BRAVO
BILLIONAIRE

As a child, Jonas Bravo saw his baby brother kidnapped
before his very eyes—and life, as he knew it, would never
be the same. Now, with another child's well-being at stake,
he was determined to fight the good fight. But to hold on
to *this* baby, he would have to marry her guardian. And
though he didn't trust her as far as he could throw her,
Jonas knew he had to let lovely Emma Hewitt into his life.
For was it possible that this woman, and this child, were
about to bring back everything he'd lost that long-ago
winter night...and thought he would never see again?

THE BRAVO BILLIONAIRE, by Christine Rimmer:
On sale in September 2001, only from Silhouette.

And coming in October, the missing Bravo baby is
alive and well...and all grown up. Find him in
THE MARRIAGE CONSPIRACY by Christine Rimmer
(SE #1423)—on sale in October 2001,
only from Silhouette Special Edition.

Available wherever Silhouette books are sold.

Silhouette®
Where love comes alive™

Visit Silhouette at www.eHarlequin.com   PSBRAV

If you enjoyed what you just read,
then we've got an offer you can't resist!

Take 2
bestselling novels FREE!
Plus get a FREE surprise gift!

Clip this page and mail it to The Best of the Best™

IN U.S.A.	IN CANADA
3010 Walden Ave.	P.O. Box 609
P.O. Box 1867	Fort Erie, Ontario
Buffalo, N.Y. 14240-1867	L2A 5X3

YES! Please send me 2 free Best of the Best™ novels and my free surprise gift. After receiving them, if I don't wish to receive anymore, I can return the shipping statement marked cancel. If I don't cancel, I will receive 4 brand-new novels every month, before they're available in stores! In the U.S.A., bill me at the bargain price of $4.24 plus 25¢ shipping and handling per book and applicable sales tax, if any*. In Canada, bill me at the bargain price of $4.74 plus 25¢ shipping and handling per book and applicable taxes**. That's the complete price and a savings of over 15% off the cover prices—what a great deal! I understand that accepting the 2 free books and gift places me under no obligation ever to buy any books. I can always return a shipment and cancel at any time. Even if I never buy another book from The Best of the Best™, the 2 free books and gift are mine to keep forever.

185 MEN DFNG
385 MEN DFNH

Name	(PLEASE PRINT)	
Address	Apt.#	
City	State/Prov.	Zip/Postal Code

* Terms and prices subject to change without notice. Sales tax applicable in N.Y.
** Canadian residents will be charged applicable provincial taxes and GST.
All orders subject to approval. Offer limited to one per household and not valid to current Best of the Best™ subscribers.
® are registered trademarks of Harlequin Enterprises Limited.

BOB01

©1998 Harlequin Enterprises Limited

Silhouette

where love comes alive—online...

eHARLEQUIN.com

your romantic books

♥ **Shop online!** Visit Shop eHarlequin and discover a wide selection of new releases and classic favorites at great discounted prices.

♥ Read our daily and weekly Internet exclusive serials, and participate in our interactive novel in the reading room.

♥ Ever dreamed of being a writer? Enter your chapter for a chance to become a featured author in our Writing Round Robin novel.

• • • • • • •

your romantic life

♥ Check out our feature articles on dating, flirting and other important romance topics and get your daily love dose with tips on how to keep the romance alive every day.

• • • • • • •

your community

♥ Have a Heart-to-Heart with other members about the latest books and meet your favorite authors.

♥ Discuss your romantic dilemma in the Tales from the Heart message board.

your romantic escapes

♥ Learn what the stars have in store for you with our daily Passionscopes and weekly Erotiscopes.

♥ Get the latest scoop on your favorite royals in Royal Romance.

All this and more available at
www.eHarlequin.com
on Women.com Networks

SINTA1R

New York Times bestselling author

JOAN JOHNSTON

is celebrated for her emotional, dramatic stories told
with a strong sensuality and a decided Western
flavor. Don't miss these Whitelaw stories!

HAWK'S WAY
ROGUES

HONEY AND THE HIRED HAND
THE COWBOY TAKES A WIFE
THE TEMPORARY GROOM

"(Joan Johnston) does short contemporary
Westerns to perfection."
—*Publishers Weekly*

Available at your favorite retail outlet.

Silhouette®
Where love comes alive™

Visit Silhouette at www.eHarlequin.com
PSHWR